PEOPLE

NO WONDER SHE WAS PALE WITH TERROR

Mallory probably found him more frightening than some of the monstrously possessed characters in his novels. A crazed stalker, hunting down a helpless woman in a back alley in San Francisco late at night…

Liam swallowed another laugh. He might be crazed, but Mallory Powell was hardly helpless. She was wealthy enough to attend charity balls and celebrated enough to be photographed for the newspapers. She ran a restaurant that was named after her. And she had the power to heal Liam—or to destroy him.

He watched her back away from him, then turn and sprint to her car, as if afraid he might tackle her from behind and haul her off to have his way with her. She ought to know he would never force her to do anything—even if his life depended on it.

She ought to know, he thought as she climbed into her car, revved the engine and blinded him with the high beams of her headlights, that he would never have to force her to do anything. She might not need him the way he needed her, with his soul as much as his body. But she wanted him. He knew it, she knew it, and she knew he knew.

Weddings by De Wilde™

Barbara Keiler is acknowledged as the author of this work.

ISBN 0-373-82543-9

A STRANGER'S BABY

A Stranger's Baby

JUDITH ARNOLD

Harlequin Books

TORONTO • NEW YORK • LONDON
AMSTERDAM • PARIS • SYDNEY • HAMBURG
STOCKHOLM • ATHENS • TOKYO • MILAN
MADRID • WARSAW • BUDAPEST • AUCKLAND

If you like your fiction light and cheerful, *The Unborn* is not for you. In his latest novel, Liam O'Neill serves up a tale of revenge and bitterness that offers no easy answers, no quick fixes, no reassurance that good will always illuminate the darkest shadows of the heart.

O'Neill relies not on flashy special effects, gallons of gore or cheap thrills to frighten his readers out of their wits. The real horror in *The Unborn* derives not from the hero's quest for vengeance but rather from the issue central to the story: Where do our most primal urges come from? Can we overcome them? Is trust ever possible for a person shaped by violence? These questions transcend the horror genre; they are questions that plague everyone who has ever reached out to another human being in love.

After reading *The Unborn*, one can only wonder at the complex mind and tormented soul of author Liam O'Neill.

CHAPTER ONE

MALLORY POWELL'S ENTIRE future hinged on whether or not she opened the door.

A light drizzle silvered the chilly February air. Swollen rain clouds hung low in the sky, turning the city gray. Car tires hissed against the damp pavement; pedestrians hugged their trench coats tightly around themselves, warding off the damp.

The door was recessed under an overhang. The building itself was nondescript, an anonymous stucco structure on Golden Gate Street, just a few blocks from the university. No one would guess what went on inside the building, and that was exactly why Mallory had come here.

She adored her own doctor and trusted her with her life—but not with this. When a woman reached a level of renown in a small, gossipy city like San Francisco, certain medical problems had to be handled discreetly. Especially when that woman was the daughter of Leland Powell, one of the city's wealthiest financiers, and was engaged to be married to Robert Benedict, a fast-rising executive in her father's firm. Besides, her face was familiar to a substantial number of locals, thanks to her weekly cooking demonstrations on one of the city's most popular television talk shows. A woman in such a position didn't just march into a doctor's office and say, "Hi. I need an abortion."

She sighed and stared out at the rain. A shiver skimmed her spine, but she suspected it had less to do with the clammy weather than with the act she was contemplating.

She pressed her hands against her flat abdomen. She honestly couldn't believe something was living inside her, something she'd never planned on, a practical joke destiny had played on her.

She didn't believe it, but she knew it was true. Not only because the home pregnancy test she'd taken had shown positive, not only because her breasts had changed over the last two weeks, becoming tight and heavy, but because ...

She closed her eyes as another shiver, this one hot and erotic, coursed through her. Two months after she'd left the retreat, her memory of the man was still too vivid. She could still recall the feel of him, the smell of him, the taste of his kisses. She could still remember the way he'd felt locked deep inside her, his body lean and powerful, his eyes iron-gray and gold, revealing his troubled soul in a flash of passion. At that instant, she'd known that it wasn't just sex, wasn't just lust. It was two people saving each other, or else maybe racing hand in hand toward the worst sort of disaster.

The home pregnancy test had only confirmed what she'd felt at that moment, that one exquisite night when she and the man had been lost in each other, wrapped in the moonlight and their desperate faith.

She didn't even know his name.

She had to end this pregnancy. There was really no other way. Everyone was expecting her to marry Robert, and she wanted the wedding to take place. How on earth could she walk down the aisle to him if she was the mother of another man's baby?

Ever since she'd found out she was pregnant, she had barely been able to talk to her fiancé. Thank God she hadn't had to see him. She doubted she could look at him without falling apart.

The only solution was to get the problem taken care of as quickly and quietly as possible. She couldn't call her own doctor, an old friend whose father—also an ob-gyn—had delivered Mallory thirty years ago. She couldn't call her cousin Kate, who probably knew about every abortion center in the region, given that she was putting her own medical training to work at an inner-city clinic. Mallory loved Kate, but she couldn't trust her with this.

A friend of Mallory's who had been in a similar predicament a few years ago had recommended Dr. Gilman. "He charges a lot," Courtney had warned Mallory, "but he's the epitome of tact. Rumor has it his patients include all sorts of famous people who don't want anybody to find out. Actresses, politicians, philandering wives... The tabloids could torture Dr. Gilman till doomsday and he would never reveal the name of a single patient."

That was what Mallory needed: the most tight-lipped gynecologist in California. She would gladly pay whatever he charged to keep her situation a secret.

She reached for the door again, a heavy glass pane framed in chrome. The handle felt like ice, and she drew her hand away as if frostbitten.

This was ridiculous. Mallory had been pro-choice all her life. If ever a woman needed the freedom to make this choice, it was now, and she was the woman.

Yet she couldn't seem to open the door.

Tears burned the surface of her eyes but refused to spill over. She was too angry to cry. Angry with herself for hesitating, when terminating her pregnancy was the only way out. Angry with her father for admiring Robert so much that she feared what Leland might do if she broke the engagement. Angry with Aunt Grace for insisting, last December, that Mallory needed to get away and unwind before stress got the better of her. Angry with the man, the stranger, who could scramble her brain with one piercing gaze, who could touch her in such a way she didn't care who he was or who she was or what the consequences might be.

She shook her head. It wasn't his fault any more than it was her father's, or Robert's, or Aunt Grace's. Mallory had marched into this catastrophe with her eyes open. She had no one to blame but herself.

She reached for the door handle one last time, then shuddered and turned away. She couldn't go through with it. Even if walking away from Dr. Gilman's clinic meant losing the future she'd mapped out for herself, losing her father's respect, losing the chance to marry Robert . . .

God alone knew why, but as she stood in the shelter of the doorway, watching the late-winter rain lend a shimmer to the air, she was absolutely convinced that losing the baby inside her would be worse.

Lifting the hood of her raincoat over her head, she stepped out into the drizzle. She had parked her car on one of the steep side streets, and she walked cautiously down the sharply sloping sidewalk. Her sneakers had enough traction to keep her from slipping, but she felt that since she'd just decided not to end her pregnancy, she had to navigate the city's hills more carefully. She was walking for two, after all.

That thought didn't trouble her nearly as much as it should have. In fact, what troubled her most was the realization that she wasn't troubled. Her life was about to come crashing down around her, and yet she didn't regret having walked away from Dr. Gilman's office.

She was going to regret it soon enough, she acknowledged as she unlocked her green Saab convertible and slumped behind the wheel. She slammed the door shut and tried to clear her mind of everything but the immediate future.

She was pregnant. She didn't know who, or where, the father was. If he telephoned her, she wouldn't even recognize his voice. They had never spoken to each other, not even that night. Everything they'd had to say to each other, they'd said with their bodies.

But if she saw him again, she would know his rugged chin, his slightly crooked nose, his eyes clear enough to reveal glimpses of pain and hope. She would know the whisper of his sighs, his broken groans, the thick calluses layering his palms. She would know the rhythm of his heartbeat, because in one timeless instant, his pulse had echoed hers. She'd heard it. She'd felt it.

And now he was gone, out of her life forever.

If she were shrewd, she would contrive a way to get Robert into her bed—tonight, if possible. She would seduce him and then, a few weeks later, present him with the news that he was going to be a father. Of course, Robert looked nothing like the stranger, and the odds of the baby resembling him were slim to none.

Besides, Mallory wasn't dishonest. She might be reckless, she might be rebellious, she might have rocks in her head, but she prided herself on her integrity. She wasn't going to pass this baby off as Robert's.

She really had to get an abortion. There was no other way to put her life back together.

The canvas roof of her car muffled the rain, blurring the sound the way the moisture on her windshield blurred her view of the street. She lifted her car phone from its nook beneath the dashboard, pulled the scrap of paper bearing Dr. Gilman's address and phone number from her pocket, and dialed. A receptionist answered.

"Hello. This is Mallory Powell. I had a 9:30 a.m. appointment with Dr. Gilman." Her voice wavered slightly. She wondered if the receptionist could hear it.

"Yes, Ms. Powell."

"Well, I..." She swallowed. "I'm not sure I can make that appointment."

"I see." The receptionist sounded calm but sympathetic. "Are you alone?"

"Right now?"

"Yes. Can you talk?"

Mallory sank against the leather upholstery of the bucket seat. "I'm on a cellular phone, but I don't think anyone would bother listening in."

"I'm asking," the receptionist explained, "because I want to know if this is your decision or someone else's. Is someone pressuring you? A family member? The man who impregnated you?"

"Oh, Lord, no." A feeble laugh escaped Mallory. "Nobody knows. Certainly not him." She exhaled, suddenly weary and annoyed with herself for her lack of backbone. "I really—I'm not saying I won't go through with it. I just need to think about it a little more."

"I understand. It's an important decision, not one you should make in haste. You've got to be positive this is what you want or Dr. Gilman won't perform the procedure."

"I know."

"How far along do you think you are?"

"Eight weeks."

"You don't want to wait too long, Ms. Powell. After a point, the decision is out of your hands. Dr. Gilman won't treat women more than twelve weeks along. You would have to see someone else."

"I'm sure it won't come to that." At least she hoped not. She hoped, with all her heart, that in the next few days she would muster the fortitude to do what had to be done.

She just couldn't do it right now.

She promised the receptionist to make up her mind as soon as possible and said goodbye. Disconnecting the phone, she moaned, a tremulous sound that mingled with the fuzzy drumbeat of the rain against the car roof. As long as she had a piece of living tissue floating in her uterus, she wasn't going to be able to face Robert or her father. She wasn't going to be able to move ahead with her wedding plans. She wasn't going to be able to stop in at her aunt's store and be measured for a wedding gown. The bottom line was, she wasn't going to be able to contemplate her impending marriage. She couldn't forge into the future before she'd cleaned up her past.

Procrastination wasn't her style. When something needed to be done, no matter how unpleasant, no matter how regrettable, Mallory did it. She just...damn it, she just wanted to feel better about her decision.

What she needed was a drink. But it was too early in the day, and even if it were later, pregnant women weren't supposed to consume alcohol. Of course, that wouldn't matter once she pulled herself together and returned to Dr. Gilman's office. But as long as she was delaying the inevitable, she might as well act accordingly.

She drove east, toward Union Square. Her restaurant was closed on Mondays, which left her the entire day to think, to plan, to figure out how the hell she was going to get out of this fix.

If only it were as simple as the scrapes she'd gotten into as a child. She tried to remember the worst jam she'd ever been in. Probably it was the summer she was eight, when she'd been staying with Aunt Grace's family at Kemberly, and she and her twin cousins, Megan and Gabe, had run amok in the grand, antique-filled country estate. They'd been playing freeze-tag in the music room, as Mallory recalled, and Gabe had chased her relentlessly until she stumbled and crashed into a shelf, shattering a priceless Fabergé egg. Uncle Jeffrey had gone ballistic, threatening to banish all three children to their rooms for the rest of their lives, but Mallory had sobbed and pleaded with him to punish only her, because she'd been the one to break the egg. She'd owned up to her mistake then.

One way or another, she was going to have to own up to this mistake, too. She only hoped that her loved ones could forgive her the way Uncle Jeffrey had forgiven her more than twenty years ago. He'd done it grudgingly, but by the end of the week he'd been treating her the way he always had.

Aunt Grace, of course, had told her to forget that fussy old dust-collector. Mallory wondered what Aunt Grace would tell her now. *Forget that fellow from the retreat. You're under no obligation to have his child. For heaven's sake, don't ruin your life over this.*

She drove to the block where her restaurant was located. It occupied the ground floor of a building overlooking Union Square, a small patch of greenery nestled into one of the city's exclusive shopping districts. Mallory's lacked a view, but that didn't matter; people came for the food, the atmosphere and the cachet that eating there seemed to bestow on them.

She steered up the narrow alley to her private parking space behind the building. She had no intention of entering the restaurant, but it was impossible to find street parking in the neighborhood, and the garages charged usurious rates. Once she'd locked the car, she pulled her raincoat more tightly around herself, slung the strap of her purse high on her shoulder and sauntered up the alley to Powell Street.

The street was named after one of her ancestors. Powells had come west to California during the Gold Rush. They'd found their own mother lode—not the chunks of gold glimmering in the clear waters of Sutter's Mill but the profits to be made by selling food to the miners. Powells soon moved from selling smoked meats and fresh eggs to building restaurants and inns, and from there to buying and developing real estate throughout San Francisco. The family had lost most of its wealth during the Depression, but after Mallory's mother died, her father had devoted himself to rebuilding the family empire. Powell Enterprises now comprised many different businesses, and Mallory's eyes would glaze over whenever her father and Robert got to talking about this property or that mortgage company, this skyscraper or that pier.

Mallory's father liked to tease her about being a throwback, since she had returned to the family's original trade—food services. But Mallory had chosen to become a chef because she enjoyed working with food, experimenting, being creative—and because her happiest childhood memories were the times she'd spent in the kitchen with their housekeeper-cook, Emma, who had kindly taken Mallory under her wing. She knew her father would have preferred that his only child had set her sights on one of the executive suites at Powell Enterprises, but Mallory had never been the least bit interested in pushing papers around, wiring huge amounts of money here and there, wheeling and dealing and arguing over how many zeros to put on a check. She had figured she would salve her father's disappointment by marrying Robert Benedict, the up-and-coming young executive he was grooming for big things in the company.

Assuming she dealt with her little problem before Robert found out and called off the wedding.

Marrying him would be safe. He was smart, handsome, well educated and courteous, and he was the ideal son-in-law for her father. Mallory didn't exactly love him, but that was all right. He didn't exactly love her, either. But they got along well, they respected each other, they traveled in the same social circles. Robert didn't complain about her demanding hours or her high profile as a celebrity chef. He didn't think she ought to settle down and become a proper society matron or, as her father might have hoped, the heiress-apparent at Powell Enterprises. Robert seemed content with Mallory the way she was. Everyone would be happy if the two of them tied the knot, and then her father would leave her alone to run her restaurant.

Marrying Robert used to seem like the answer to all her problems. But she'd never anticipated a problem like the one she was facing now.

She strolled past the locked front door of her restaurant. Glancing at the darkened windows, she saw a ghostly reflection of herself. She didn't look pregnant. She resembled her usual skinny self, her shoulders a bit too wide, the length of her legs emphasized by her black jeans, her breasts still small despite their recent inflation. Her face was pale, but then, only people who'd escaped San Francisco for a Hawaiian vacation weren't pale in February.

She continued down the street, passing boutiques, souvenir shops, an art gallery. A cable car clanged past her, practically empty since it was off-season for tourists. Near the end of the block she reached a combination bookshop and café. She frequently stopped in there to read her newspaper over a mocha latte. Her restaurant had its own gourmet coffee brewing constantly, but one of her favorite luxuries as a restaurateur was to have someone else prepare a drink or a snack for her.

She stepped inside the shop. The amber track lights warmed her, chasing away the morning's dreariness. Tables of artfully arranged books flanked the entry on either side of her. She had to weave past them to reach the walnut-paneled coffee bar at the rear of the store.

Unbuttoning her raincoat, she shook out her hair and released a long, weary breath. The table on her left featured an array of books on self-acceptance: *Love Yourself!, One Hundred Ways to Pamper Yourself, Healing the Inner You.* She grinned and contemplated browsing among the titles on that table before she left. Maybe they would teach her how to stop simmering with rage and frustration over the mess she was in.

She strode farther into the shop, and her gaze snagged on another pyramid of books, all of one novel: *The Unborn*. Not surprising that that particular title would jump out at her—especially since it was printed across the maroon dust jacket in eerily elongated silver lettering. Below the title, in letters slightly shorter but just as striking, was the author's name: Liam O'Neill.

Mallory had never heard of him. She wouldn't have even noticed the book if its title hadn't had particular relevance for her at the moment. It was obviously a horror novel, and she never read horror novels.

She walked determinedly past the table, heading for the coffee bar. A gale of laughter behind her caused her to spin around. She noticed a young couple, heads bowed together as they scanned a book of humorous cartoons. When she turned back toward the coffee bar, she saw him.

Stacked in that perfectly arranged pyramid, tier upon tier, multiple images of the author of *The Unborn* stared at her from the back covers of his book. She knew his eyes. She recognized his hair, too dark to be blond but too light to be brown, too long to be stylish but perfectly suited to him. His nose, with its intriguing bump near the bridge, and his chin, strong and angular enough to balance his nose. His mouth, hinting at a wistful smile, and his sad, proud eyes.

Oh, God. It was the man, the stranger.

The father of her baby.

LIAM O'NEILL SLAMMED the ax blade-down into the chopping block. He had split enough logs to last the rest of the winter. He had probably split enough to last the rest of the century, but that didn't matter.

What mattered was that he was sweaty and his lungs were heaving and the muscles in his back felt well used. What mattered was that he'd chopped enough wood to hold off the demons for another day.

He yanked a bandanna out of the hip pocket of his jeans and mopped his face. Fog banked in over the bluff, snagging in the needles of the wind-twisted pine and redwood that surrounded his property. He was hot now, but if he stayed outdoors much longer he'd be shivering.

He pulled the flannel shirt from the hook on the door to the shed, shoved his arms through the sleeves and scooped up the logs he'd split. He stacked most of them inside the shed—his woodpile rose nearly as high as his shoulders—and gathered what was left into his arms. Then he trudged across the yard, added the newly cut wood to the box on the back porch, and entered the kitchen, his thick-soled boots thudding hollowly against the plank floor.

He had built the cabin on top of an abandoned stone cellar. A carpenter in town had helped him, occasionally with a hammer and nails but mostly with his expert counsel. "You'll want your hall a little wider," he had pointed out. "You don't want to get claustrophobic, and a narrow hall will do that to you. Put your studs closer together—it'll make the house more solid. Triple-glazed windows may be overkill, but you'll save a lot in heating costs."

Liam hadn't cared about saving money. He'd cared only about the labor. He'd wanted to work, ceaselessly. He'd wanted to put his brain on hold and construct something physical, something that would last.

It took him a year to complete the house, working days. Nights, he worked on his demons.

For a hand-hewn cabin, his home had come out pretty well. His closest neighbors lived a quarter-mile down the road, and enough forest separated their house from his that he didn't need curtains for privacy. Whenever the coastal fog let up, sunlight streamed through his triple-glazed windows, which, combined with the wood-burning stove, kept his rooms so warm he never needed to rely on the backup furnace.

He scrubbed his hands at the sink, doused his face with water and filled a heavy ceramic mug with coffee from the pot he'd set up to brew earlier that morning. Once he'd downed some caffeine, he would hike down his long, unpaved driveway to the mailbox to pick up the two newspapers he was now subscribing to. He'd been receiving the local rag ever since he moved to the near-wilderness of northern Marin County. But a month ago, as part of his tentative return to the real world, he had started taking a San Francisco daily, as well. It had proved to be a smart move.

He used to be a news junkie, once. Back at Berkeley, he'd devoured the San Francisco and East Bay papers, the campus newspapers and all those goofball tabloids people were always handing out for free on Telegraph Avenue. He used to read every article, every word, even the classifieds. In those days, he had believed the human race was more interesting than any fiction.

He was trying to get back to that point. Five years was long enough—or so everyone kept telling him. But healing was a slow process. He was a cripple learning how to haul himself off the floor, how to take his first step, how to maintain his equilibrium.

He still stumbled a lot, but for the first time, he could almost picture himself back on his feet.

That week at the retreat had made the difference, he conceded, cupping his hands around his mug and gazing out through the kitchen window at the winter brown grass that stretched between his house and the woods, flattened beneath the oppressively dank air. The coffee's dark aroma floated up from the mug, invigorating him. He hadn't been aware of the scent of coffee before that week. He hadn't been aware of the heft of a mug in his hands, the weight of an ax arching over his head. He had been in a trance until then. For five long years he'd been among the walking dead. And if those few friends who hadn't been scared off by him hadn't urged him to go to the retreat, he might still be missing the simple pleasures of coffee and physical toil.

But for some reason he'd gone. Never in his wildest imaginings would he have pictured himself booking a reservation at a former ashram in Sonoma, taking a vow of silence, purging his soul. He had a pretty strange imagination, but it had never encompassed anything quite that far out.

Yet he'd done it, because nothing else had worked and he'd grown tired of his emotional paralysis. He couldn't say for sure that he'd been strengthened by the clear skies, the sharp coastal peaks and the pungent fragrance of the evergreen woods surrounding the retreat. He suspected that the freedom from having to listen to other people telling him things had helped. But what had truly cured him was...

The woman.

Mallory Powell.

He was still thinking about her two months later. Constantly. Obsessively. He recalled the way she used to charge the air whenever she entered a room, the way she moved like a dancer, or maybe a gymnast, her limbs slender and her face girlish. She wasn't outrageously beautiful. Some might not even find her pretty. But she had been riveting, her eyes green and gray, the color of the Pacific Ocean at dusk, her hair the color of the sky on a moonless night. She'd smelled of jasmine. She'd glowed with an inner luster, like a pearl. Wherever she'd been at the retreat, that was where he'd wanted to be, too.

The last night, he'd followed her. He had wanted to talk to her, but she was taking the retreat's vow-of-silence policy to heart. So he'd made love to her instead. Nothing in the rules of the retreat forbade that.

He wasn't sure what she had done to him, but she'd done *something*. Something that heightened his senses, brought him back to full consciousness, keyed him in to his feelings. Something that made him crazy with yearning whenever he thought about that wordless night, when the only sounds were the singing of the crickets and the hum of the wind and the sweet, choked gasp she'd made when her body had convulsed around him.

She'd left the retreat before dawn the next morning, and the desk had refused to tell him her name or anything about her. He'd had no idea whether he would ever see her again. But he was still driven by the need to be where she was.

And thanks to a society column photo in the San Francisco daily last week, he might actually be able to be with her once more.

The phone rang. Turning from the sink, he reached for the wall extension and lifted the receiver. "Hello?"

"Liam? It's Hazel. I didn't wake you, did I?"

Hazel was his agent in New York. A prim woman in her late fifties, she carried herself with the mildly addled air of a headmistress at an exclusive prep school for girls. But Liam knew her well enough not to be fooled. She was one of the sharpest literary agents in the business, and she was more than able to keep track of the time difference between her coast and Liam's.

"It's nine o'clock," he said, indulging her. "I've been up for hours."

"I get so confused," she said. He smiled. Nothing confused Hazel. "How's the new book coming?"

"It's coming." Liam knew she hadn't telephoned him to discuss his current work-in-progress. He never talked about his stories while he was shaping them. They were too dark, too dangerous. If they were exposed too soon, they might evaporate, like nightmares at dawn.

He sipped his coffee, waiting for Hazel to explain why she'd phoned. "I just got a call from Creighton," she reported, referring to Creighton Daggett, Liam's editor. "He says *The Unborn* is doing phenomenally. They're already going back for a second printing."

"The first print run was too low," he said.

"The first print run was fifty thousand higher than the print run for your last book. This one's flying off the shelves. According to Creighton, people are buzzing about how a certain horror writer up in Maine is looking over his shoulder and getting nervous."

Liam chuckled politely. He didn't really care how well his book sold, and he didn't consider himself in competition with other authors. He simply wrote his novels because he couldn't seem to do anything else, and then he shipped the manuscripts to Hazel, and then checks arrived in his mailbox.

The Unborn was his third horror novel. The first one was an abomination, a wretched excess of grotesque emotion, so awful he hadn't even considered showing it to anyone other than an old colleague of his from Berkeley. His friend had taken the manuscript home one night, and two weeks later had confessed to Liam that he'd sent it to his mother's roommate from college, Hazel Dupree, who just happened to be a literary agent in Manhattan.

Back then, Liam hadn't cared. He hadn't cared about the manuscript, about his friend's mother's college roommate, about publishers and earnings. He hadn't cared about anything.

But he'd kept writing, because it was either write or go even more insane than he already was. And the second book had come out better, and the third—*The Unborn*—better yet.

"The thing is," Hazel was saying, "Creighton says the publisher would really, really like it if you would do just the teeniest bit of promotion on this book."

"It's flying off the shelves," he reminded her. "What do they need me to do promotion for?"

"Nothing major," Hazel assured him. "Just a couple of newspaper interviews, maybe. A TV show or—"

"No."

"Liam. Just consider it, all right? You're on the cusp of superstardom—"

"I don't give a flying—" He caught himself and chose a less obscene phrase. "I don't give a damn about superstardom."

"And I know how you treasure your privacy. But this is the big time, Liam. The publisher wants to put everything it has behind your book. One of the things it has is you."

"I wrote the book. That ought to be enough."

"In this day and age, it rarely is. Just one TV show. Something local. One of the San Francisco stations. Think about it, Liam, would you? If it doesn't kill you, maybe you could do a second TV spot in L.A."

"No."

"The publisher would set everything up beforehand. There would be no hardball questions. Just fluff. You wouldn't have to answer anything you'd rather not talk about. Just push the book a little. San Francisco is a friendly town. They won't bite you."

"No."

"Did anyone ever tell you you were a hardheaded bastard?"

A smile that was really more a grimace twisted his mouth. Lots of people had called him a hardheaded bastard. Especially Jennifer. God, he missed her calling him that.

And he was not going to go on some happy-talk TV show and discuss her, or his past, or why he wrote such bleak, bone-chilling books.

"No, Hazel. Tell Creighton no."

"He's not going to be happy."

"It's not my job to make him happy. It's my job to write books that fly off the shelves. And it's your job to tell him no for me."

"All right. I'll tell him. The things I do for you," she muttered, laughter filtering through the receiver. What Liam was asking her to do wasn't so onerous, and they both knew it.

He said goodbye, hung up, took a long swig of coffee and thought about San Francisco. He thought about last week's newspaper. It had been crammed with the sort of stuff that filled most major city dailies: political intrigues, international unrest, gang shoot-outs, ethnic wars, terrorist bombings, everyday horrors that made his own fictions seem pathetically weak in comparison. He'd flipped through the pages, searching for something to boost his spirits. Somehow, he'd stumbled onto the society page.

He refilled his mug with coffee now and left the kitchen for the room where he wrote his books. It was a small, simple den with a desk, a computer, a supply cabinet and a wall taken up by floor-to-ceiling shelves that contained books far better written than any of his. On his desk, exactly where he'd left it, was the society page he had clipped out of last week's paper.

The article detailed a fund-raiser for the San Francisco Ballet. It was illustrated with black-and-white photographs of men dressed in tuxedos and women in haute couture gowns, artfully posed in groups and doing their darnedest to look as if they were having fun. The CEO of a hospital and his wife, Caterina. The president of a university and his wife, Suzanne. Investment broker Niles

Madison, his wife, Pamela, and their daughter, Caroline. Mallory Powell, owner of Mallory's on Union Square, and her fiancé Robert Benedict.

He set down his mug on the desk, lifted the article and stared at the photograph just as intensely as he'd stared at it the day he'd first seen it and every day since then. It featured a slim, elegant woman, her black hair flowing loosely past her shoulders, her face upturned, her smile unconvincing. She had on one of those black dresses that looked like lingerie, held up by two string-thin straps on her pale, angular shoulders. Her eyes were sharp, as if she saw more than she would ever admit. Her slender fingers rested on the arm of the mannequin-handsome man identified as Robert Benedict.

A low curse tore from Liam's throat. He'd recognized her the instant he'd seen the picture, and he'd spent the last week studying it, studying her and trying to figure out what to do. She was the woman from the retreat, the woman who had saved him, who had loved him, who one glorious night had denied him nothing but the sound of her voice. The woman who had fled before the sun had risen the next day, as if she'd been unable to face him. The woman who had run away without telling him her name.

Mallory Powell. Mallory Powell, owner of Mallory's— and her fiancé.

Still holding the newspaper clipping, he returned to the kitchen, lifted the phone receiver and punched in Hazel's number. Her secretary answered, and he demanded to speak to Hazel. His gaze veered back to the grainy photo in his hand, the photo of the woman who had found the life inside him and cut it loose.

The woman and her fiancé.

"Liam?" Hazel sounded bemused.

"Tell Creighton I'll do it."

"Do what?"

"I'll go to San Francisco," Liam said. "Tell him I'm going."

CHAPTER TWO

"OKAY, REUBEN, what have you got?" Mallory asked.

Reuben Cortes rolled up the rear door of his truck and beamed at her. "I got stuff you wouldn't expect to see in February," he said, his smile bright and tantalizing. He reached into the back of the truck and pulled out a small crate of portobello mushrooms. "This, you expected."

"This, I need," she told her produce supplier. Portobello mushrooms were a staple on her menu. Reuben had proved adept at keeping her supplied with them—as well as numerous other staples. He also brought her produce particular to the seasons, and sometimes he surprised her with out-of-season goodies that Mallory's could offer on its "Specials" menu. Mallory never knew the entire range of ingredients she was going to have at her command on any given day. Being flexible kept her fresh.

She didn't feel fresh today, though. She'd been awake for most of the night. Wishing to distract herself from her dilemma, she had foolishly started to read *The Unborn,* the novel by Liam O'Neill. She never should have bought it, and having bought it, she never should have read it. It was so scary she could only assume its author was seriously unbalanced.

And she was carrying that unbalanced man's baby.

The logical half of her brain insisted that she end her pregnancy as soon as she could. The emotional side of her brain—the side she tried not to pay much attention to—told her that, besides being the sexiest man she'd ever met, Liam

O'Neill was some sort of genius, if his novel was anything to judge by, and she wanted to keep his baby regardless of logic and common sense.

"I have greens here." Reuben's voice dragged her attention back to the alley, to his truck of goodies, to the distant rumble of traffic on the street and the chatter of her assistant chefs in the kitchen, their voices audible through the screened back door. Reuben lowered a crate of romaine into her arms. She passed it along to Burt, her kitchen manager, and he lugged the vegetables inside.

"Where's my surprise?" she asked, forcing enthusiasm into her voice. Wiry and energetic, Reuben was the best supplier she'd ever worked with. He relished springing his surprises on her, and usually she was thrilled by them. She didn't want to hurt his feelings by behaving less than eager.

"Patience, *bonita*." He unloaded carrots, squash, parsley, scallions. Mallory checked the items off on her inventory list and passed the bags and crates along to her squad of kitchen workers. Onions. New potatoes. Peppers from Central America. Garlic from a farm south of San Jose. These were the winter vegetables she was used to working with.

Reuben paused, as if to signal he was finished delivering her order. Mallory played along as best she could. "Okay, Reuben. I guess that'll do it for today."

"I guess so," he answered, his dark eyes glinting with amusement. "Except for this." He reached deep into the back of the truck and produced a small wooden crate of tomatoes. Not winter hothouse tomatoes, those pinkish spheres as hard as tennis balls, but real, red, sun-ripened beefsteaks, so fresh she could still smell the vine on their stems.

"Oh, my God. Where did you get these?" The sight of such delicious-looking tomatoes in February was enough to jolt Mallory out of her fatigue.

"Don't ask. I had to sell my sister to get them."

"They're gorgeous! Is this all I can have?" She estimated that there were only about three dozen tomatoes in the box.

"Don't be greedy. You should worship the ground I walk on, getting these for you."

"You're right. I should." She kissed Reuben's cheek. "You're a sweetheart. I'll try to buy your sister back for you."

"Don't do me any favors." He grinned wickedly and stretched up to slide the truck's rear door back into place. "I'll see you tomorrow."

After she waved goodbye to Reuben, she carried the tray of tomatoes into the kitchen. The room was already bustling; Burt was overseeing the simmering stocks that would form the bases for her sauces, and an assistant chef was sorting through the vegetables Reuben had delivered. Everyone in the kitchen wore white linen toques and tunics, starched and as yet unstained. Laboring within the room's spotless walls, surrounded by stainless-steel surfaces and illuminated by bright overhead lighting, Mallory's staff looked almost like medical personnel presiding over a surgery.

The atmosphere of the kitchen, however, was more playful than one would expect in an operating room. The small stereo in the corner was blasting out the latest Pearl Jam CD, and two young apprentices, fresh out of culinary school, were flirting with each other as they filleted the salmon and albacore Burt had picked up at the wharf earlier that morning.

An awed silence descended upon the room as first one and then another of Mallory's assistants noticed the gorgeous tomatoes she was carrying. "Mother Mary," Burt whispered with exaggerated reverence. "Who'd you kill to get those?"

"I didn't kill anyone. Reuben sold his sister," Mallory answered, setting the small crate on a counter and hiding her weariness behind a smile.

"He should have sold his mother, too," Burt remarked, studying the case intently. Plump and boyish, Burt looked like the kid brother Mallory would have loved to have had—quick on his toes despite his bulk, and mentally just as agile. As Mallory's second-in-command, Burt ran the kitchen and kept the other chefs organized, freeing Mallory for the creative work of assembling each day's ingredients into unique menus. "There aren't enough tomatoes here to do anything useful with."

"I'm sure we can think of something," she said.

"A sauce?"

The two apprentices booed loudly. Mallory laughed. She agreed with their assessment. To waste such fresh, firm tomatoes by stewing them into a sauce would be sacrilegious.

"Well, you haven't got enough to use them in salads," Burt said, justifying his suggestion.

"How about we slice them into thin wedges and garnish each entrée with a wedge?"

Burt eyed the exposed sprinkler pipes overhead, and then the other cooks in the kitchen. "See?" he boomed. "That's why this place is called *Mallory's* and not *Burt's*. She's brilliant, ladies and gentlemen."

Ordinarily, Burt's teasing amused her. But she was too exhausted to feel amused right now, too troubled, too queasy. The bright red of the tomatoes made something clutch in her belly. Too little sleep and too much worry combined to cause her stomach to roil.

No, it wasn't too little sleep or too much worry. The same problem that provoked her insomnia and her worry was causing her nausea now. Mallory was suffering from morning sickness.

Gritting her teeth, she managed to fake another smile as she ducked out of the kitchen. A short hall led to her private office and the staff bathroom. She headed directly into the lavatory and locked the door behind her.

The queasiness began to ebb. Her head stopped swimming; her knees stopped trembling. Bracing herself against the sink, she peered into the mirror above it and grimaced. Her complexion was the color of skim milk, and her eyes were framed in gray shadows. Her hair hung in a limp braid down her back, emphasizing the hollows in her cheeks. Wasn't a woman supposed to gain weight when she was pregnant? Mallory had lost two pounds in the past two days. Not surprising, given her utter lack of an appetite.

When a crate of mouth-watering tomatoes could make a woman feel like throwing up, the situation was obviously dire. She was going to have to pull herself together and do what had to be done. Soon. Now.

Sighing, she filled a paper cup with water and drank it in small, controlled sips. When she was sure the water wasn't going to return on her, she took a deep breath and exited the bathroom. There, standing in the doorway to her office, was Robert Benedict.

Damn. She hadn't realized things could get any worse.

Robert's attire informed her he'd come directly from his office. The suit was Armani, the tie Dior, the shoes Bally. On Robert, the executive uniform looked right. He had the height and polished looks to carry it off. Indeed, on those rare occasions when he dressed down, he always seemed kind of uncomfortable to Mallory.

Of course, his elegant apparel pointed up her own drab appearance. Cooking was a messy business, and under her tunic she wore a plain cotton shirt and machine-washable khakis. But one of the things that made Robert the perfect husband for her was that he didn't care about what she wore to work—or, for that matter, where she worked or when. Running a restaurant entailed long, erratic hours.

Mallory was never going to have a normal routine, punching in at nine and out at five so she could be home for dinner with her husband or available to go out with him on a moment's notice. To her father, this was a grievous flaw, but Robert didn't seem to mind.

"Have you got a minute?" he asked, flashing her a smile that could melt the polar caps.

"Sure." Her own smile, no doubt, could curdle cream. She was relieved that Robert didn't comment on it.

He stepped aside to let her enter her office ahead of him. It was a utilitarian room barely big enough for her desk, a computer and a couple of chairs. The walls were decorated with framed certificates lauding Mallory's accomplishments as a chef, and photographs of some of her more elaborate creations. She sank into her upholstered desk chair and tried not to glance at the photograph on the opposite wall of a crabmeat mousse surrounded by plum tomatoes. For some reason, tomatoes triggered adverse reactions in her stomach that morning.

She leaned back in her chair, trying to position herself so the window wouldn't throw the morning light directly onto her face. She knew she looked like hell. She would prefer if Robert didn't notice.

Luck wasn't with her. "Are you okay? You look ghastly," he said.

She smiled feebly. "Just an upset stomach."

"I've been worried about you. You've sounded funny on the phone, too."

"I'm not feeling my best. But I'll be over it soon." *If I ever get my act together,* she added silently.

Apparently her vague explanation was enough for Robert. He settled into the chair across the desk from her, stretching his legs and beaming beatifically. He was a remarkably handsome man. People often pointed this out to Mallory, as if they suspected that she lacked the taste to appreciate his smooth, high forehead, his arrow-straight nose, his perfectly groomed brown hair and practiced smile. Her friend Courtney once described him as "John Kennedy-esque." Her cousin Kate had said he reminded her of one of the emergency-room doctors on a popular TV hospital drama. "You know, the one with no morals," she had elaborated.

Mallory was in no position to judge anyone's morals. "So," she said, putting as much energy as she could into her voice. "What brings you here?"

"The folks from the Hong Kong consortium flew in yesterday. I'm spending the day showing them some investment possibilities. I'm supposed to meet them at the Mark Hopkins in a half hour." He glanced at the gold watch adorning his wrist, then returned his smile to Mallory. "I thought I'd stop by on my way and say hello. We haven't seen each other in a while."

Mallory knew better than to believe Robert had stopped by to say hello. It was typical for her and her fiancé to go for days, sometimes weeks, without seeing each other. In fact, she believed the principal reason their relationship flourished was that they didn't need each other's constant company. They didn't crave it. They liked each other, enjoyed each other, and survived rather nicely without each other.

Mallory assumed that for some people, true love was a fine thing. But she simply couldn't imagine it for herself. Her mother had died when she was only four, and her father had seemed content to immerse himself in his work, rebuilding the Powell fortunes. That was where he found his satisfaction—not in love but in work. Her cousin Megan had been in love with that turkey Edward Whitney, and he'd jilted her. And what had seemed the most perfect love match—her aunt Grace's marriage to Jeffrey DeWilde—had ended after thirty-two years.

Really, what was the point in all that messy emotion? Robert was clever, he was acceptable to her father, and he respected Mallory. Passion didn't have to be a part of it. When a woman got caught up in passion . . . terrible things happened.

Like unplanned pregnancies.

"Actually," Robert said, sidling toward his real reason for visiting the restaurant, "there was something I wanted to talk to you about."

Mallory encouraged him with a nod.

"I was wondering..." If his smile grew any brighter, she would need her sunglasses. "Would it be a big problem if we moved the wedding date up to, oh, say, September?"

"September?" she blurted out, jerking upright. "You're kidding, aren't you?"

"Umm . . . no, I wasn't kidding."

"September? Robert, you can't be serious! We've got the St. Francis booked for December 28, remember? We've got everything reserved for then!"

"I'm sure they'd return the deposits—"

"Who cares about the deposits? We'd never be able to find another place so soon. Besides, there's so much planning to do. Aunt Grace would die if she didn't have the time to plan the wedding adequately."

"Aunt Grace isn't the one getting married," Robert pointed out, a hint of steel behind his velvet tone.

"Aunt Grace is still in shock over the way her son eloped and denied her the opportunity to plan his wedding. I can't deprive her now. She's got all these fittings for my gown lined up, and..." Mallory groaned. In all honesty, she would be just as happy to buy one of those cotton Mexican wedding dresses and exchange her vows with Robert under a tree in Golden Gate Park. But Powells didn't do things that way. They had an obligation, as members of the city's social aristocracy, to put on a grand and extremely expensive show when the occasion was as significant as a wedding.

September was out of the question. Mallory and Robert had agreed to wed right after Christmas. She had thought the holiday atmosphere would add romance to the occasion, and he had liked the tax ramifications of being able to file jointly for the entire fiscal year, even though he would be married for only a few days of that year.

She couldn't begin to calculate the tax ramifications of a September wedding. As for romantic, how romantic could a woman in her ninth month of pregnancy be?

Cripes. If she didn't take care of business soon, by September she'd be as big as an eighteen-wheeler. Wouldn't that make for a fine wedding? Aunt Grace would have to have one of her designers fashion a maternity gown for Mallory, who would waddle down the aisle and probably go into labor in the middle of the service....

"What's so funny?" Robert asked.

Nothing. Nothing in the world was funny, and Mallory struggled to erase her smile. "September is out of the question, Robert. My father would never—"

"It was your father's idea."

"What?"

"He and I were talking the other day about the Drew Financial Services acquisition he's been working on. Everything's going to be in place by the end of December, and then January 2, he's going to announce the acquisition. Things are going to be hectic, Mal. It's just not a good time for you and me to go traipsing off on a honeymoon. Your father is going to need me here in town." Robert's smile was almost smug.

Mallory couldn't blame him for taking pride in his position as her father's right-hand man. Leland Powell was a major player—arguably *the* major player—in San Francisco's financial world, and Robert had worked hard to earn his place at Leland's side. He'd put in the hours and done the drone work. Even now he accepted such menial tasks as chauffeuring a group of Hong Kong businessmen around town all day, doing whatever it took to add a chunk of California real estate to their international portfolios. Robert deserved everything he'd achieved at Powell Enterprises.

But it rankled to think he had discussed his honeymoon with her father before he'd discussed it with her. Robert and her father talked all the time, every day, taking great delight in sharing strategies and analyzing business decisions. They didn't have to plan Mallory's honeymoon, too, did they?

"I can't get married in September," she said tersely. It might well turn out that she couldn't get married at all, if she didn't do something to remedy her situation—a situation that was her own fault, not Robert's. She couldn't resent him for the pressure she was under.

She could resent him for rearranging her wedding with her father behind her back, though. She glowered at his finely chiseled features, his impeccable clothing, his annoying self-assurance. She had agreed to marry him, to make him as vital to the Powell family as he was to the Powell family fortune. But she wasn't going to let him railroad her.

"It really would make life easier," he noted.

"Not for me, it wouldn't."

His smile faded slightly. "I know January is your slow period here at the restaurant. But how would you feel if I had to call your father three times a day during our honeymoon?"

"How do you think I'd feel?" she snapped. She would feel lousy. She would feel neglected. She would feel, as she had occasionally felt during the months Robert had put a serious effort into courting her, that he was marrying her out of convenience, not out of love.

But wasn't convenience why she was marrying him, too? Hadn't she accepted his proposal because she knew he would never ask her to change, or to abandon her restaurant, or to be something she wasn't? And because her father approved of Robert, maybe—God willing—he might eventually approve of her, too.

It suddenly struck her as quite sad. She wished real love could happen to her, everlasting, blinding, irrational love. Love that approached the passion she'd felt one crazy night at the retreat—only she would feel it for someone she knew, someone she cared about, someone who was actually a part of her life. Someone who didn't write novels about murder and revenge.

She had long ago given up on ever experiencing a love like that. Maybe some women were lucky enough to create that kind of bond with a man, but Mallory was thirty years old, and she wasn't expecting any miracles.

She closed her eyes, willing her anger away. As it waned, another emotion took its place, something warm and delicate and oddly surprising. Maybe she wasn't expecting a miracle, but a miracle had occurred, anyway. A different kind of love, flowing out instead of in, a love that demanded to be given, not received. Mother love.

No. She couldn't let herself think that way. She couldn't afford to feel maternal. She couldn't wreck her life over such a foolish sentiment.

Yet it soothed her, transforming her red rage into cool blues and greens that washed through her, tranquilizing her. Who cared whether she got married in September or December? Who cared if she got married at all? She was going to have a baby.

"Mallory?"

Her eyes flew open and she forced them to focus on Robert.

"I thought you were falling asleep on me."

"Just thinking," she said.

"About September?"

"About..." *Don't do anything rash,* her mind clamored, but the words pressed against her lips regardless, anxious to be voiced. "About whether maybe we ought to put the wedding on hold."

Oh, God. She'd said it. She'd actually said it.

And it had sounded . . . reasonable.

Robert appeared nonplussed. He shifted in his chair and cleared his throat. "Put our wedding on hold? Until after New Year's, you mean?"

There went his tax ramifications, Mallory thought with a small grin. "Put it on hold indefinitely."

"Now, Mallory, let's not get drastic here. All I did was make a suggestion. Obviously, you don't like it. If you really want the wedding after Christmas, that's when we'll have it."

"I'm serious, Robert. Maybe we ought to reconsider the whole idea."

"Oh, come on." His tone was heavy with irritation. "One thing I've always admired about you is that you don't throw tantrums. I really think—"

"*I* really think I've got to think," she said, feeling more and more certain that she was doing the right thing, that having this baby would make her happier than marrying Robert. It was insane, and surely she would snap out of this strange, blissful mood soon enough. But as she spoke the words, as she contemplated the idea, her queasiness vanished and her strength returned.

"Mallory. We've known each other for years. What more do you need to think about? We're a match made in heaven."

"I don't know," she said, not wanting to hurt him. She had already shocked him to the point where he was almost as pale as she was. If she told him she had engaged in an inexplicable fling with a stranger in December and gotten pregnant as a result, he might faint dead away. "Look, Robert, I've got things to do. So do you. Your Hong Kong clients are waiting for you."

He checked his watch again and winced. "We're not done, Mal. We obviously need to talk."

"Yes." She rose to her feet when he did. He hesitated before dropping a light kiss on her cheek, as if he feared she no longer loved him.

She *did* love him, in her own peculiar way. She loved his dependability, his steadiness, his refusal to stand in her path. She loved his courtly manners and his rapport with her father. So what if he didn't ignite fires inside her? She'd known what those fires could feel like. She'd felt their heat once, and look where it had gotten her.

She would come to her senses soon. This wedding would happen. Gazing up into Robert's troubled brown eyes, she offered him a smile, wishing she could reassure him.

Wishing she could reassure herself.

FROM THE SMALL TERRACE outside his room at the Hyatt Regency, Liam could see the bay beyond the Embarcadero Freeway. The water was the color of a turquoise stone. It shouldn't have been that blue, not on an overcast day, not in February.

The sight might have transfixed him if he didn't have other things on his mind. Four times since he'd checked in, Hazel had telephoned him, running coast-to-coast interference because she didn't trust him to speak civilly to Creighton Daggett and the publisher's public relations people in California. Two newspaper interviews had been lined up for tomorrow, he'd been scheduled to appear on a local television talk show, and book signings had been arranged in San Francisco, Oakland and Berkeley.

The thought of returning to Berkeley ought to have preoccupied him. But the telephone calls, the rush-rush plans, the extraordinary fact that a mere week after he'd told Hazel he would do some promotion, he was in a hotel room in downtown San Francisco with a view of the bay...

There was only one view he wanted to see, one person he wanted to talk to.

He abandoned the terrace and went back into his room. The phone was ringing again, but he ignored it, moving directly to the desk and yanking the telephone directory from the drawer. There, in the yellow pages under "Restaurants," he found Mallory's, on Powell Avenue.

It was three-thirty. He didn't know whether the restaurant would be open yet, and he didn't care. For the first time since...God, practically since forever, he was smiling. Looking forward to something. Thinking about a woman who wasn't dead. Thinking about sex.

He ran a comb through his shaggy hair, grabbed his leather jacket from the back of a chair and pocketed his room key. In the mirror he looked like himself—a bear crossed with a lion, fierce and untamable. But that hadn't bothered her at the retreat. She hadn't objected at all to his crooked nose and his jutting chin and the way his hair defied him, lying every which way, and the way he held himself in, always prepared to defend himself against pain, always ready to pounce before he was pounced upon. She hadn't objected one bit.

Recalling the way she hadn't objected, he felt a stirring below his belt.

He pointedly reminded himself that she was engaged to be married. The society photo in the newspaper had identified the man with her as her fiancé. Robert Benedict, a well-dressed, well-pressed escort, no doubt rich and stable and sane. A man who could bring her all kinds of happiness, which was more than Liam could ever do.

So what? If that night at the retreat had been even remotely as magnificent to her as it had been to him, she would want to see him again. Damn it, *he* had to see *her* again, if only to prove to himself that he hadn't dreamed the whole thing.

He rode the elevator down through the central atrium of the hotel. He wasn't used to hotels, or cities, or civilization in general. In a former lifetime, he would have felt at ease in such surroundings. He didn't exactly feel uneasy now. He just felt detached, as if the potted trees and the sky-lights and the boxy sofas and marble floors were flat scenery, a video arcade game in which he was the protagonist journeying across the screen.

Mallory had made him feel three-dimensional. For those few wordless days they'd shared at the retreat, for that one intense night, she had made him feel whole. He hadn't even had to know her name to come alive in her presence.

The hell with her fiancé. Liam wanted her to make him whole again.

The doorman summoned a cab for him, and he stuffed a bill into the guy's hand. The cab navigated the steep roads to Union Square, climbing up and down San Francisco's famed hills. At last they reached the urban park cutting a rectangle out of one of the city's prime neighborhoods. Elegant department stores and boutiques huddled around the park. Chic women and men strode purposefully along the sidewalks. It was too chilly for anyone to linger and browse.

After paying the driver, Liam got out and looked around. Mallory's stood facing away from the square, its front door overlooking the heavy traffic of the street.

His heart drummed, loud but steady in his chest. He assessed his mental state and decided he wasn't worried. He would walk into the place and see her, and if she didn't recognize him...

If she didn't recognize him, he would assume the world had come to an end. There was no way she would fail to recognize him. No way she would look at him and not feel the gut-deep charge, the surge of awareness, the magnetic pull. It wasn't something either of them had had any control over in December. He saw no reason to believe they could control it now.

Straightening his shoulders, he stalked down the street to Mallory's, feeling an affinity for the brave meteorologists who flew airplanes into the eyes of hurricanes. Liam knew that if he saw her, if he touched her, he would get sucked into the storm, tossed by it, blown to bits. Yet he couldn't stop himself. He needed to feel as much as he'd felt that one night.

A young man—practically a boy, really—stood at a podium inside the restaurant's front door. He was dressed in a green silk shirt and black jeans, his hair a tight nap of curls covering his head. "May I help you?" he asked in dulcet tones.

Liam surveyed the entry, the walls covered in silk the same green as the maître d's shirt, the floor a veined gray marble that opened into an expanse of black carpet beyond the inner doorway. A black ceramic urn stood in one corner, holding what appeared to be stalks of dried wheat.

It had been years since Liam's last visit to a fancy restaurant. He occasionally went to Smitty's in town for a burger and a beer, but nothing like this. For all he knew, urns filled with wheat were de rigueur at all the high-class eateries these days.

"I'd like a table for one," he told the kid.

"Do you have a reservation?"

"No."

"I'm afraid all our tables are reserved for this evening. If you'd like to wait and see if someone cancels...but that hardly ever happens," the kid said, less boastful than matter-of-fact.

"Have you got a bar? Could I buy a drink?"

"Well, we do have a small lounge, but—"

"Fine. I'll go sit in the lounge." He knew he was coming across as gruff and stubborn, but he didn't care. He wasn't here to impress a postpubescent bouncer. He was here to see Mallory Powell. Which, he supposed, would be easier to do if he simply stormed the kitchen. But God knew, he didn't want to scare her into a bad reaction. There were sharp knives in restaurant kitchens. He had to exercise caution.

The young maître d' seemed miffed, but he reluctantly pointed out a cozy area just inside the door where a few low-slung leather sofas nestled among more urns filled with wheat stalks. Liam nodded his thanks and entered the lounge. The sofa was lower than he'd realized; he nearly lost his balance as he sat.

A cocktail waitress approached, smiling deferentially. "Can I get you something?" she asked.

He asked for an Anchor Steam beer.

The waitress seemed in no hurry to leave. "You look familiar, but I don't think I've ever met you before. Have you been here recently?"

He shook his head, not wishing to get into a conversation with her—and definitely not wishing to consider himself familiar-looking. He assumed the waitress had seen that photo of him on the back of his books. He'd fought against having his picture put on the dust jackets, but Creighton and his crew had prevailed. Liam had refused to go to a professional photography studio for the portrait, however. He'd had a friend take a snapshot of him.

Smiling impassively at the waitress, he repeated his request for an Anchor Steam.

She took the hint and backed off, her gaze remaining on him until she reached the sleek black bar at the opposite end of the lounge. She spoke to the bartender, who glanced over at Liam and frowned in thought, then smiled and murmured something to her.

Oh, great. Terrific. Who would have thought Mallory's would be the meeting place for the San Francisco chapter of the Liam O'Neill fan club?

Liam had wanted to remain anonymous, at least until
he'd checked out Mallory's establishment, gotten a feel for
it—and maybe gotten a feel for her before he actually saw
her. He had wanted to lie low and sip a beer, maybe eat
some of her food—assuming it involved more than wheat
stalks—before he took her in his arms and said, "I need
you. I need to feel the way you made me feel. I need to
know I'm still alive, and you're the only woman who can
prove to me that I am."

If nothing else, he wanted to talk to her. He wanted to
hear her voice, hear her speak his name, hear her tell him
that she had needed him as much as he'd needed her that
night, that he hadn't been insane to believe something special had occurred between them, something as essential to
her as it had been to him.

The bartender accompanied the waitress across the
lounge to where Liam was sitting. "You're Liam O'Neill,
the author, aren't you," he said.

Liam swore under his breath. "Yes," he muttered. He
didn't want to be gawked at. It wasn't as if he were a movie
star or a politician or anyone worthy of note. He was a re-
cluse, a hermit, arguably psychotic, and he was currently
fixated on a woman he hardly knew, a woman who might
be appalled to discover him drinking a beer in her restaurant. He didn't want to make happy talk with these people.

After a moment, they retreated. The bartender smiled as
if to say, *No problem—we'll leave you alone.* The waitress
waltzed through a swinging door into the kitchen.

Mallory might be in there. The waitress might be shouting to everyone, including Mallory, that Liam O'Neill was
right that minute sipping an Anchor Steam in the lounge.
Not that his name would mean anything to her. If she'd
read his earlier books, she would have recognized him at the
retreat, but she clearly hadn't had any idea who he was,
other than a drifting soul who had tethered himself to her,

anchored himself, become solid and human in her arms. As far as she was concerned, Liam O'Neill could be anyone—which was the same as being no one.

So he knew that whoever had cracked the kitchen door open a half inch but remained behind it, in the shadows, peeking out at him, couldn't possibly be Mallory Powell.

CHAPTER THREE

SHE KNEW. NOT CONSCIOUSLY, but in some dark, dangerous part of her soul, she knew he would be waiting for her. Surely his appearance at Mallory's hadn't been a coincidence. People didn't come to Mallory's for a beer.

Or two beers. Two beers that he'd managed to nurse for hours. She'd been certain that he would invade the kitchen once he'd finished his first beer, or at the very least buttonhole some of the waiters and interrogate them about her, but he hadn't. He had only sat on the couch, his eyes hard, his hands wrapped around the frosty brown glass of the beer bottle, his glass ignored on the cocktail table before him.

She had risked a couple of glimpses through the kitchen door after Cynthia had romped inside and announced to the cooks that none other than Liam O'Neill, the horror novelist, had just ordered an Anchor Steam in the lounge. Several of the waiters had never heard of Liam O'Neill, and Burt had sniffed haughtily about the tawdry state of publishing, when a writer of spine-chilling trash like O'Neill could be treated like a celebrity. Mallory had peered through the porthole window in the door in time to see him drain the second bottle and place it carefully on the table. Then he'd stood, stretched his lean, strong body and pulled several bills from his wallet. After leaving the money on the table by the empty bottle and the unused glass, he'd departed.

Mallory knew better than to assume that once he was out of her restaurant he would be out of her life. Perhaps he had a dinner date somewhere else; perhaps he'd checked out her menu and decided nothing looked appetizing. Perhaps he thought the place was overpriced.

Whatever his reason for leaving, it didn't alter the fact that he'd found her. For some reason, he had gone to the effort of tracking her down. And now that he knew where she was, he would be back.

She tried to put thoughts of him out of her mind as she oversaw the kitchen and prepared her entrées during the dinner crunch. But God, what a day it had been: the tomatoes, her first hint of morning sickness, Robert's unwelcome visit, his attempt to change their wedding plans, her transient whim about scrapping the wedding altogether.

And then this: Liam O'Neill. In San Francisco. In her restaurant. In her world, in her life. In her way.

She insisted on sending everyone home and closing the restaurant by herself. The demand didn't spark anyone's curiosity; she was often the last person to leave Mallory's at the end of a long day. But tonight, closing up the restaurant was only a delaying strategy. She was going to have a confrontation with Liam O'Neill sooner or later. Even if he wasn't waiting for her outside the restaurant tonight, he would be back tomorrow, or the next day. Or he would ferret out her home address. Or he would learn about her weekly TV appearance on "What's Up?", and he would barge in on her at the studio. One way or another, she was going to have to deal with him, face-to-face.

Logic told her he *might* be outside the restaurant that night. Instinct told her he *was* outside. As she locked the cash and credit-card receipts into the safe for tomorrow's bank run, as she double-checked the walk-in refrigerator and the ovens, as she turned off the lights one by one throughout the dining hall, the lounge, her office and the

kitchen, she discerned Liam O'Neill's nearness, almost as
if he were a fragrance, a rare scent only Mallory could
identify. She felt his presence the way she'd felt it at the retreat, subliminally. Her nervous system quivered with the
unwelcome knowledge that he was somewhere close by. The
skin at the nape of her neck tingled. Her pulse thumped.
Heat seeped through her muscles, making them feel heavy.

It had been that way with him right from the start. Before she'd known his name, who he was, what he did...
Practically from the moment she had arrived at the retreat, she had felt connected to him, on his wavelength,
picking up his signals. She hadn't wanted to, but it had been
beyond her control.

Beyond his, too, she suspected. Why else would he have
bothered to seek her out in San Francisco? He was a horror novelist, for heaven's sake. Surely he enjoyed a rich,
rewarding life. He didn't have to amuse himself by tracking her down. He could have consigned her to his memory,
filed under "One-Night Stands," and let it go at that. She
wasn't about to slap him with a paternity suit.

In fact, she wasn't even going to let him know that paternity was an issue between them. She was going to call Dr.
Gilman and take care of the Liam O'Neill paternity crisis
without involving him. It was her choice, her life, and she
wasn't going to give him—a perfect stranger—the option of
meddling in her personal decisions. He wasn't going to
know about it at all.

Surely he had no idea of the consequences of their tryst.
He had to have come after Mallory for another reason.
Perhaps that pull, that connection, that instinct—whatever it was—that had drawn them to each other at the retreat was drawing him to her now.

She could still remember the first time she'd felt the attraction. It had crept up from behind and wrapped around
her, an immutable force that scared her but intrigued her
even more. She had thought, the morning after they'd

made love, that if she raced home to San Francisco before she saw him again, she would be free, cured of the mindless passion that had briefly overtaken her.

Silly thought. Knowing that Liam had found her made her wonder if she would ever be cured. Her reluctance to let Dr. Gilman take care of her condition made her wonder, too. Ending her pregnancy would put the entire affair in the past for good. It would release her from the most calamitous result of Liam's hold on her. She didn't want him in her life. She never had.

A man was the last thing she'd been looking for when she drove to the retreat last December. Quite the contrary. She had been seeking a respite from the whirlwind of wedding plans that kept buffeting her and blowing her down. She didn't want to think about marriage, or love, or Robert, or her father, or any other man.

The retreat—a collection of low, rustic buildings, hiking trails and gardens hidden within the woods of northern Sonoma County—had been built as an ashram in the seventies. Idealistic hippies had gathered there to practice meditation and live communally. In the eighties, a charismatic con artist had taken over the retreat, ripped off his followers and absconded to Nepal two steps ahead of the feds. A group of Trappists had taken title to the property and converted it into a monastery. Somewhere along the way, taking a vow of silence had become one of the requirements for entrance.

A few years ago, the monastery was purchased by a private outfit and turned into a secular retreat, but the vow of silence remained. Lay people discovered the therapeutic benefit of escaping from their rat-race lives for a few days and listening to nothing but soothing music, the whispers of their hearts and the wind in the trees. Word spread around the Bay Area that spending a few days at the retreat was more salubrious than six years on the couch unloading to a psychiatrist, more invigorating than body massage and aromatherapy at an exclusive health spa, more relaxing than locking oneself into a closet and listening repeatedly to the *Chant* CD.

By last December, Mallory was strung tighter than a zither. What with her wedding to plan, and the pressures of her recent contract with "What's Up?", the still-raw shock of Aunt Grace's separation from Jeffrey DeWilde and her father's subtle disapproval of her for not being the executive-minded child he'd always wanted, she was desperate to get away for a while. When she'd heard about the retreat in Sonoma, she had liked the sound of it. *Retreat* was precisely what she wanted. She made a reservation, packed a small bag and headed north, promising her loved ones she would be back in four days.

The silence of the property had enveloped her as soon as she turned the engine off and climbed out of her Saab in the unpaved parking lot. She heard nothing but the breeze and the ancient creaking of the sequoias towering in a wall-like perimeter around the cluster of buildings. In contrast to the quiet, her sneakers sounded deafening against the loose gravel of the lot as she crossed to the main building, a low, Asian-inspired structure of pine, glass and cedar.

In the outer room she checked in, signing not only the registration card but also a written pledge not to speak on penalty of expulsion from the retreat. The clerk took an imprint of her credit card, and then a mute staff member led Mallory out of the main building and through a courtyard to her guest room, an austere square cell with pale walls, straw matting on the floor, a lamp, a three-drawer dresser and a narrow bed.

Not much more than the Trappist monks would have enjoyed, she thought with a smile. She hadn't come here for luxuries, though. She had access to more luxury than she could ever want in San Francisco.

The retreat had offered her what she couldn't find in the city: Tranquillity. Serenity. Refuge.

Liam O'Neill.

The first time she saw him was right after she'd unpacked her few belongings into the chest of drawers and
wandered across the courtyard into one of the common
rooms. The hushed lilt of a flute curled through the air. A
few people were seated here and there on the carpeted floor.
A couple of people stood. A barefoot woman performed a
private ballet, her eyes closed.

Typical California weirdness, Mallory thought with a
smile . . . and then she saw him.

She couldn't have pinpointed exactly what it was that
pulled her attention to the man seated in the darkest corner of the room, his back against the wall, one leg extended along the floor and the other drawn up so he could
rest his forearm across his knee. But the instant their eyes
met she felt something click inside her, a light switch snapping on and illuminating her from within. The light burned,
igniting a tremor of sensation along her nerve endings.

Who was he?

Just a man, she told herself. Just another guest at the retreat, someone who, like her, had handed over a credit card
and signed a pledge of silence. Although he was seated on
the floor, he gave the impression of largeness—not bulging muscle or fearsome height, but a powerful solidity that
made him impossible to ignore. He had a face that could
have been carved out of stone—not marble but granite,
something harsh and unforgiving. His hair was the color of
the dried wheat with which she decorated her restaurant, a
mix of blond and brown with a few strands of white; the
man looked as if he'd managed to avoid a hair stylist for at
least a decade. His eyes were metallic, gray and gold, re-
flective but not the least bit welcoming. He wore a thick
flannel shirt and faded jeans.

He could have been a lumberjack resting after a hard day
of felling trees with a chain saw in the surrounding forest.
But Mallory assumed he was someone like her, someone

who needed to cleanse his system of all the stresses the real world had imposed on him. He looked angry, even desolate, yet she sensed a glimmer of hope in his gaze as it met hers across the airy room.

They didn't have words with which to get acquainted. All they had was that peculiar, demanding awareness of each other. In what was either the most sensible or the most foolish act she had ever committed, she walked across the room and lowered herself onto the floor next to him. There they sat, listening to the translucent song of the flute, feeling the nearness of each other.

She soon discovered that she would experience the same reaction every time she was in a room with him: the heat, the tremor along her nerves, the erotic thrill of being in the presence of this man. Even if her eyes were closed, she would know the instant he entered a room, or a garden, or a glade where she was relaxing. She could practically calculate his distance from her and visualize his movement toward her. Whenever they found themselves in the same place, they wound up together, side by side, sitting or walking or finding a comfortable position in which to meditate. At meals, they would dine facing each other across the long picnic-style tables. They would watch each other eat. They would smile at each other, and search each other's eyes, and lower their silverware at exactly the same time.

Mallory had never had any dealings with men like him. As the daughter of Leland Powell, she generally socialized with business executives with pristine pedigrees. At the restaurant, she worked with funky, spunky young guys, dramatic types, epicurean artists and part-time students.

Rough-hewn lumberjacks? Never.

There was something almost palpably sexual in the way he looked at her, in the way she responded to his looking at her. It took all her strength not to speak whenever his gaze merged with hers. If she hadn't signed the pledge of silence, she would have told him...she wasn't sure what. Maybe to stop looking at her and keep his distance. Maybe to look deeper, to move closer, to yield to the strange force that bound them together.

Yet without the luxury of speech, they still knew how to find each other among the sprawl of buildings, at the art studio, in the library, on the hiking trails, in the gym. When they were with each other, they said with their eyes what they couldn't say in words. When they were apart, in their own rooms at night, Mallory would dream of him, picturing his broad shoulders, his sleek chest, his long, athletic legs...imagining what his hands would feel like against her skin, what his mouth would feel like against hers.

She had never considered herself particularly lustful; her lovemaking with Robert had always seemed rather neat and precise. She didn't mind it, but she didn't consider it terribly exciting, either. In her dreams about the stranger, sex *was* exciting—so exciting that when she met him in the dining hall for breakfast the following morning, she would feel herself blush.

So what if she did? Once she left the retreat, her fantasies would be history. She wasn't going to apologize for indulging in daydreams about the man. And that was all it was: fantasy. Make-believe. In a few days she would be back home, fielding frantic calls from Grace about what sort of fabric she wanted for her gown, what color scheme for the reception, what vintage champagne for the bridal toast....

Once she returned to San Francisco, she would never think about him again.

The night before she was scheduled to leave, that realization depressed her. Would she really have to put an end to her delicious fantasies? Would she have to pretend she hadn't met a man who could make her feel restless in her own skin, make her ache merely by glancing at her, make

her breath catch in her throat and her heart jitter unsteadi-
ly because she desired him in an insane way?

She knew the answer. And it depressed her even more.

All the tension the retreat had drained from her began to
return. Too edgy to sleep, she climbed out of bed and threw
open her window. The night was uncommonly clear, the air
gilded by a three-quarter moon.

She donned a sweater and jeans and left her room, hoping a quiet walk through the gardens of the retreat would
help her to unwind. Moonlight rimed the stone paths that
wove through the winter gardens and into the forest. She
ambled slowly, amazed at how still the shrubs sat in the
calm night, how sweet the air smelled so far from the hus-
tle-bustle of the city. The night was cool but not cold.

And then she felt his presence again. Startled, she turned
and saw him on the path behind her.

He must have followed her. In the distance behind him
she saw the compound, the common buildings and resi-
dences, the gardens and the encroaching woods. Her gaze
narrowed on him as he closed the distance between them,
one resolute step at a time, until he was less than an inch
from her.

Just as she had known he was there, she knew that he
would kiss her. It seemed preordained, a moment destiny
imposed upon them. He slipped his arms around her and
his mouth—the mouth she'd dreamed about since she'd
arrived at the retreat—brushed against hers, so gently she
was surprised. He was so big, so powerful-looking, yet his
kiss undermined her with its tenderness.

He leaned back and peered into her upturned face. She
felt tiny in his arms, even though she was taller than average.

He opened his mouth to speak. Before he could, she
pressed her fingertips to his lips. This retreat was about silence, about listening to the inner voice, the soul. If he

spoke, she would speak, too—and once she heard her own voice, it would smack her back to reality.

The reality was, she was betrothed to Robert Benedict in San Francisco. She was going to marry him because it made more sense than not marrying him and suffering her father's unspoken displeasure, and because if even the most romantic marriages in the world could die, as her aunt Grace and uncle Jeffrey's had, Mallory had every reason to doubt the existence of romance.

But tonight it existed. In the silence, in the tacit understanding she shared with this stranger, Mallory experienced her first taste of romance.

He took her hand and continued with her along the path until they reached a gazebo at the far end of one of the gardens. He ushered her inside the hexagonal shelter, pulled her into his arms and kissed her again.

This kiss wasn't gentle. It wasn't questioning. It was hard and hungry, and it made her shiver and sigh and cling to him because her legs suddenly felt weak. His lips urged hers apart and his tongue thrust deep into her mouth, stealing her breath, conquering her.

She was deluged by a flood of heat. She wanted to melt against him, to shape her body to him. Through her sweater she felt the hard contours of his chest, lean muscle and rigid bone, far more exciting than her feeble fantasies of him. When she leaned back, she saw the spill of moonlight over the angles of his face and the harsh lines of his nose and jaw, illuminating the desire burning in his gaze.

She rose on tiptoe and kissed him again. This time she was the hungry one, stealing back everything he'd stolen from her. She kissed him greedily, aggressively, lovingly. He sucked in a shaky breath, then slid his hands under her sweater and up the smooth skin of her back.

They didn't need words to undress each other. They didn't need permission or agreement. It was understood, expressed by their eyes, their hands, their mouths touching a newly exposed spot, a ridge, a hollow.

She traced her fingertips along his naked chest. His skin was hot; his muscles rippled in the wake of her caress. The breath rushed from his lungs as she reached for his belt buckle and unfastened it. His mouth crushed down on hers as he yanked off his shirt, kicked off his jeans, tugged off her sweater and slacks.

His hands were simultaneously rougher and sweeter than she had imagined, stroking, kneading, learning her body. He lowered his mouth to her throat, her breasts, her belly, then fell to his knees before her and cupped his hands around her bottom, drawing her against his lips.

She wanted to cry out. She had never before been kissed that way; she had never before felt so aroused, so vulnerable. She bit her lip, refusing to break her vow, refusing to let her voice intrude on something so intense.

The man rose to his feet and guided her to one of the upholstered benches built into the walls of the gazebo. He kissed her as if he were dying and she were a life force, his only link to the world. He slid his hand between her legs, exploring with his fingers what he'd already tasted with his tongue. She stroked him as well, delighting in the hardness and heat of him until at last he drew her legs up around him and plunged into her. Their bodies moved together, peaked together, descended into the darkest heaven together.

She had never felt anything more natural, more vital...more right.

And now he was here. In the alley behind Mallory's, in downtown San Francisco, waiting for her.

She spotted him through the screen door into the alley. Fog smothered the crescent moon overhead, but a bright floodlight glowed above the door, lighting the alley and the small parking area. Her Saab was the only car in the lot right now, and Liam O'Neill was the only person.

He was leaning against the green convertible. A less observant person would have considered his posture almost lazy, but Mallory knew—she sensed—that he was on full alert, watching for her.

He had on jeans faded to a soft baby-blue, and a brown bomber jacket that had been worn to within an inch of its life. The zipper lay open to reveal a dark shirt underneath. His hands were buried in his pockets, his hair pale and shaggy, his eyes fixed on the door.

She could race back into the restaurant, locking the inner door behind her, and wait for him to leave. But he wasn't going to leave—or if he did, he would come back. Dealing with him now seemed as inevitable as making love with him at the retreat two months ago.

Setting her jaw and swearing that she was going to stay in control, here on her own turf, she hoisted her purse strap higher on her shoulder, shoved open the screen door and pulled the inner door shut behind her. He pushed away from her car and started toward her. She remembered his long, powerful strides. The last time they had carried him to her, she'd wound up naked in his arms, loving him—and getting herself knocked up.

She ordered herself not to think about that. If she thought about it, she might inadvertently let something slip. God only knew how he'd react if he learned she was pregnant. He might think he owned her, or at least had the right to make demands.

She would have to be very careful not to let down her guard. She would simply act gracious and polite, and unmoved. Despite the fact that his nearness prompted that familiar tingling sensation, despite the fact that her blood was singing in her veins and her breath growing shallow as his steps brought him closer to her, closer... She was going to have to treat this as if it were a chance meeting with an old acquaintance. She couldn't give anything away.

She opened her mouth, primed to speak his name. But her voice seemed trapped in her throat, and no sound came out. Only a faint, desperate sigh as he closed in on her, as his gaze bore down on her, as he circled his arms around her and covered her mouth with his.

He knew how to disarm her, all right. With one kiss, one deep, searing kiss, he had stripped away her defenses.

Almost as soon as the kiss began, he ended it, drawing back and inhaling sharply. His eyes were as hard as she remembered them, glinting gray and gold.

"Say my name," he murmured.

She flinched. Partly she was stunned by his voice, deep and husky, more a whisper than a sound. But beyond that... How could he know she knew his name?

The same way she knew his presence. On some intuitive level, they read each other. God help her if he read more than she wanted him to.

"Liam," she said, half a moan, half a plea. "Liam."

CHAPTER FOUR

SOMETHING WAS WRONG.

Something was right, too. She knew his name. And she kissed him every bit as wildly as she'd kissed him two months ago. And her kiss had the same wild effect on him.

But something was wrong, too. She looked ashen, her skin almost chalky, her eyes glassy, her cheeks gaunt. She looked as if she were in as much trouble as he'd been before he met her—and after he'd lost her.

Well, sure she was pale. She had just been more or less jumped by a guy in an alley. That she had somehow learned Liam's name didn't mean she knew him from a mugger.

He wanted to reassure her. But before he could say anything, she started talking.

Her voice was deeper than he'd expected, throatier. Sexier. He had thought she would have a high, piping voice. Maybe that was because the first time he'd seen her he had been listening to ethereal flute music, and he'd simply expected her to have a voice like a flute.

He had to remind himself to pay as much attention to her words as to her voice. "I realize you must have gone through a great deal of effort to find me, Mr. O'Neill. I appreciate that. I don't know why you bothered, but I suppose I should be flattered. However, it wasn't necessary. I think we can both agree that what happened last December was an aberration, and we need to put it behind us and move forward...."

He suppressed a laugh. Although her voice was level, her tone utterly reasonable, she was in fact babbling. It occurred to him that she was on the brink of hysteria.

"We both have our own lives to live. The retreat was just one of those things. Being there was a—a detour. A vacation from reality. I wasn't myself there. I wasn't thinking. I mean, one of my reasons for going to that place was to stop thinking for a few days, to give my brain a rest. I'm sure that's true for you, too. What happened was a mistake—"

"No," he said. Babbling and borderline hysteria were well and good, but he wasn't going to stand by in silence while she denied the truth. "What happened at the retreat *wasn't* a mistake."

"Yes, it was. I should never have…" She drifted off, her eyes dark and troubled, staring past him as if she couldn't bear to meet his gaze.

"You never should have what, Mallory?"

She glanced nervously at him. She had the most beautiful mouth, he realized, soft and pink and full. He wanted to kiss her again, and he knew she would kiss him back if he did. But to his regret, talking was more important than kissing right now.

She continued to peer up at him, her anguish evident in her pinched lips and dark, troubled eyes. He supplied the words she obviously couldn't bring herself to speak. "We shouldn't have made love?"

"It wasn't love," she whispered. "How could it be love? We didn't even know each other."

"We knew enough."

"No. No, we didn't." The more rational she sounded, the more panic-stricken she looked. She adjusted the shoulder strap of her huge leather handbag, not an easy thing to do with her hands clenched into fists. "I don't know why you found me. I don't even know *how* you found me—"

"From the newspaper."

"What newspaper?"

"The San Francisco newspaper. It published a photo of you and your fiancé at a ballet fund-raiser a few weeks ago."

"My fiancé," she repeated dully, lowering her eyes as if her shoes had suddenly become the most fascinating sight in the world. Her lashes were thick, shockingly black in contrast to her pale complexion. "I'm engaged to be married."

"I hope you're planning to have an open marriage." Liam knew he shouldn't tease her, but he wanted her to meet his gaze once more.

His goading worked. Her eyes flashed angrily as she lifted her chin and glowered at him. "No. I'm not planning to have an open marriage. I really wish you would go away, Mr. O'Neill."

"You know my name," he pointed out, his own anger wrestling with his relief that, after two long months, he was actually touching her again. It was ridiculous—to say nothing of hypocritical—that she should pretend she had no interest in him when she obviously had enough interest to find out who he was. Even before she'd kissed him just now, before she knew he was in San Francisco, she had somehow learned his identity.

The truth she was trying so hard to ignore was that she was as caught up in her memory of last December as he was. And this wasn't only about memories. It was about the present, too—and maybe the future. The heat they'd generated minutes ago, when he had kissed her, was enough to ignite the heavens. If Mallory were being honest, she would acknowledge that.

But she wasn't being honest, with him or with herself. And it bothered the hell out of him. "Why did you find out my name?" he asked.

"I learned it by accident," she said. "I saw your book in a store. It had your picture on the back, and I recognized you. It wasn't as if I was deliberately searching for you, Mr. O'Neill—"

"Liam," he corrected her quietly, relaxing his hands on her shoulders when he realized that she was shaking. He doubted she was cold. The night was relatively mild—warmer than that fateful night in December when they'd both bared themselves to the moonlight and each other. If she were cold, he would wrap his arms around her to warm her. But her shivering was a result of panic, nerves running amok, and if he wrapped his arms around her, he suspected she would fall apart completely.

Perhaps she truly loved her fiancé, and whatever had happened between her and Liam had indeed been a momentary blunder. Perhaps what he had considered immeasurably profound had meant nothing to her.

Perhaps he had come all this way for nothing.

No. It had to mean something to her. The way she'd kissed him tonight proved that.

"I didn't come here to cause you problems," he told her.

"I don't know or care what your intentions are, Mr. O'Neill—"

"Liam."

"Liam." She sighed. "It doesn't matter. Your being here *does* cause problems."

"I'm here because being away from you causes problems for me." He didn't like to reveal so much. But unlike Mallory, he wasn't going to ignore the truth.

She eyed him skeptically. "What kind of problems?"

He ran his thumb gently along the taut line of her jaw, and then across her sweet, tempting lips. It took every ounce of his willpower not to kiss her again. One of the problems Mallory Powell had been causing him over the past two months made itself felt in the most physical way, causing his groin to tighten, his muscles to constrict. "I want you," he whispered.

"Liam." He heard a catch in her voice. "I'm sorry, but..." She sighed again as he traced her tremulous lower lip once more. Her eyes glinted with fear. "Please..."

"Please what?"

She swallowed, then ran her tongue over her lip where he'd caressed her. A faint moan escaped her. He knew she was as aroused as he was. "Please leave."

"I'm not going to hurt you," he promised.

She averted her gaze once more, as if aware of how transparent she was. "I'm going home," she murmured, easing out of his embrace. "Good night."

Without her in his arms, he felt bereft. But he couldn't force her to stay with him. He supposed he ought to count his blessings that she'd said good-night and not goodbye.

She must have understood that it *wasn't* goodbye. Liam would be back. If not tomorrow, then the next day or the next. He had found her once. He would find her again.

No wonder she was pale with terror. She probably found him more frightening than some of the monstrously possessed characters in his novels. A crazed stalker, hunting down a helpless woman in a back alley in San Francisco late at night...

He swallowed another laugh. He might be crazed, but Mallory Powell was hardly helpless. She was wealthy enough to attend charity balls and celebrated enough to be photographed for the newspapers. She ran a restaurant that was named after her. And she had the power to heal Liam—or to destroy him.

He watched her back away from him, then turn and sprint to her car, as if afraid he might tackle her from behind and haul her off to have his way with her. She ought to know he would never force her to do anything—even if his life depended on it.

She ought to know, he thought as she climbed into her car, revved the engine and blinded him with the high beams of her headlights, that he would never have to force her to do anything. She might not need him the way he needed her, with his soul as much as his body. But she wanted him. He knew it, she knew it, and she knew he knew.

Sooner or later, she would stop running from the truth.

"SMELLS GOOD," Alex called up to her.

She sat on the terrace of her condo, which occupied the second floor of a hacienda-style building perched on one of the twisting mountain roads overlooking the neighborhood of Sunset. On a morning as clear as this, she could see glimpses of the Pacific Ocean beyond the roofs of the buildings that spread westward below the hill. The early sun was behind her, blanketing her terrace in taupe shadows.

She directed her gaze from the ocean to the sidewalk beneath her terrace, where the man who owned the apartment directly above hers stood. Alex Stowe was clad in sweat-drenched jogging shorts and a T-shirt, his silver hair curling with moisture and his arms akimbo. His face was baked to a golden sheen, and the muscles in his legs stretched taut.

"What smells good?" she called down to him.

"Your coffee. Offer me a cup, and I'll say yes."

Mallory smiled. No matter what her mood, Alex always had a way of making her smile. He was so easygoing, so relaxed, so at peace with himself. If she hadn't known better, she would have taken him for an overaged surfer-bum rather than a nationally renowned architect. She also would have guessed that he was closer to forty than his actual age—fifty-eight. At the moment, Mallory felt older than Alex looked.

"I'll give you some coffee if you take a shower first," she called down from the terrace. "I'm not going to have you traipsing through my apartment dripping sweat."

"What? You don't like my *eau de sueur?*" he quipped, sending her a smile and then vanishing through the building's front door.

She rose from her canvas director's chair and adjusted the sash on her robe. It wasn't yet seven o'clock, much too early to be out of bed. But she'd given up on getting any more sleep.

She'd been awake most of the night, kicking her sheets, punching her pillow, telling herself she was too exhausted to figure out the rest of her life—but trying to figure it out, anyway. After several hours, she'd surrendered to insomnia, turned on her bedside lamp and finished reading Liam O'Neill's book.

That had been a strategic mistake. Once she'd reached the end of the story, she had been too chilled to close her eyes. Did the frightening obsessions of Liam O'Neill's fictional hero relate to Liam in a personal way? Was his tale of death and vengeance a reflection of his dreams? What kind of mind did it take to cook up such a weird plot? How was it possible that the same man who wrote *The Unborn* could reduce a sensible, feet-on-the-ground woman like Mallory to a mass of mindless desire?

Once her thoughts had wandered in that direction, they never wandered back. She remembered the way he'd made love to her last December. She remembered his kiss in the alley behind her restaurant. She cursed the way that one kiss had demolished her composure and made her crave more—more of him.

She left the terrace for her kitchen to warm some muffins for Alex—and for herself, too, she scolded silently. She wasn't hungry—she hadn't been hungry in days—but she was going to have to start taking better care of herself.

She arranged several whole-wheat muffins on a cookie sheet and slid it into the oven. Her kitchen was bright, with a broad window, a butcher-block center island, lots of clean work spaces and polished white appliances. But she couldn't take credit for having baked the muffins herself. Even at Mallory's, baking wasn't her area of expertise.

Once the muffins were heating up, she headed down the hall to her bedroom to get dressed. Except for the spectacular view and the expensive address, her condo was modest, a two-bedroom unit furnished in muted earth tones. She could afford a bigger place, but she didn't want it. Robert often talked about buying a Victorian in Pacific Heights once he and Mallory were married, but she had no idea what they would do with a big house. Fill the extra bedrooms with children?

She paused in the doorway of her spare bedroom. She used it as a study, although it doubled as a guest room. How would it work as a nursery?

A lump filled her throat. She couldn't imagine having this baby without imagining the baby's father. Closing her eyes, she pictured the way he'd loomed above her in the alley last night, the way his gaze had penetrated her defenses, the way his mouth had felt against hers. It didn't make sense that he could arouse her so intensely when she didn't even know him.

She was going to have to convince him to leave town before he learned that she was pregnant. She couldn't let him find out and impose his own wishes on her, either to continue the pregnancy or to end it. What if he sued her for custody once the baby was born?

Dear God, he was a total stranger. How could she let him take her baby?

Assuming she had the baby.

Groaning, she stalked the rest of the way down the hall to her own bedroom. She had already showered, so she simply threw on a pair of jeans and an oversized fisherman's sweater. By the time she was done brushing out her hair, the oven timer was buzzing and the doorbell was ringing.

If she didn't adore Alex Stowe, she would hate him for being so chipper when she felt like a soggy dishrag. Freshly showered and shaved, he smelled of mint and milled soap;

like her, he had on neat blue jeans and a sweater. "You're doodling today," she guessed, letting him in and closing the door behind him. She knew that when he was meeting with clients, he wore expensive suits, but when he was going to spend his day sketching ideas at his drafting table, he dressed casually.

"Doodling to my heart's content. Boy, it smells wonderful in here. Did you bake me something?"

"The bakery down on Noriega baked you something. All I did was warm it." She led the way to the kitchen and removed the muffins from the oven. After arranging them in a napkin-lined basket on a tray, she glanced up to find him thumbing through Liam's book, which she'd left on the breakfast table when she'd arisen to brew herself some coffee.

"I didn't know you read horror fiction."

"I don't."

Alex closed the book and smiled at her. "O'Neill's stuff is pretty nerve-tingling. I read his last book and loved it. How's this one?"

"Nerve-tingling." She filled an insulated decanter with coffee and set it on the tray next to the basket of muffins. "Let's go out to the terrace. It's such a lovely morning."

"There's genuine sunshine for a change," Alex agreed, striding ahead of her to open the sliding door.

Stepping out onto the terrace, she lowered the heavy tray onto a small glass-topped table between two chairs, then busied herself pouring the coffee. "What are you doodling these days?" she asked, eager to talk about anything other than herself.

Alex helped himself to a muffin and lounged in the chair across from her. "Carlisle Forrest asked me to submit a design for them."

"The hotel people? They're cousins of mine, you know."

"Is there anyone of importance in this town you're not related to?" Alex chuckled. "Well, they're planning to open a hotel in Atlanta. I made a presentation for them already, but they asked for some alterations in the design. They like my stuff, for some reason."

"I can't imagine why," Mallory joked, chuckling at his overwhelming modesty. Alex's architecture graced the major capitals of the world. He was known for his soaring towers and his ability to design buildings that blended in with their surroundings. It didn't surprise her that a luxury hotel chain like Carlisle Forrest would call upon Alex Stowe and Associates to design the chain's new Atlanta hotel.

Like Mallory, Alex could afford to live elsewhere. In fact, he owned a home in Aspen and a co-op in Manhattan, as well as his ex-wife's house in Santa Fe. The Santa Fe house had been featured in *Architectural Digest* a while back. He'd designed it for his wife as a "going-away" present in honor of their years together. They'd had one of the friendliest divorces Mallory had ever heard of.

"So tell me," he said, directing the conversation back to her, "when did you start reading horror novels?"

Mallory busied herself with a muffin, trying to split it in half but instead breaking it into a mess of crumbs on her plate. She sighed at her own clumsiness. "I'm not a big fan of the genre," she admitted. "I just... I was in the bookstore the other day, and that book caught my eye."

"What is it about?"

She shot him a quick look. He was leaning forward, evidently eager to hear all about Liam O'Neill's new masterpiece. If she evaded his questions, she would arouse suspicion, so she picked at the crumbs of muffin and described the story. Maybe if she talked about it, it wouldn't seem so scary to her. Maybe Liam wouldn't seem so scary.

"It starts with a woman who's nine months pregnant," she said. "The woman gets murdered. But the doctors are able to save her baby. The thing is, before he was born, the baby heard the murder take place. Through the woman's skin, inside her womb, he heard the voice of the murderer and the argument that led up to the murder. But of course, he heard all this before he was even born. He didn't understand language in any conscious way. He had no idea what it was he was listening to."

"I'm getting the chills already," Alex murmured.

Mallory smiled and forced herself to eat a small lump of muffin. "The baby's mother was never married, so no one knows who his father is. The baby gets adopted, and he grows up in a nice, normal, middle-class family. But there's this memory haunting him of a voice and an argument and the sound and the feel of his mother being murdered—although he doesn't realize what it is he's remembering. He has these terrible flashbacks. The book tries to describe what the unborn child felt when his mother was being murdered. It's..." She shuddered. "It's really spooky."

"It sure sounds it. So, what happens to this kid?"

"He grows up. But he's obsessed with the sound of the murderer's voice. He has to find the owner of that voice and wreak revenge, even though he doesn't know why." She shuddered again. Retelling the story gave her the chills—especially when she thought about the perverse intelligence the book's author must have possessed to concoct such a tale. Alex grinned and shook his head. "Liam O'Neill is amazing."

"What makes you say that?"

"It's a fantastic story, don't you think? It taps into all those primal fears about whether what happens to us before we're born determines who we wind up becoming in life. We all have compulsions we can't explain, right? Like a fear of dogs, or claustrophobia, or bursting into tears whenever you hear a certain passage of Bach's B-minor Mass. Or just some compulsion to do something. You don't know *why* you have to do it. All you know is if you don't do it, you'll die."

Mallory bit her lip and gazed out at the leafless trees bordering the sidewalk below the terrace. Making love with Liam had been like that, a compulsion, totally without logic. She still couldn't figure out why she'd felt so irresistibly drawn to him. Yet her attraction to Liam had driven her to uncharacteristic acts.

"You think these irrational compulsions result from what happened to people in the womb?" she asked.

"Who knows? It's a fun theory, though."

"I'm not sure *fun* is quite the word for it."

"Let me guess—O'Neill's novel kept you up all night. You look beat."

She nodded. "I was having trouble falling asleep. I thought reading would help me to unwind."

Alex guffawed. "A Liam O'Neill book is definitely not the thing to read when you can't sleep. Next time, fix yourself a glass of warm milk and read something by Dr. Seuss."

"Thanks for the advice," Mallory muttered, smiling to blunt the edge of exasperation in her tone. She wasn't going to reveal to Alex that Liam's story hadn't been the only thing keeping her awake all night. Yesterday evening, just to be sure, she had taken a second home-pregnancy test. It had confirmed the result of the first test. She had her own "unborn" inside her.

Could it hear her? Did it know her voice? Had it heard Liam in the alley last night, promising that he would never hurt her, whispering that he wanted her? Had it felt the heat that seared her body when he had kissed her? Had it reacted to the sudden rush of her heartbeat—the same rush she was experiencing now, merely thinking about him? Did it know her anger, her arousal, her fear?

She had no reason to assume it did. But in her mind, it was now a conscious being. And as the sun climbed higher in the morning sky, burning away the night mist and clarifying the world around her, Mallory realized she wasn't going to go back to Dr. Gilman.

It wasn't logical. It wasn't sensible. Maybe it was simply another irrational compulsion. But her decision was made: she was going to keep her baby.

"THAT WAS WAY COOL." The bookstore manager, an emaciated young man with a ponytail and a goatee, took down the placard in the window of his University Avenue shop. "We don't always get a mob like that. Celebrity bios always draw a crowd, or memoirs of a hacker or something. But fiction? We usually don't get a turnout like you got."

Liam said nothing as he pocketed his pen and flexed his fingers. He had signed more than ninety books in the last two hours. As tiring as that had been, it had been even more exhausting putting his brain on ice for those two hours, smiling at each person in line, expressing thanks for their having bought *The Unborn,* asking each person his or her name and inscribing it on the title page along with his own ragged signature. He'd pulled it off, but now his head was throbbing from the exertion.

"Can I get you anything else?" the store manager asked, reaching for the empty water glass at Liam's elbow. "We've got coffee out back, and—"

"No, thanks." Liam unfolded himself from the metal chair at the card table the manager had set up near the entrance to the store. His joints were stiff from sitting for so long. His right shoulder ached. The fingers of his right hand were nearly numb from having gripped the pen so tightly.

"Well, I'm sorry we ran out of books. I usually order just twenty-five or so when it's a novel. But you're not an author who makes the scene very often, so I ordered more. And I guess you've got quite a following on the campus."

"I guess I do." Liam wasn't in the mood to make small talk with the guy, but courtesy demanded it.

"I heard a rumor you used to teach at U.C., Berkeley."

"I did," Liam said tightly. He *really* didn't want to have this discussion.

"No kidding? What'd you teach?"

It had been an eon ago. Liam had done everything in his power to eradicate his memories of those days. He had to think for a minute. What the hell had he taught? "Modern American Lit.," he finally recalled.

"No kidding? We've got a huge literature section—"

"I've got to go," Liam said, not bothering to check his watch. He shook the manager's hand and thanked him for the successful book-signing, then exited through the rear door into the parking lot behind the building.

The car his publisher had arranged for him was waiting there, the driver immersed in a copy of *Entertainment Weekly*. Liam slung his leather jacket over his shoulder—it was surprisingly warm for late morning in February—and donned a pair of sunglasses. He tapped the window, jolting the driver, who tossed down the magazine and edged open the door.

"I'm not ready to go back to San Francisco yet," Liam said. "What's your schedule?"

The driver glanced at the dashboard clock. "I'm supposed to get you to the bookstore in Oakland at two. Other than that, I'm free."

"I want to take a walk," Liam said. "I'll be back in an hour. Maybe less. Can you wait?"

The driver peered up at him. "I'll go grab a sandwich and meet you back here at one."

"Fine." Liam pivoted and sauntered out of the parking lot to the sidewalk.

Five years. Five years since he'd walked along these Berkeley sidewalks teeming with students and professors. Sidewalks alive with noise and energy. Sidewalks filled with unseen danger.

But that was the way it was with danger. Some perils were easy to see and avoid. Others inched up on a person and grabbed him from behind. Others rose up out of tranquillity like a tsunami, crashing over unsuspecting victims and dragging them down. Or they arrived as innocently as a car cruising down the street.

He had been on campus when it happened, finishing a lecture on the Beat poets. Later, he would reconstruct where he'd been: at the front of a lecture hall, discussing the rhythms of Allen Ginsberg's *Howl*. At the precise moment, the very instant that innocent-looking car had jumped the sidewalk and destroyed everything Liam loved, everything that had ever mattered to him, he had been pointing out how Ginsberg used consonants to create an agitated tempo.

Liam used to care about things like the way a poet used consonants.

It had occurred not far from where he was standing right now. Just a few blocks south of the campus, at the corner of Telegraph and Derby. He knew he should turn around, but his legs carried him forward, past bicycle riders, past students lugging bulging backpacks, past refugees from the sixties, past merchants and shoppers and carefree spirits. He kept going, another block and then another, until he reached the exact spot.

The shops looked the same. He wasn't sure that particular boutique had been there five years ago, but it didn't matter. The street artisans looked the same, their wares arrayed on folding tables along the sidewalk. Earrings. Tooled leather belts. Silk-screened T-shirts. According to the police report, several street vendors had been at the corner when that innocent-looking car had careered up over the curb like the hand of death, reaching out to grab whoever was convenient. They'd witnessed it, and their statements had told Liam more than he wanted to know.

He had been just a short walk away—yet an unfathomable distance. Too far to stop fate, to get in its way and hold it back. Too far to do the one thing he was supposed to do, the most essential thing a father could ever do for his child.

He had finished his lecture on Allen Ginsberg and returned to his office. The English department chairman had been waiting for him there, a grave expression on his face. Before Liam could unlock his office door, Wally had guided him down the hall to his own office and closed the door behind them. "There's been an accident, Liam," he'd said.

Liam stared at the corner now, waiting for emotion to sweep over him. He saw no sign of what had happened five years ago, no indication that two people had died and taken Liam's heart and soul and reason for living with them. No scars marked the curb, no memorial hung from the lamppost. The only scars were inside Liam, where his heart and soul had been torn out. The only memorial was what he wrote every day, stories of rage and vengeance, of doom and grief.

A year ago, he couldn't have brought himself to come back to this corner. Two months ago, he couldn't have. But then he'd met Mallory.

Why had she changed him? How had she made it possible for him to stand here without screaming, without blacking out and throwing things and hating God? He had no idea. All he knew was that two months ago he would have rather walked the circumference of the planet on his hands than come to this corner in Berkeley, where a musician strummed a guitar and girls and boys eyed one another with lusty interest, where people shopped and tossed coins into the guitarist's open case and went about their lives.

For some reason, in some way, Mallory Powell had given Liam the strength to return to this corner without letting his memories destroy him. She might not understand why he'd had to find her, why, if she ran away, he would find her again and again.

The answer was here. This busy intersection in the center of Berkeley held his pain—and Mallory somehow made the pain go away.

CHAPTER FIVE

MALLORY ENTERED her aunt's bridal shop with the leaden step of a naughty child marching to her punishment. She knew her lunch with Aunt Grace was going to go poorly, and not because her digestive system was in rebellion again—in fact, once she'd made up her mind about the pregnancy, her appetite had returned stronger than ever. But she was about to do something very foolish with her life, and her aunt was going to be furious about it.

The store had a way of soothing Mallory, though. Stepping inside the showroom, with its gentle pastel decor, the rose carpeting, the quiet cream walls and esthetically arranged showcases displaying bridal accessories, Mallory felt her tension wane. Although she regretted that the new store, Grace, was founded on the ashes of her aunt's dying marriage, Mallory adored the shop. She also adored the fact that Aunt Grace was living in San Francisco.

Grace DeWilde had been the closest thing to a mother Mallory had ever known. Her real mother had died of an aneurysm, leaving behind a four-year-old daughter and a husband utterly at a loss about what to do with the scrappy little girl he'd always assumed his wife would raise. In a ranking of the world's most inept parents, Leland Powell would easily place in the top ten. He loved Mallory, but he was the first to recognize his strengths and his weaknesses. His strengths lay in the world of finance, his weaknesses in the world of warm-and-fuzzy bonding.

Mallory had always considered it proof of her father's love that he shipped her off to England every summer so she could visit with his sister, Grace, her husband, Jeffrey, and the cousins. Leland Powell was sensitive enough to realize that Mallory needed a mother figure in her life, someone besides Emma, the housekeeper. Mallory needed a family—and the DeWildes were a real family.

During the long, dreary school year in San Francisco, she felt isolated. The apartment on Nob Hill was a large but lonely place for a young girl whose father was preoccupied by the demands of rebuilding Powell Enterprises and restoring the family's wealth. But summers meant the De-Wildes.

Mallory's twin cousins, Megan and Gabriel, were her age, and she used to pretend the three of them were actually triplets. Kate was a baby the first summer Mallory had gone abroad, and Mallory had adored spoiling her, diapering her, taking her for walks and playing pat-a-cake, activities Megan and Gabriel had found boring. Mallory had wished she could have had a baby sister around often enough for it to become boring. At least she could pretend she had a baby sister during her summers with the De-Wildes.

Often, while Grace and Jeffrey worked at their store in London during the week, the children would stay with a governess and the rest of the staff at Kemberly, the grand family estate in the country. Kemberly was a mind-boggling place to a California native accustomed to apartment living. The manor's stone walls had stood centuries longer than the earliest white settlements in California. At Kemberly, a girl could dream of princesses and wizards, of magic gardens and knights in shining armor. Mallory treasured the time she spent there.

But sometimes Grace and Jeffrey brought all the children to London. And while their city home wasn't anywhere near as conducive to dreaming, Mallory was happy there, too. As long as she could feel a part of the loving, noisy, two-parent DeWilde family, she was happy.

Grace used to let the children visit the London DeWilde store when they were in town. But the bridal emporium had always intimidated Mallory in a way Kemberly never did. Kemberly had seemed like a stage set, a fantasyland, but the store was real. People worked there, shopped there, spent scads of money there. Its Edwardian decor—the mahogany counters, the gilded doors, the dense wool carpeting, the guards discreetly positioned throughout the showrooms—lent the place a grim, stuffy ambience, leaving Mallory with the impression that weddings were a ponderous, somber ritual, not an occasion for joy. And the famous DeWilde tiara on display in the London store had always given her the willies. It was so ornate and glittery she'd been afraid to stare directly at it, because maybe it would blind her. She'd always felt she was entering a museum when she stepped inside DeWilde's—and well-bred children knew that they had to be on their very best behavior in museums.

Grace's shop in San Francisco wasn't anything like that. Its light, fresh atmosphere could convince even the most hesitant bride that a wedding was a festive celebration, not a solemn duty.

The mother and daughter seated on one of the sofas, reviewing a portfolio of gown designs with a consultant, seemed in a festive mood. Mallory forced herself to smile in their direction as she strode past them to the elevator.

The mere act of smiling perked her up. Maybe she shouldn't expect the worst. Maybe her aunt would be surprised but not dismayed by her news. Maybe she would not only accept it but would volunteer to run interference with Mallory's father.

"In your dreams," Mallory muttered to herself, stepping inside the elevator and pressing the second-floor button. Grace had had conniptions when Gabriel had chosen to elope with Lianne Beecham. She was not going to take Mallory's news sitting down.

Mallory reminded herself again of the time she broke the Fabergé egg at Kemberly. Grace had recovered from that disaster well enough, hadn't she? And Mallory had brought a tote bag full of goodies from her restaurant for her in-the-office picnic with her aunt. Good food might lead to forgiveness.

She left the elevator for the suite of offices from which Grace was managed. Her aunt's high-energy assistant, Rita Mulholland, bounced past Mallory with a grin, shouting "Hi!" over her shoulder. Mallory gazed after her, admiring her chic red suit. Compared to Rita, Mallory felt dowdy in her jeans and sweater.

A woman who worked in the offices of a bridal boutique had to look chic, Mallory reminded herself. And a woman who slopped around in veggies, meats and sauces had to dress with practicality in mind. She was going to feel a whole lot dowdier once she had to start wearing maternity fashions.

The notion made her laugh. That it didn't make her weep convinced her she'd reached the right decision, regardless of how her aunt was going to react to it.

She tapped on the door to Grace's office, then nudged it open. "Aunt Grace?"

"Mallory!" Grace cried, rising from her chair to greet her niece with a hug. Several loose papers drifted from her desk to the floor, but Grace didn't stop to pick them up. Her desk was a mess, but she'd never really liked to work at a desk, anyway. Her favorite place to work was in bed, with documents spread around her and a telephone at her elbow.

Mallory returned her aunt's exuberant hug, managing not to drop her tote in the process. "Careful, Aunt Grace," she warned, holding the bag away from her aunt's back. "I've got shrimp in here."

"Shrimp! You are a sweetheart!" Aunt Grace relaxed her embrace, stepped back to appraise Mallory and frowned. "You look dreadful. Have you been ill?"

Mallory chuckled, not only at her aunt's bluntness but at the hybrid accent that carried traces of both England and California. "I haven't been ill, Aunt Grace, but we do have a lot to talk about."

"Indeed we do." Grace led the way across her office to the striped satin sofa and chairs arranged around a coffee table near the window. "It seems like years since I last saw you."

"Two weeks," Mallory corrected her, carrying the tote bag over to the table.

Grace seated herself on the sofa, impeccable in her designer silk suit, her blond hair perfectly styled, yet beneath the elegant exterior she fairly sparkled with gleeful impatience. "Well, then—what other delectables are in that bag of yours? Did you bring any of that splendid coffee?"

Mallory pulled a thermos out of her bag. "I don't remember what I brought last time. Today we had a Kenyan roast in the maker."

"That'll do. Do you know, Mallory, I believe I'm reverting to my American roots. I haven't had an afternoon cup of tea in days, and I don't miss it. Now, tell me, where are those shrimp?"

Smiling, Mallory unpacked the container of marinated shrimp, a second container of cold steamed asparagus, and a small foil-wrapped bowl of fruit. From the bottom of the bag she dug out paper plates, plastic utensils, cups, napkins and a bag of herb-flavored rolls.

"Oh, heavens. You do spoil me." Aunt Grace sank onto the sofa cushions, gazing blissfully at the food. "If you hadn't suggested this luncheon, I would have wound up ordering out for a sandwich. Or skipping lunch altogether."

"Burt yelled at me for filching the best stuff. The shrimp always sells well at lunchtime. He told me I should have taken the country paté. People aren't ordering paté the way they used to. Everyone's so health conscious."

"As you and I are. To your health!" she said, lifting a shrimp by its tail as if it were a glass and she were drinking a toast. She popped the succulent pink curl into her mouth and sighed in contentment. "Luscious. Now, tell me—how have you been?"

Mallory fussed with the thermos, unscrewing the top and pouring steaming coffee into the two cups. She had come to the store specifically to tell her aunt how she was, but she hated to spoil Grace's cheerful mood.

"First you tell me," she stalled. "How are you?"

"Absolutely lovely. Buried in work, and I adore it."

"And Gabe and Lianne? Have you heard from them recently?"

"Gabe and Lianne are expecting. I'm to be a grandmother."

Mallory nodded. She'd heard the news from Megan, but she wanted to hear it from Grace herself, to see how her aunt felt about it. A shadow passed over Grace's face, and then she smiled wistfully.

"You're not happy about it?"

"I'm thrilled beyond words. But it breaks my heart to think I shall have a grandchild in England while I'm living halfway around the world."

"They'll come and visit," Mallory assured her, almost adding, *And you'll have my baby to pamper. You'll be an honorary grandmother to my child.* But she sensed her aunt's mixed feelings were based on more than just her physical distance from Gabriel and his wife. No doubt she had dreamed of becoming a grandmother with Jeffrey by her side. Nothing could change the fact that she and Jeffrey weren't going to share this special blessing.

"I gather Gabe and Lianne are doing splendidly." Grace popped another shrimp into her mouth and managed a convincing grin. "And Megan is soldiering along in France. And Kate...well, you know as well as I do what she's up to."

Mallory detected a glint of disapproval in her aunt's gaze. "I admire Kate," she said defending her cousin. Kate seemed to resent Mallory at times, probably because Mallory got along with Grace better than Kate did. But Mallory spoke from the heart when she said, "Thank God there's an idealist among us. The rest of us have made careers catering to the rich. She caters to the poor."

"I admire her, too, Mallory, but honestly! All those years of college and medical school, and there she is, working in that squalid clinic in the seediest section of the city. I'm not saying she shouldn't help poor people. I just worry for her safety. And whenever I dare to express my concerns, she tells me I don't respect what she's doing."

"She's been working there for a while, and nobody's hurt her yet."

Grace sniffed. "I just don't see why she can't affiliate herself with a nice, safe hospital and let ambulances bring the poor people to her."

"You're a snob, Aunt Grace," Mallory declared, as blunt as her aunt.

Grace laughed. "So I am. But now, tell me, when are we going to put our heads together and move forward on your wedding? I've seen some sketches by a new designer that are just wonderful. Her gowns are sleek and daring, perfect for a woman with your physique. I'd really like you to have a look at them. Also, your attendants. Have you figured out how many you want? Too bad Gabriel's child will be a newborn—too young to participate. If you ask me, you'd be better off forgoing a flower girl than including Robert's niece. Leland tells me she's quite the whiner. A prodigious brat. I'm afraid she'll spoil everything if you—"

"Aunt Grace." Mallory held up her hand to silence her. Her gaze rested on the bowl of blueberries and chunks of melon. She wanted to gorge on the fruit, just to fill her mouth with natural sugars so that what she said would come out sweetly.

"What is it, dear? Have you and Robert argued about his niece? I promise you, I shall back you to the hilt if Robert insists on including her."

"No, Aunt Grace. It's not that."

Grace finally set aside her own agenda and studied Mallory. Her eyes reflected her worry. "Oh, heavens. You have bad news for me, don't you."

"I'm not sure if it's *bad*," Mallory fibbed, smiling with more optimism than the moment could sustain. "I'm pregnant."

Grace said nothing for a moment. Then she pressed her hand to her chest and inhaled deeply. "Oh, my."

"'Oh, my' is right."

"I suppose I should be relieved that it's nothing worse."

Mallory burst into laughter. "Meaning, it's pretty damned bad?"

Grace laughed, too, a weak, shocked laugh. "Well, it certainly takes me by surprise. Whatever were you thinking of? You're a modern, intelligent woman, Mal. Surely you know how to avoid such things."

Mallory shifted uncomfortably on the sofa. "Surely I do," she said, unintentionally imitating her aunt's diction. "But even modern, intelligent women make mistakes."

Grace pursed her lips and shook her head. "I suppose it's Robert's fault as much as yours. I certainly would have expected some restraint from him."

"Robert isn't—"

"But I suppose people who put off marrying until they're thirty might behave like teenagers throughout their twenties. And I'm not so old I don't understand what hormones can do to a person."

"Aunt Grace, I—"

"When are you due?"

Mallory sighed, resigned to letting her aunt control the conversation for now. "September."

"Well. This can be dealt with. You and Robert can have a quick civil ceremony now, and then proceed with your end-of-the-year gala. Most ministers will perform a religious service for a couple who have already been married at town hall. And by December, you should have your figure back, if you watch your diet during your pregnancy. We can still proceed with the gown. This is not insurmountable."

"It's not Robert's baby," Mallory announced.

Grace lapsed into another silence. "Oh, my," she whispered, glancing at Mallory's flat abdomen. Her cheeks darkening, she lifted her stunned gaze to Mallory. "Not Robert's?"

Mallory shook her head.

"Dear God."

"I think I prefer 'oh, my.'"

"Oh, my," Grace obliged, then laughed even more faintly. Mallory closed her eyes, grateful that Grace hadn't erupted in anger. But then, she must have known deep down that her aunt would respond with soul-deep concern rather than rage. "Oh, Mallory...I don't know what to say. Who *is* the father?"

"That's not important," Mallory answered quickly. She refused to let Liam O'Neill enter into it. This was *her* baby, *her* problem. *Her* decision.

Grace looked perturbed. "Isn't it, though? You've been with a man behind Robert's back. What man would have done this to you?"

"Really, Aunt Grace, I'd rather not talk about him."

"Has he broken your heart?" At that possibility her aunt flared with indignation. Grace's loyalty brought a blur of tears to Mallory's eyes. "If some beast treated you wrongly, sweetheart, if he hurt you in any way—"

"No, Aunt Grace. No. He didn't hurt me. Really. He has nothing to do with it."

"Well, I should hardly think that's the case. You're a very independent woman, Mallory, but this man had to have had *something* to do with it."

"You know what I mean."

Grace sighed and pushed herself to her feet. She paced in a circle around the spacious office, stopping to pick up some fallen sheets of paper near her desk. She paused there, staring across the room at Mallory, bracing herself on the back of her chair. "What does Robert have to say about this?"

"He doesn't know yet."

Grace's gaze seemed to turn inward, to her own thoughts. Mallory could almost hear the gears whirring in her brain. "If only he didn't have to find out. There is such a thing as too much honesty, Mallory. Trust me when I say that too much honesty can destroy a marriage."

"The only way he wouldn't find out is if I ended the pregnancy."

Grace sighed. "Mallory, I don't know how to advise you in this. It's a terribly difficult decision you have to make."

"I've made my decision, Aunt Grace."

"I see. Well, raising a child alone can't be easy, not when you work such long hours. And certainly, if Robert was never apprised of the situation, your marriage could move forward. I imagine you've found a discreet doctor...."

Dr. Gilman, Mallory thought pensively. Less than a week ago, Dr. Gilman had seemed the answer to all her problems. But the more she'd thought about it, the less she'd cared for that particular answer. "I'm not going to get an abortion."

"You're not?" Grace's eyes widened.

"I don't want to."

Grace seemed stunned. "You don't want to? But you've always been pro-choice. Militantly so, if I'm not mistaken."

"I still am. But you know what? Pro-choice means I have the right to choose. And this is my choice." Grace still looked dazed, as if she couldn't quite believe what Mallory was saying. "Granted, it's not the logical choice, or maybe even the smart choice. But once I made up my mind, I felt at peace. I know I'm throwing a monkey wrench into everyone's plans—especially my own. But while I was considering ending the pregnancy, I couldn't sleep, I couldn't eat, I could barely think straight. And once I made my mind up not to end it, I felt better. Everything fell into place inside me. My heart was telling me that this was right."

"Oh, Mallory." Grace shook her head sadly. "I'm sure your heart is telling you all sorts of silly, frilly things. It isn't telling you what raising a child requires. It isn't telling you what losing Robert would do to him—or your father, or *you*. Surely you can't expect Robert to marry you when you're carrying another man's baby."

"It's *my* baby," Mallory argued. "And Robert has the freedom to make his own choice, just as I do. For all I know, he may marry me, anyway."

"How can you possibly believe he'd do that?"

"Aunt Grace, you know he and I aren't the romantic match of the century. We like each other well enough, and marrying each other seems like a practical step. For him as much as for me."

"*Practical?* Haven't you ever heard of love?"

Mallory snorted. "You loved Uncle Jeffrey, and look what happened. Love doesn't guarantee a damned thing."

"Oh, my." Grace reflected for a moment, her expression growing simultaneously more sympathetic and more astute. "You love that baby's father, don't you. Whoever he is . . . you're in love with him."

"No!" Mallory protested vehemently, not wishing to analyze why the mere suggestion that she might love Liam O'Neill would disturb her so much.

Grace must have realized that she'd touched a nerve. "Who is he, Mal? Can you tell me?"

"I'd rather not. It's no one you know." Her eyes brimmed with fresh tears. She was too embarrassed to explain what had happened between her and Liam O'Neill last December. There *was* no explanation. It had been another instance of Mallory listening to her heart, and she ought to have learned from that mistake.

Yet her heart told her it *hadn't* been a mistake. Even if Liam was a madman, a crackpot, a conjurer of demented stories. Even if she knew nothing about his background, nothing about his life. What they'd shared at the retreat hadn't been love, but it hadn't been a mistake, either. "I'd rather not talk about him," she said quietly, shaken by the truth. "It doesn't matter."

"Once that baby is born, it will matter." Grace shook her head. "Good Lord, Mallory—I always thought you had your head on straight. It sounds to me as if you've given no real thought to this at all. What will you do if Robert refuses to marry you?"

"I'll stay single."

"And how will you juggle the restaurant and the baby?"

"I won't be the first single parent in the world. I was raised by a single parent, don't forget."

"And if this is anything to judge by—" Grace gestured in the direction of Mallory's womb "—he did a terrible job of it."

Mallory forgave her aunt's bitter words. Grace was just as upset as Mallory had expected, and the truth was, her father certainly could have done a better job raising her. She wouldn't fumble the job of rearing her child the way he had, though. She would raise her baby so it would know how very much it was loved **and** wanted. It would never be lonely the way Mallory had been lonely.

Standing, she crossed the room to her aunt, who looked suddenly quite frail. "Don't be sad, Aunt Grace," she murmured, wrapping her arms around Grace and hugging her tight. "This will all work out, some way or another."

"I wish you could have said it would work out for the best. But I'm not convinced it will."

"I'm not, either," Mallory admitted, smiling against her aunt's shoulder. "I may regret this decision for the rest of my life. But it's the only decision that's right for me."

"I pray to God it is." Grace's voice caught in her throat, but when Mallory leaned back to peer into her face, Grace shook her off with a casual wave. "I'm fine, really. Just so many things going on these days, so many changes."

"Come to my house for dinner, Aunt Grace. How about it? Monday night. We'll have a nice quiet meal and talk, and we won't think about the restaurant or this store, or marriages or love or anything. How about it?"

"Will we talk about the baby, at least?"

"As long as you aren't going to try to talk me out of having it. It's my decision, Aunt Grace. I want that clear."

"It's as clear as Waterford crystal, my dear." Grace smiled crookedly. "Will you make shrimp?"

"If you'd like."

"I'll be there."

Mallory kissed her aunt's cheek. Grace was entitled to be distressed. But if an invitation to dinner at Mallory's home was enough to console her, she couldn't be *that* upset.

HE STAYED AWAY from Mallory that night. He could easily have gone back to her restaurant again and cornered her at closing time as he had last night. But he didn't want to scare her away or pressure her. He didn't want her to think all he was after was another passionate interlude with her.

On the other hand, he wasn't sure what, beyond passion, he *did* want. But something was at stake between Mallory Powell and himself, something more than physical desire, and he had to figure out what it was.

Meanwhile, he had to get himself together for another bout with fame. Tomorrow morning, he was scheduled to appear on a local television talk show called "What's Up?" to promote *The Unborn*. Hazel had assured him that whoever was going to interview him on the show would go easy on him. "Just be your usual charming self and you'll sail through it," she'd said with only the slightest touch of sarcasm. Charm had never been Liam's long suit.

He stretched out on the king-size bed in his room. The TV inside the wall cabinet was tuned to a sitcom, but he lay on his back with his eyes closed, ignoring the hum of the ventilation system and the predictable bursts of hilarity from the laugh track.

He reminisced about the corner in Berkeley where he'd made his pilgrimage earlier that day. It had looked so normal, so mundane. Yet his own personal earthquake had originated from that very spot. That corner had been the epicenter, sending fissures throughout the ground beneath him. It had cracked, shattered, opened a great, bottomless darkness under his feet, and he'd fallen in.

He was still amazed he'd found the strength to return to the spot—and even more amazed that he could think about it now without succumbing to blind emotion. Where was his anger? Where was the gut-wrenching bitterness he always experienced when he thought of that corner, that fateful day, the horror that made the gruesome plots of his books seem anemic in comparison? Why couldn't he remember Jennifer's face, and John's? Why couldn't he feel the rage, the helplessness, the bitterness?

Mallory Powell.

Why her, of all people? What did she have that no one else he'd met in the past five years had had? What strange, miraculous power did she possess that could nullify his fury? Why her?

Why couldn't he have been cured by someone more like him? Someone from a similar blue-collar background, perhaps. Someone whose father, like his, had arrived in this country a dirt-poor kid desperate for an opportunity. Colm O'Neill had fled the turbulence of Northern Ireland and wound up in the Irish-immigrant community of Boston, where he'd met the American-born daughter of an older Irish immigrant and married her. Liam's parents loved each other, and they'd struggled together, his mother working as a hotel chambermaid and his father driving a cab so they could raise their son for better things.

Always, there had been story and song in his home, always the rhythm of his father's brogue, the lilt of his mother's sweet voice. But Liam O'Neill had not been groomed to become a professor of Modern American Literature at the University of California. It was Jennifer who had introduced him to the Beat poets, to the macho energy of Kerouac and the irony of Salinger, the gutsy humor of Mary McCarthy and Dorothy Parker. It was Jennifer who had opened his eyes to so much—to literature and to love.

So why couldn't he picture Jennifer now? Why could he see only Mallory Powell, a high-born woman who appeared at charity balls? How could someone like her bewitch him? Not just bewitch him, but make him feel alive— and happy about it.

Damn, but she turned him on. Even here, alone in his bland hotel room, with the chatter of the television droning in the background and the swirled texture of the plaster ceiling spread above his eyes, he thought about Mallory Powell...and the mere thought of her turned him on.

Whatever she was doing to him, he needed it as he'd never needed anything before. And he wasn't going to leave her alone until he'd figured out what it was.

CHAPTER SIX

"YOU'RE LOOKING a little pale," Cassie said. "Why don't we add some more red to your cheeks?"

Mallory's smile bounced off the mirror to the production assistant, whose artfully made-up face was reflected alongside hers in the glass. Mallory didn't like wearing tons of makeup, but she hated to disappoint Cassie, a twenty-two-year-old intern who really wanted to feel she was contributing something important to the world of San Francisco television. Cassie had already sprayed Mallory's hair so it wouldn't fluff around if she moved her head. Usually when she did the cooking show, she wore it pulled into a French braid—Cassie made the most even French braids in the world—but for today's show, Mallory had chosen to wear it loose, held back from her face by a satin headband the same vivid turquoise as her roll-neck tunic. Black leggings completed the outfit. It was simple and homey, just like the food Mallory planned to feature today on her eight-minute segment of "What's Up?"

She was feeling upbeat. Hopeful. Almost cheerful. Liam O'Neill hadn't returned to the restaurant last night. He hadn't lurked in the alley, waiting to test her shaky resistance to him. The madman who'd written the horror novels had left her alone—which was exactly what she wanted.

She'd telephoned Robert from the restaurant after leaving Aunt Grace's store yesterday. She wasn't about to inform him of her pregnancy over the phone, but she wanted to set up a time to meet with him, as she had with her aunt.

His secretary had informed her that he was in Los Angeles on business.

Typical, she thought with a wry laugh. Robert's taking off on an out-of-town business trip without bothering to inform her was nothing unusual. She wasn't hurt. He didn't have to clear his travel plans with her. But it was only one more bit of proof that whatever kept the two of them together, it wasn't passion.

Love just didn't work, she concluded grimly, sinking deeper in her chair as Cassie appraised her in the vanity mirror. Look at her cousin Megan and her fiancé, Edward, who had abandoned her at the alter. Look at Aunt Grace and Uncle Jeffrey.

Look at Mallory and Liam. No, *Robert*. Mallory and *Robert*.

"You really do need a touch more color on the cheeks," Cassie murmured as she dabbed a cosmetics brush into a jar of powdered rouge. "The lights on the set are going to bleach you out."

"Fine," Mallory conceded with a wan smile. "Go ahead and turn me into a painted woman." She didn't want to think about love right now. She wanted to think about cooking, which rarely disappointed the way love did.

"I hear you're doing your show on comfort food," Cassie said, highlighting Mallory's cheekbones with a dusting of pink. "It doesn't sound like your usual stuff."

"It's not." Most of the shows she did simplified a gourmet cooking technique—how to flambé desserts, how to use roux as a base for various sauces and stews, how to make pasta dough in different flavors and colors. She often instructed her audience on impressive yet easy recipes they could whip up in little time and use to dazzle their families and friends. "What's Up?" offered her airtime every week so she could address the average midday television viewer, teaching that viewer how much fun cooking could be.

Not just fun, but satisfying, fulfilling, therapeutic. Cooking brought Mallory more gratification than just about anything else she did. The only thing she could think of that was more pleasurable was...

A memory of that night at the retreat with Liam O'Neill flashed in her mind. And the more recent memory of his kiss in the alley behind the restaurant. A whisper of heat echoed inside her, steamy and hypnotic, darkening her cheeks more effectively than any powder in Cassie's box of cosmetics. Just one kiss from that man, one touch from a virile stranger...

Oh, yes, it had been pleasurable. But definitely not therapeutic. Quite the opposite, she thought, glancing down at her chest and wondering whether anyone other than she could see that her breasts were larger than they used to be.

Pregnancy was an odd thing. Well, not odd if a woman was married and settled and planning for it. But for Mallory, who hadn't even considered having children when she'd agreed to marry Robert, the very idea that she was carrying a cluster of cells inside her that could evolve into a baby seemed peculiar—and maybe just a bit gratifying, too.

When she'd been preparing her script for today's show, she had been in what could only be called a nesting mood. She had been ruminating on babies, and mommies, and...comfort food. She had scrapped her original idea— adventures in the world of salad greens—and faxed her producer a script about oatmeal and mashed potatoes.

"Are you going to talk about peanut butter? That's my favorite comfort food," Cassie said, placing the brush back in her cosmetics case. "When I've got PMS I eat it by the spoonful. Super-chunky."

"You should buy fresh-ground peanut butter," Mallory recommended. "Or you can grind your own if you've got a food processor. Buy shelled, unsalted peanuts, dump them down the chute and pulverize them into a nice, coarse paste.''

"Yes, Chef Powell," Cassie teased, lifting her hand to her brow in a mock salute. She glanced at the wall clock and then at the speaker bolted above the door. Through the metal mesh came the television station's current sound-track, a game show. "What's Up?" was taped in the morning and then shown from noon to one. It featured light news, celebrity interviews, movie reviews and Mallory's weekly *What's Cooking?* segment. If ratings meant anything, "What's Up?" was just the sort of show Bay Area residents liked to watch while they ate lunch.

"I guess I'm as gorgeous as I'll ever be," Mallory joked with a final glance at the mirror. She stood, rolled her shoulders and gave her head a gentle shake to loosen her hair from the sticky grip of Cassie's hair spray. "Let's get this show on the road."

Cassie trailed her down the corridor to the kitchen studio where she taped her segment. It was a few doors away from the studio that contained the show's principal set. Originally, the producer had considered having Mallory perform her kitchen wizardry on the main set, but the logistics had proved that impossible. A functional kitchen set could not be rolled into place in the cramped studio where the bulk of the show was taped.

Mallory entered her TV kitchen, which looked as if it had been lifted from a sixties sitcom. Swiss-dot café curtains framed the fake window; the center island at which she worked featured a gray plastic surface with black veins marbling it; and the stove was electric, although Mallory hated cooking on an electric range. The producer had promised her that if her cooking segment was a hit, he'd build a new set for her, with a gas range.

Glaring lights hung from the grid of steel beams above the tiny work area. One camera sat on a trolley in the sea of darkness extending in front of the work counter, and another dangled from the ceiling above the range.

Mallory surveyed her work area. One of the other production assistants had laid out the ingredients Mallory had brought for today's show, as well as the precooked dishes. The pots and bowls she was planning to use in her segment were arranged correctly.

"Hey, gorgeous!" the cameraman shouted to her from the shadows beyond the illuminated kitchen set. "You ready to do a lighting check?"

"As long as you don't tell me I look pale," she called back to the man lurking in the shadows behind the main camera. She positioned herself at the counter and watched the silhouetted camera roll and crane, focusing on her.

A row of monitors hung from the ceiling behind the cameraman. One screen showed her—and she was pleased to see she didn't look all that pale. In fact, she thought she looked rather good. Her smile seemed natural; her eyes sparkled. The turquoise of her sweater and headband created a striking contrast with her creamy complexion and black hair.

She looked well rested, too. Last night, she'd slept soundly, because instead of spending her evening reading Liam O'Neill's novel of dementia and rage, she'd skimmed a fashion magazine before drifting off. She'd dreamed about her baby, warm and cuddly dreams about a perfect little being nestled in her arms, gurgling and smelling of baby powder and gazing up at its mother in wonder and love, the same wonder and love Mallory felt whenever she thought of having this child.

For the first time in ages, she had awakened smiling. No one could tell her she looked like hell today.

The monitor next to the one on which she appeared showed the game show the station was broadcasting at the moment, but without the audio. The third monitor showed Sheila Robbins, one of the co-hosts of "What's Up?", smiling perkily and speaking directly to the camera. That monitor's audio was on, allowing Mallory and her cameraman to hear the show as it was being taped.

"Thanks for that report from Mount Tamalpais," Sheila was saying. "Coming up later this hour, during our regular *What's Cooking?* segment, Chef Mallory Powell is going to discuss the emotional benefits of comfort foods. What a lovely combination—comfort and food." She turned to her co-host, Roger Magnus, who sat beside her at a sleek desk in front of a stylized painting of the Golden Gate Bridge. "I read somewhere that eating chocolate releases those happiness enzymes in the brain—endorphins, I think they're called."

Roger chuckled. "True chocoholics don't need a biochemical excuse. They just eat the stuff."

"And go berserk if they can't get it, just like any other addict. I've had some experience with chocolate withdrawal, so I know whereof I speak. Well, Mallory will probably turn comfort foods into something healthy. You know how nutrition-conscious she is."

"Gee," Roger said with a nostalgic smile, "I can still remember a time when I didn't know the fat content of every bite of food that went into my mouth."

"Well, that's what I love about *What's Cooking?* Mallory makes healthy food that also tastes good. I tried that recipe she demonstrated last week for fat-free pasta sauce, with all those chunks of tomato in it."

"Was it good?" Roger appeared impressed.

Sheila giggled guiltily. "It was fabulous. And then I pigged out on garlic bread dripping with butter—but that's another story." She turned from Roger back to the camera. "Before we step into the kitchen with Mallory, we have a special guest to welcome today." The camera followed Sheila as she crossed from the desk to the interview sofa, continuing her introduction as she walked. "Those of you who seek out the darkest corners of the human heart will know this man's name. He's a reclusive writer, a creator of characters who scare us all the more because they're so recognizably human. This author knows the monsters that dwell within our souls, and his latest book is scaring the heck out of readers all across the country. We're very lucky to have with us Liam O'Neill, who wrote the hot-selling new novel *The Unborn*.''

Sheila had reached the sofa, where Liam O'Neill was standing. Mallory dropped the spoon she'd been fidgeting with and swallowed a gasp as his familiar face filled the screen. If she'd been able to tear her gaze from the monitor to look at her own image on the other screen, she had no doubt she would have looked as pale as the bowl of beige oatmeal on the counter in front of her.

Liam O'Neill on "What's Up?"? Why hadn't anyone told her?

Well, why *should* anyone tell her? The producers never cleared their guest list with Mallory. She faxed in her script, then showed up at the studio and taped her segment. One time, she'd made a point of meeting a movie star who'd appeared on the show to promote his new film, and she'd presented him with a slice of the pear tart she'd made. He'd devoured it and asked her to marry him, and everyone had laughed, no one harder than Mallory.

She wasn't going to prepare a treat for Liam, that was for sure. She only hoped she could duck out of the studio after her segment without having to come in contact with him. She'd made up her mind about the baby—but she'd also resolved that Liam O'Neill wasn't going to have the opportunity to cast a vote, yea or nay. It was *her* decision, *her* body, *her* choice, and no stranger with a deranged imagination was going to interfere in her life.

Dressed in a collarless gray shirt and black jeans, the stranger with the deranged imagination looked demonically handsome, both menacing and far too seductive. His hair framed his face in a wild mane of tawny waves, and his eyes glinted like polished steel. His smile as he shook Sheila's hand was lethal.

On the monitor, Mallory watched as he and Sheila sat on the sofa together. The camera zeroed in on the table before them, where his book was prominently displayed.

"Liam, I understand you hate doing interviews," Sheila acknowledged. "But unlike the hero of *The Unborn,* I swear I'm harmless."

He smiled again, cool and restrained.

Sheila looked relaxed enough for both of them. "I'm sure you must get asked this quite often," she said, "but where do you get your ideas?"

"From my brain," he replied.

Mallory would have laughed if she weren't so flummoxed. When he hadn't shown up at the restaurant last night, she had stupidly thought he had gone back to wherever it was he came from. His words the night before had implied that she wasn't the least bit free of him, and in a very real sense, the life growing inside her meant she and Liam would never be completely separate from each other. But if he'd originally intended to keep after her, last night had misled her into thinking he'd changed his mind.

She might have taken comfort in the realization that he'd come to San Francisco only to promote his novel on "What's Up?" But Sheila had just announced that he hated interviews. And if he'd come only to do the show, he wouldn't have arrived several days in advance and stopped in at Mallory's for a couple of beers—and a stolen kiss from her at closing time.

Face it, Mallory—he came for you. For all she knew, he'd agreed to do the show deliberately to get at her. If he couldn't bother her at Mallory's, he would bother her at the studio.

The truth was, he didn't have to go anywhere or do anything to bother her. Merely viewing him on the monitor bothered her. Seeing his troubled eyes, listening to his deep, gravelly voice, watching the motions of his lips—the lips that had skimmed her body and awakened her soul last December, and then reminded her, two nights ago, of everything that had happened at the retreat... All he had to do to bother her was exist.

"Well, that's quite some brain you've got," Sheila Robbins observed. "According to readers and book critics, the most frightening thing about *The Unborn* is the very ordinariness of the characters. They're everyday people. That's part of what freaked me out about this story—that the hero seems so normal."

Liam stared at Sheila. Evidently, he felt no obligation to respond.

Gamely, she plowed ahead. "Do you consider yourself normal?"

He laughed, a soft, throaty chuckle that carried only a hint of sarcasm. Then he offered a cryptic answer: "I'm a writer."

"You used to be a professor," Sheila said. "Right across the Bay Bridge, at U.C., Berkeley."

Mallory flinched, knocking an empty pan off the counter. The loud clatter as it hit the floor failed to rattle her. She was too stunned by the idea of Liam O'Neill as a university professor.

"That was another lifetime," he said laconically.

"What was your field of study?"

"As I said," he repeated firmly, his eyes flinty and his hands unnaturally still against his knees, "that was another lifetime."

Mallory knew Sheila would have to back off from her line of questioning. "What's Up?" was supposed to be lighthearted chitchat, not investigative journalism. If Sheila wanted authors to come on her show, she had to treat them nicely.

But Mallory didn't have to abandon the subject. She tried to visualize Liam teaching in a college classroom. He seemed too... intense. She couldn't picture him presenting an esoteric lecture on Hegelian philosophy or scribbling unfathomable calculus problems across a chalkboard, or conducting a chamber orchestra, or giving dramatic readings of Euripides' plays. In fact, she couldn't picture him standing in front of a lecture hall and discussing *anything*. He seemed too tightly wound, too threatening. Too virile.

"I've heard rumors that Hollywood is interested in *The Unborn*," Sheila went on.

"I've heard those rumors, too," Liam said, then smiled again. Even though his smile hid a lot, it showed off his rugged handsomeness. It occurred to Mallory that she wanted to see him smile in person, not on a TV monitor. And then it occurred to her that she shouldn't want to see him at all.

"Any idea who'd play the hero? Brad Pitt, maybe? Keanu Reeves?"

"The book really doesn't have a hero," Liam argued. "The main character is a psychopathic murderer."

"Yet the reader cheers for him, because we recognize why he commits murder. There's a genuine sense of underlying justice in this book. He's trying to avenge a terrible wrong."

"In other words, you think his murderous impulses are actually moral?" Liam was still smiling, but his smile seemed less defensive now, more mischievous. Mallory smiled, too. She hardly knew him, yet it seemed just like him that he would turn the tables on Sheila, posing the questions so she would have to answer them, as if he and not she were the talk-show host.

She accepted the role-reversal with equanimity. "Actually, after reading *The Unborn*, I was left pondering the meaning of morality. It's kind of a surprise, the way the philosophical ambiguity creeps up on you. You're left with the idea that maybe the moral questions your novel leaves unanswered are more horrifying than the blood and gore."

Liam's smile was even broader. His eyes sparkled with amusement. Mallory's breath caught in her throat. She had responded to his physical attributes—far more than was wise—but she'd never before acknowledged the heart-melting warmth in his face. When he smiled that way, not his cold, skeptical smile but a smile of genuine humor, the harsh lines and angles of his face softened into something gentle and beckoning.

Gazing at him on the monitor above the camera, she felt her heart trip over itself and her abdomen tense. The man could turn her on even when all she wanted from him was a quick disappearing act.

"Five minutes, Mallory," Cassie called out from a dark corner of the studio.

Yanking her attention from the monitor, Mallory scanned the work counter, trying to collect her thoughts and remember what she was supposed to be doing: not obsessing on Liam's unnervingly potent smile and the news that he had once been a professor at U.C., Berkeley, but planning her segment on comfort foods. She bent down to collect the pan and spoon she'd knocked onto the floor and placed them back on the counter. She inventoried her ingredients, her precooked dishes and her copy of the script, tucked discreetly out of camera range on the counter, even though the TelePrompTer would scroll her speech before her while she spoke. Reassured that she had everything properly organized, she let her gaze wander back to the monitor.

"So, Liam, what's next for you?" Sheila asked. "Are you working on a new book?"

"Yes."

"And enjoying San Francisco, I hope?"

"Oh, yes." He seemed to stare straight through the monitor at Mallory. "San Francisco is very special to me."

"Really? What do you think makes this city special?"

Liam continued to stare directly at Mallory—at least, it felt that way to her. Given his deep contemplation of his answer, she knew he wasn't going to resort to the usual clichés about the hills, the cable cars, Fisherman's Wharf and the Golden Gate Bridge. "I have . . ." He paused, his eyes searching, as if he could see Mallory in the camera lens. "Emotional ties to this city."

"That sounds intriguing," Sheila murmured. "What kind of ties?"

"Emotional ones," he said, at last turning to look at her.

His expression must have been forbidding, because she had the good sense to back off with a laugh. "Well, Liam, once again I'd like to thank you for stopping by "What's Up?" And remember, folks—" Sheila lifted his book into camera range "—*The Unborn*, by Liam O'Neill. This book will give you sleepless nights. You have my word on it."

The monitor switched from Sheila to Roger at the desk. "After these messages, we'll be back with Mallory Powell, who'll tell us what's cooking on 'What's Up?' Don't go away!" The monitor switched again, this time to a taped commercial.

"Two minutes, Mallory," Cassie announced.

Emotional ties? Mallory thought frantically, her hands trembling slightly as she lined up her utensils on the counter one more time. Was *she* the emotional tie he was referring to?

For God's sake, she wasn't tied to him. At least not in any way he could possibly know about. Just because he made a riveting impression on TV didn't mean Mallory wanted any connection to him.

"One minute, Mallory."

She took a deep, steadying breath and stared at the camera. The opening paragraph of her script appeared in large, clear print on the TelePrompTer, and she skimmed it, praying for the words to crowd out all thoughts of Liam O'Neill.

"Thirty seconds."

The monitor showed Roger Magnus peering attentively into the camera. "Welcome back to this Thursday edition of 'What's Up?' As you know, on Thursday we feature *What's Cooking?* with our resident chef, Mallory Powell. I believe she's got a different kind of show for us today. Mallory?"

The camera's red bulb flashed on before her, and Mallory's face replaced Roger's on the monitor. *No more Liam,* she commanded, shaping a smile. *Forget about him. You're on.* "Hi," she said brightly. "It's mid-February, it's been a long winter, and who cares about how to whip up the perfect meringue? When it's chilly and foggy outside, what we need is to be warm and cozy inside. And in the kitchen, that means comfort food."

HE SAT IN THE SMALL greenroom lounge across the hall from the studio, gaping at the television monitor on the table beside him. There was Mallory, presiding over a kitchen—somewhere in this building—and discussing oatmeal. The shock of it made Liam laugh.

Actually, he'd pretty much recovered from his initial shock. It had jabbed him in the gut while he'd been standing by the sofa on the set, roasting beneath a bank of sizzling lights and watching two offensively pretty people yammer about Mount Tamalpais while he waited for his turn on camera. When he'd heard Sheila mention *Chef Mallory Powell,* he'd flinched, then fought the temptation to storm across the set, grab the pert TV hostess by the shoulders and demand that she tell him where Mallory was, right then, that very instant.

But he'd kept his cool. He'd behaved as Creighton Daggett and Hazel and all the other publishing bozos in New York wanted him to. He'd made nice with the TV lady, he'd talked, he'd answered her questions using reasonably grammatical sentences. Cripes, he deserved a medal.

Instead of a medal, his reward was this: watching Mallory on television.

She looked...*amazing*. There was no other word for the impact she had on him, even through the filtering medium of television. The vibrant turquoise of her sweater made her eyes appear bluer and warmed her cheeks, turning them the pink-and-gold hue of a ripe peach. Her hair hung loose past her shoulders, a stark, lustrous cascade of black.

She was talking about oatmeal. And Liam O'Neill—a man whose idea of gourmet cooking was to use Dijon mustard instead of the regular kind on his ham-and-cheese sandwich—was hanging on her every word.

"I know you hated oatmeal when you were a child. *I* hated it, too. But let me tell you a secret about oatmeal...."

Yes, he wanted to shout at the television. *Tell me your secret.*

"When you're a grown-up, oatmeal tastes pretty good. It's the easiest thing in the world to make—rolled oats, a pinch of salt and boiling water." The camera showed her dumping the ingredients into a pot. "Stir it and let it boil until it gets thick. There's nothing to it. That's one of the wonderful things about comfort foods—they're easy. Easy to make, easy to eat—and they make you feel all warm and mushy inside."

You make me feel warm and mushy, too, Liam thought, then amended that. Warm, yes. Mushy, no. She made everything inside him go hard and tight.

"You might want to add brown sugar to your oatmeal to give it flavor, but of course that's got lots of calories. No fat, but it *is* fattening. Instead, try sweetening your oatmeal by stirring in some thin-sliced apples sprinkled with cinnamon and nutmeg. Or slice a banana into your oatmeal. You can stir in all-fruit jam or dates and nuts. Nothing tastes more comforting on a raw, wet day." She held up an already cooked bowl of oatmeal with sliced apples arranged prettily across the surface.

"The next comfort food I want to talk about," she continued, "is mashed potatoes. Ah, I can hear you all sighing nostalgically now. When was the last time you had mashed potatoes?"

Liam snorted. Potatoes had been a mainstay in his diet when he was growing up. To him, the greatest luxury in the world was having rice or spaghetti instead of potatoes at dinnertime.

"I don't boil the potatoes, because that makes them watery. Instead, I bake them in a hot oven for about an hour, an hour and fifteen minutes. Then I cut the skins in half and scrape out the potato. Save those skins—" she held up some hollowed-out skins "—so you can serve the mashed potatoes in them. Forget the butter. That's what makes them fattening. Instead, mash them with a little skimmed milk, and then flavor them with chopped fresh chives, fresh-ground pepper, paprika, minced garlic, whatever you like. Chop in some water chestnuts for crunch. Be creative. One of the great things about comfort foods is that they're kind of bland, so you can add all sorts of flavors. There's no right or wrong when it comes to comfort foods.

"A production assistant was asking me, just before the show, whether I was going to discuss peanut butter. I wasn't planning on it, but peanut butter is her comfort food. What's yours? Chicken soup? Easiest thing in the world. And some doctors believe it really can cure a host of ailments."

Liam leaned back in one of the small vinyl chairs furnishing the lounge. Chicken soup. Mallory Powell was turning him on by talking about chicken soup.

Nearly ten minutes were up. She turned briefly from the camera to lift a platter on a counter behind her, then turned back to the camera and revealed the plate with a flourish. The broad glass dish was heaped high with chocolate chip cookies. "True confessions," she admitted, her sheepish smile ratcheting up his arousal another notch. God, she was gorgeous when she smiled. Particularly *that* smile, a touch apologetic, a touch bashful... a touch wicked. "You all know how I like to emphasize good health in cooking. But sometimes you've just got to splurge. Especially when we're talking about comfort food, the special foods we reach for when life is stressing us out and getting us down. So here's my confession—sometimes the only thing that will bring me comfort is a hot, sweet, chewy, homemade chocolate chip cookie. If this is the route you're going to take, then I say, forget the fat. Forget the calories. Forget everything but how wonderful chocolate chip cookies are." She lifted one from the plate and took a lusty bite out of it. A contented sigh escaped her. "That's it, folks. I'm comforted! This is Mallory Powell, telling you what's cooking. Back to you, Sheila and Roger."

The camera returned to the set where Liam had appeared. Sheila was grinning covetously. "I want one of those cookies!" she whined. "Someone go steal that plate from Mallory!"

"Yeah! She can keep the oatmeal," Roger chimed in. "We want those cookies!"

"I bet you do, too," Sheila addressed the viewing audience. "Hot from the oven, sweet and chewy. Thanks for whetting our appetites, Mallory. Coming up next..."

Liam hoisted himself to his feet and strode out of the greenroom. He didn't want a cookie. He wanted the hot, sweet chef who had just whetted his appetite. And if he didn't track down her kitchen studio right away, she might leave the building before he could find her.

He glanced down the hall one way. It was ruler-straight, well lit, flanked by heavy black doors with On Air lights above them, none glowing. He glanced down the other way and saw the On Air light turn off above one of the doors. It swung inward, and a young man with a clipboard and a headset bounded out, followed by a woman barely out of her teens, carrying a familiar-looking plate of cookies.

Followed by Mallory, blinking in the hall's bright light. A smudge of chocolate stained her lower lip, and a few golden crumbs hovered in the corner of her mouth.

Liam realized, with growing hunger, that he wanted to taste one of those cookies, after all. He wanted to taste the crumbs clinging to her lip, the smear of chocolate. He wanted to taste the woman who could bring him comfort like nothing else in the world.

CHAPTER SEVEN

SHE HALTED SEVERAL FEET from him. "I had no idea you were going to be on the show," she said. Her voice was taut, her eyes round with panic. Obviously, she didn't want to see him.

But what the hell. She hadn't wanted to see him in the dark alley behind her restaurant, either—until he'd kissed her. For those few incredible minutes when his mouth crushed down on hers, she'd wanted to see him, all right. She'd wanted to see him with enough passion to tilt the earth's axis.

"I had no idea you were going to be on it, either," he told her. Above him a fluorescent light buzzed. Important-looking people raced past them, chattering into cordless phones and carrying plastic cups of coffee. Liam had things he wanted to say to Mallory, but this hall wasn't the place to say them.

He reached for her hand. She didn't shrink from him, but as his fingers closed around hers, she seemed to twitch slightly. Her hand was cold and stiff. Her eyes widened even more as he pulled her toward the open door to the green-room lounge.

As soon as they were both inside, he closed the door. The monitor was still on; Sheila and Roger, effervescent with excitement, were discussing tomorrow's guests. Without releasing Mallory's hand, Liam strode across the room and shut it off.

Her fingers moved within his clasp; the heat from his palm seemed to thaw the ice in them. Gradually, almost imperceptibly, she began to relax. Her eyes remained fixed on him, her ebbing panic replaced by wariness.

"We have to talk," he said, trying not to let the residue of her chocolate chip cookie distract him.

"There's nothing to say."

"There's too much to say. That's why we're both afraid to say it."

"I'm not afraid of you." The faint tremor in her voice contradicted her words.

The cookie crumb was driving him insane. So was her scent—an odd mix of floral perfume, melted chocolate and tart apples. He tightened his grip on her, pulling her into his arms. "Why fight it, Mallory? We're crazy for each other. You know it as well as I do."

"I'm engaged to be married."

"He's not worth it."

Her eyebrows shot up. Amusement filtered through her skepticism, dimpling her cheek. "How would you know what he's worth?"

"He's probably worth millions," Liam muttered. "After all, he appears in the society pages with you."

"I wasn't referring to—"

"But money is irrelevant."

"Yes."

He gazed down into her eyes. They were so clear, so bright they seared his retinas, as if he were staring into the sun. "Do you love him?"

"Liam, I don't think—"

"Do you love him?" he repeated.

She glanced away. "Yes."

He wondered if she was aware of how bad a liar she was. She might as well be wearing a neon sign that flashed Not True whenever she uttered a falsehood. "If you loved him so very much," he pointed out, "you wouldn't have come to me in the gazebo."

"I didn't come to you. You came to me."

"You received me." *Received him?* Cripes, that sounded so archaic. But at least he was speaking honestly. "What kind of claim does he have on you? You aren't even wearing an engagement ring."

"He hasn't—we haven't had a chance to pick one out yet."

"That's all I want, Mallory—a chance. Get to know me. Don't marry him until you know for sure."

"I *do* know for sure," she murmured, turning her gaze back to him. She searched his face, openly questioning, openly wondering. The truth burned in her eyes: she didn't love Robert Benedict. She wasn't at all certain what to do about Liam, but her uncertainty had nothing to do with love for her fiancé.

"I'm asking for a chance," he whispered, lifting his hands to her jaw and using his thumbs to tilt her face upward so he could gaze directly at her—so she would have little choice but to gaze at him. "That's all I'm asking for. A chance."

"A chance for what?" Her voice was even more hushed than his, barely a breath of sound in the small room.

He could think of a million answers, none of which would persuade her to trust him. Instead, he did the one thing guaranteed to make her distrust him completely. He lowered his mouth to hers.

He tasted the chocolate on her skin, warm and bittersweet. He tasted fear and desire, loneliness and need. He tasted the shivery rush of yearning that softened her lips against his, made them caress his and mold to his and part to welcome his tongue.

He'd been with women since the accident. Yet none of them seeped under his skin the way Mallory did. None of them insinuated themselves so deeply, so personally into his psyche. He couldn't begin to guess why she, of all the women in the universe, should be the one to lure him back to life, to make him willing to risk feeling something more than the momentary release of sex. He had no idea what she did to him, or why. All he knew was that he would fight any resistance she put up, any way he could, for the chance to place his heart at risk.

Right now, she wasn't putting up any resistance at all. Her mouth opened fully to him and she clenched her hands against his upper arms. Sighing, she closed her eyes and gave herself fully to the kiss, her tongue dueling with his, her breath a quiet moan deep in her throat as he slid his hands to her hips and pulled her hard against him. If her response was anything to go by, she was as willing to risk everything as he was.

He moved his hands lower, cupping her bottom and guiding her against him. A shudder racked her and she moaned again. Whatever he was doing to her, he was doing ten times as intensely to himself. He was ready to burst—out of his trousers, out of his skin. It was glorious torture, pressing the heat of her against him. If only they were somewhere far away, in a garden under the moon, with no one to see or hear them ...

Like the punch line to a stupid joke, the door swung open and a young fellow with a headset wrapped around his neck peeked in. "Oops!" he exclaimed. "Sorry—I was looking for someone."

Before Liam could speak, the guy vanished, slamming the door shut behind him.

Mallory hid her face against Liam's shoulder. "This is wrong," she said.

"No. It's very right." He skimmed his hands up to her waist, to her sides, along the arch of her ribs. His thumbs traced the curves of her breasts.

She shook her head but didn't back away. "Liam, please ..."

"I want you so much I can't sleep," he confessed. "I can't write. I can't concentrate." He followed the rounded swells of her flesh, feeling her heat through her tunic, wishing he could tear it off and massage her breasts, knead them, kiss them until she was too aroused to argue with him. "All I think about is that night—"

"Don't." Her voice emerged thick and throaty.

"It was so good, Mallory. So good between us."

"It can't happen again." At last, she eased out of his embrace. Her face was flushed, her hair mussed. Breaking from him, she paced the lounge as if anxious to burn off her tension. "That technician saw us. This is a disaster."

"Who cares what he saw?"

"*I* care. I work in this town, you know. I have to appear on that TV show every week."

"Why?"

"Why?" She halted in her circuit around the room and gaped at him. "What do you mean, why?" she repeated, evidently stunned.

"Why do you have to appear on the show? Do you need the money? The publicity?"

She opened her mouth and then shut it. Her eyes, startlingly bright, never wavered.

"It's a valid question, Mallory. Why do you have to do the show? Why do you have to marry Robert Benedict?"

"Don't twist me around this way!" she stormed. "You don't understand anything about my life."

"I want to."

"Do you? Well, here's what *I* want. I want you to stay away from me. I want you to go home, wherever that is, and lead your own life, and chalk last December up to a pleasant memory."

"*Pleasant?*" He wanted to roar in protest at her understatement, but she was already so spooked he kept his voice low and calm, only the slightest bit ironic. "*Pleasant* isn't the word I'd use to describe it."

"Well, that's all it was. Just one of those things." She reached for the door and twisted the knob, then turned back to him. Her expression was plaintive. "Go home, Liam. Please. Just leave me alone and go home." Her eyes glimmering with moisture, she cast him a wistful parting look before she stepped out into the hall.

He watched her leave, aching to call after her that home was no more his desolate cabin up north than it was Berkeley, or Ann Arbor, or Boston. Home was nowhere he could think of, because home had to do with love and family, and his life was devoid of both. Yet when he looked at Mallory, when he held her, when he kissed her...he almost had a hint of what home could be.

Damn it, he was going to get past her lies. He was going to force her to get past them with him. Too much was at stake for her to walk away from him, frustrated and miserable at the choice she'd made.

She might say she wanted him to leave her alone. But he wasn't going to, not until she could convince him it was the right thing to do.

BY THE FOLLOWING MONDAY morning, she realized that Liam O'Neill was gone.

She had spent the last few days figuratively glancing over her shoulder, watching for him, expecting him to materialize out of thin air and resolving to be ready, no matter where or when he finally showed up. Locking the restaurant at night, she searched the alley's shadows for him. Strolling down the street to the bookstore for a mocha latte, she surveyed the crowds for him. Whenever a cable car clanged past her, she scanned the passengers, certain she was going to glimpse his face, his long, tawny blond hair.

But she didn't see him. And with each passing day, she felt...*better,* she swore to herself. Relieved. Free of his charismatic pull, his impassioned words, free of the fierce power of his kisses.

She was glad he was gone. Now, at last, she could start making plans.

Her first order of business was to talk to Robert. She had telephoned him from the restaurant Sunday evening, hoping to find him home from his business trip to Los Angeles. But he wasn't there. She had considered calling her father to ask him Robert's whereabouts, but the idea that her father might know more about her fiancé than she herself did was appalling, even if it happened to be true.

She would have to tell her father about her situation once she'd figured out where she stood with Robert. If Robert decided to stand by her, her father would, too. But if, as was much more likely, Robert rejected her... She knew her father wouldn't embrace her the way Aunt Grace had. Her father didn't understand messy passion. He didn't understand anything that couldn't be rationalized or calculated or printed on paper. He had always claimed to understand Grace's marriage to Jeffrey DeWilde, because Jeffrey had been the rich scion of a dynasty and Powells were destined, whether through marriage or through hard work, to regain their stature in the world. It would never have occurred to Leland Powell that his sister Grace had married for love.

Nor would it have occurred to him that his daughter should marry for love. Love didn't fit into his agenda, not once he'd recovered from the devastation of losing Mallory's mother.

Mallory sensed that in his awkward, detached way, her father did love her. But he didn't approve of her. All she'd ever wanted from him was acceptance and paternal pride, a smile and a hug and a few words: "You're doing great, Mallory, and I respect everything you've accomplished in your life."

Fat chance he'd ever say that, now that she had decided to have an out-of-wedlock child while simultaneously sending that child's father packing.

She would sound Aunt Grace out at dinner tonight. She had invited her aunt to come to her condominium at around five-thirty; that would give them the entire evening to relax and talk. By now, Grace must have gotten over her shock at Mallory's news. Any residual turbulence could be smoothed over with a delicious shrimp dinner.

She left the apartment early Monday morning, driving down to the docks of Fisherman's Wharf to buy fresh shrimp. She did enough regular business with the shrimpers and fishermen there that they welcomed her like an old friend. She enjoyed shooting the breeze with the shrimpers, who woke up in the wee hours to dredge the chilly waters of the bay, who dressed in slickers and wool and smelled of deep salt water. They weren't people she would ever meet on the society circuit, at the latest fund-raiser or charity ball. They weren't people she would run into outside Powell Enterprises' steel-and-glass skyscraper on Montgomery Street. Yet she felt comfortable with them, the way she felt comfortable with Burt and her apprentices and waiters at the restaurant, or with Cassie and the interns at "What's Up?" Or with a brutally honest, unpretentious horror novelist named Liam O'Neill.

Preposterous! She didn't feel the least bit comfortable with Liam. Whenever he was around, it was all she could do to keep her mind functioning. The instant he touched her, her brain turned to oatmeal—and unlike the oatmeal she'd glorified during her TV appearance last week, this mental oatmeal wasn't a comfort. It was just...trouble.

She was thrilled about his having left town. Really. She was jubilant. Ecstatic.

She bought way too much shrimp, because the shrimpers were giving her such a good price. She would have to cook it all; shrimp tasted bland if it wasn't cooked fresh. She didn't worry about having too much, though. Whatever she and Grace didn't eat tonight, she would pack up in a doggie bag for her aunt to take home with her.

From the wharf, Mallory journeyed across town to one of the green markets, where she bought vegetables not quite as exciting as what Reuben Cortes was able to get for her—but then, Reuben had connections she couldn't begin to dream of. She purchased a head of spinach, an assortment of mushrooms, fresh chives, leeks, plum tomatoes and winter pears. A few days ago, browsing among the booths and tables heaped high with fresh produce might have made her queasy. But she felt healthy now, and her appetite was blossoming like a rose in April.

She was going to have fun with this intimate dinner party, she decided. She was going to cook and schmooze with her aunt and not even think about Liam O'Neill. She wasn't going to think about his eyes, as hard and metallic as rivets, able to pin a woman down and demand her attention. She wasn't going to think about the friction of his callused fingertips against her skin, and the heat and hunger of his mouth as it took hers. She wasn't going to think about the way his hips felt against hers, seeking, pressing, promising a rapture she had never known before she'd met him, or since. She wasn't going to think about his low, dark voice, demanding that she give him a chance.

She wasn't going to waste another second of her life thinking about him.

By midafternoon, she was happily ensconced in her kitchen, surrounded by pots and pans, ingredients and aromas. A fresh tomato sauce simmered on the stove; a pound and a half of basil-flavored pasta dough waited to be cranked through the linguine die of her pasta-maker. Her windows were open to let in the mild afternoon air, and her CD player spilled Bonnie Raitt's mellifluous blues from the living room speakers. As Mallory shelled her boiled shrimp, she hummed along with the music. Love might have found Bonnie Raitt in the nick of time, she thought. And love of a different kind—she glanced down at her belly—had found Mallory, too.

She'd taken her chance, and she was prepared to accept the consequences. But she wasn't going to take any more chances now. She couldn't. She had a baby to think about. She had to save her heart for the new life inside her, not wager it on Liam O'Neill.

Whom she absolutely, positively was *not* going to think about anymore.

Her doorbell rang. A glance at her wall clock told her it was too early for Aunt Grace to have come. Unlike Mallory's restaurant, Grace was open on Mondays, and Aunt Grace reigned over her shop like a benevolent despot. Even though Rita Mulholland was fully capable of managing the store, Grace liked to be a part of everything that went on there.

Mallory wiped her garlic-scented hands on a towel and crossed to the foyer. Squinting through the peephole, she discovered Alex Stowe on the other side of the door.

She swung it open. "Alex! What are you doing here?"

"Following my nose, as usual. I smelled garlic and started salivating like one of Pavlov's dogs." He was dressed neatly but casually in khaki trousers and a pine green shirt. His smile was enigmatic. He held his hands behind his back, tempting Mallory to glimpse around him to see what he was hiding from her.

"Alex, Alex, Alex." She clicked her tongue and laughed. "A person might think you were starving to death upstairs. What would you do if you didn't have me to feed you?"

"I'd feed myself and wish I was eating your dinner instead of my own," he said with exaggerated self-pity. "Actually, I come here bearing gifts." With a flourish, he brought his hands forward to display a bottle of champagne. "I've just won the commission for the new Carlisle Forrest building in Atlanta. You're looking at an architect with a very big project on his drafting table."

"Oh, Alex! That's wonderful!" She gave him an exuberant hug.

"I thought I'd take a chance and see if you were available to drink a toast to me. But since you're so busy making snide remarks about my inability to feed myself—"

"Stay for dinner," she blurted out, then bit her lip and considered the rash invitation. A moment's contemplation reassured her. She did want Alex to stay. So what if his presence would make it impossible for her to discuss her future with Aunt Grace? Maybe that was just as well. Mallory had to figure out her future for herself, by herself—and she wouldn't be able to do that until after she'd spoken to Robert. It would be just as well if the evening didn't center on her current predicament.

Alex was a sweetheart, and she honestly loved feeding him. He always appreciated her culinary skill, and he never demanded anything more of her than her company. She doubted Aunt Grace would mind if he joined them. As a matter of fact...

Still smiling, Mallory accepted the bottle from him and cast him a quick, assessing glance. He was looking particularly dapper tonight, his hair a thick silver mass, his excitement about the new commission giving his eyes an unusual radiance.

What if Alex and her aunt...

No. Mallory refused to play matchmaker. She couldn't even straighten out her own love life—she wasn't about to meddle in Grace's. Or Alex's.

And yet...

The idea was preposterous. Grace still hadn't healed from the wounds Jeffrey had inflicted on her. And Alex Stowe relished his bachelorhood. There was absolutely no potential for anything between him and Grace. Absolutely none.

By the time she'd dismissed the notion, he had wandered ahead of her into the kitchen. "Oh, my God!" he howled, as if he'd discovered a bloody corpse on the floor. "You're hosting a party and you didn't invite me!"

"I was hosting a dinner for two, and now it's a dinner for three because I *did* invite you," she retorted, following him into the kitchen.

Alex stood near the center island, gazing in awe at the food preparations cluttering her counters and stove top. He spun around at her entrance, his smile contrite. "I'm interrupting a dinner for two? Why didn't you tell me? You don't need a chaperone."

"You aren't interrupting anything, Alex. It's just my aunt. Please stay. You'll love her."

"Your aunt? The famous expatriate?" His eyebrows flickered up and down, playfully lecherous. Mallory had told him about Grace—or, more accurately, about the DeWilde empire and her aunt's decision, upon separating from Jeffrey, to found her own bridal shop in San Francisco. "Is she going to slap my hand if I use the wrong fork?"

"No. *I'll* slap your hand."

He pouted. "Do I have to practice proper etiquette?"

"Aunt Grace raised three kids. She's used to rowdy behavior. I think she can handle you."

"Ah." His smile deepened. "Any woman who can handle me deserves a medal."

"I guess I deserve a medal, then," Mallory teased, crossing to the stove to give her sauce a stir. "If you're going to stay, make yourself useful." She slid the bottle of champagne into the refrigerator, then handed him an apron and steered him toward the pasta-maker. "Your job is to cut off the strips of linguine when they reach a reasonable length. Every eight inches or so. Can you handle that?"

"Eight inches and it gets cut off? Hmm." His eyebrows began twitching wickedly again.

"Watch it." Mallory brandished a knife. "You're already testing *my* tolerance for rowdiness."

"I have to get the rowdiness out of my system before the queen of the weddings arrives."

"Get cutting that linguine," Mallory ordered him, reaching for the garlic. She was feeling a lot more excited about dinner now that Alex was going to be a part of it. No longer was it going to be about her and her predicament, a predicament she would really rather not think about, because thinking about it meant thinking about Liam O'Neill.

Whom, she swore on a sleek white bulb of garlic, she wasn't going to think about ever again—or at least not for the next couple of hours.

BY LIAM'S ESTIMATION, there were at least one hundred Powells listed in the San Francisco telephone book, more than a few of them identified with the first initial *M.* Then, too, it was always possible she didn't live in the city.

He had spent the weekend at home, ostensibly trying to get some writing done on his new book, but mostly trying to come up with a new strategy for gaining Mallory's trust. He wasn't used to courting women—even before his marriage, courting hadn't been the way he related to women. He would meet a lady, and if the mood was right, the attraction real and mutual, he would go with it.

Then he'd met Jennifer, and he'd no longer had to worry about the right way to capture a woman's interest.

He didn't want to capture Mallory's interest. Hell, he already had her interest, and more. What he wanted—what he *needed*—was to persuade her that his selfish yearning to feel as much as he'd felt last December at the retreat was more important than anything going on in her life.

Selfish was the word, all right. He was demanding that she drop her fiancé, her plans, everything that mattered to her—just because if she didn't, he would lose his mind.

Given the stakes, he wasn't going to give up. For the first time in five years, he had discovered something worth fighting for. Maybe that was what she'd stirred inside him—the will to fight.

Monday morning, he headed back to San Francisco, a warrior marching to battle, prepared to put himself on the line once more. He took a room at the Hyatt Regency, since he knew the place, and unpacked everything in his suitcase—a few changes of clothing, toiletries and the newspaper society page describing the fund-raiser for the San Francisco Ballet at which Mallory had been photographed, standing with her Ken doll of a fiancé. Liam studied the photo for a moment, then looked up the telephone number of the San Francisco Ballet. "Can I speak to someone in fund-raising?" he asked the receptionist who answered his call.

After the requisite eternity on hold, he was connected with an unctuous woman who seemed to think he was interested in sending her a tax-deductible check. "Actually, I'm trying to reach one of your benefactors," Liam explained. "Robert Benedict."

"We don't give out personal information about our benefactors," the woman said.

"That's all right—I don't want personal information. I just want to be able to reach him. Do you have a work number you could pass along?"

"His work number..." She stalled.

He pressed ahead anyway, figuring it couldn't hurt. "I've been a big fan of the ballet all my life. I especially like the way your company interprets—" he scrambled for a ballet he could name "—*The Nutcracker*. I take my class of third-graders there every year," he added, hoping she would consider a schoolteacher less threatening.

His ploy worked. "Well, I do have a work number here for Mr. Benedict, at Powell Enterprises." She recited the phone number. Liam jotted it down on a sheet of hotel stationery.

After thanking the woman, he hung up. Powell Enterprises, he pondered, staring at the phone number. Powell Enterprises must be connected to Mallory in some way. He couldn't believe that Mallory Powell's boyfriend could have landed a job at a company called Powell by coincidence.

He considered dialing the number, then thought better of it. Thumbing through the San Francisco directory, he found a listing for Powell Enterprises in the business pages. The address was Montgomery Street, and the telephone number matched the number the lady at the ballet had given him.

A few short blocks from the hotel, Liam located the company, which occupied the top five floors of a tower in the heart of the city's business district. He had never understood why people built skyscrapers on a fault line, but San Francisco had its share of them. What would happen to the Powell he cared about if the Big One hit? Who was the Powell of Powell Enterprises? What the hell *was* Powell Enterprises, anyway?

Stepping out of the elevator on the twenty-fifth floor, he knew at least something about Powell Enterprises: it was lucrative. The reception area had the electrically charged aura of a company where great sums of money exchanged hands. The carpet was plush enough to deaden his steps as he approached a receptionist posted behind an elegant, geometric desk carved from a solid block of redwood.

"Hi," he said, offering his best smile to the young, chic woman behind the desk. "I'd like to see Robert Benedict."

"Do you have an appointment?" she asked, batting tastefully mascara-darkened eyelashes at him.

"No. But I'll only take a minute of his time."

"And your name is...?"

"Liam O'Neill."

"What is this in reference to?"

"Ballet."

The receptionist eyed his scruffy leather jacket, his jeans and his thick-soled leather shoes. Liam's apparel did not shout *ballet*. Still, she did her job, lifting her telephone receiver and tapping several buttons on her console.

"Mr. Benedict?" she asked, her gaze never wavering from Liam. Her fingernails were long and square, tipped with white enamel. "There's a gentleman here named Liam O'Neill who wants to speak to you about the ballet. He doesn't have an appointment." She listened for a minute. "Okay. I'll tell him." Lowering the phone, she glanced dubiously at Liam's hands. Toughened from years of carpentry and wood-chopping, they were the antithesis of balletic. "Mr. Benedict can spare you about five minutes, but you'll have to wait," she said, then pursed her lips in mild disapproval.

"Fine." Liam crossed to the sofa of glove-soft leather. Copies of *Forbes* and *Business Week* lay in a neat fan-shaped display on the glass-topped coffee table in front of the couch. Liam lifted one and pretended to read it.

High finance held no interest for him. According to Hazel, *The Unborn* was making him rich, but growing rich had never been one of his objectives. He liked not having to think before he spent money on something, not having to budget and scrimp. Other than that, accumulating wealth seemed a rather boring pursuit.

He checked his watch. Two-thirty. He wondered how late Powell Enterprises stayed open, how long Robert Benedict was going to let him cool his heels. He wondered how enamored of the ballet the guy was. Did Benedict donate money because Mallory wanted him to? Or because Powell Enterprises encouraged its employees to be charitable?

Liam reached the end of the magazine without having absorbed more than a half-dozen words. He checked his watch. Two-forty.

The receptionist appeared extremely busy behind her desk, riffling through papers, pushing buttons on her phone, tapping the keyboard of the computer on the counter behind her. Every time Liam glanced at her, she swiveled her chair away from him. Twice, she wasn't quick enough, and he caught her staring at him. Both times, she blushed.

Two-forty-six. He leafed through another magazine, scrutinizing advertisements for state-of-the-art laptops, leather briefcases and excruciatingly fancy pens. BMWs were touted, mutual funds lauded. He reached the last page of the magazine. Two-fifty-eight.

The receptionist cleared her throat. "Mr. O'Neill? Mr. Benedict will see you now."

Carefully arranging his face to reveal nothing, Liam rose and followed the stylish receptionist down a long hall, around a bend to a heavy oak door. She knocked timidly, then inched it open. "Mr. Benedict?"

Over her shoulder, Liam glanced into the spacious corner office. Its two walls of glass displayed a vista that included the TransAmerica Pyramid and glimpses of the bay. But the view was less important than the man rising from the massive mahogany desk angled diagonally between the two glass walls.

Robert Benedict was tall and unbearably clean-cut. He could have modeled for the BMW and mutual fund ads in the magazines with which Liam had occupied himself for the past half hour. Robert's dark hair was meticulously barbered, his suit meticulously tailored, his smile meticulously bland. "Thank you, Ellen," he said, dismissing the receptionist, who slipped past Liam and disappeared down the hall.

Robert stood and extended his right hand. "Mr. O'Neill, is it? Come on in." Even his voice was meticulously smooth.

How could Mallory love this guy? Kissing him would be about as exciting as sucking skim milk through a straw.

Still, he worked for Powell Enterprises. If the connection between him and Mallory was about love, it was also about something else.

Liam entered the office, hiked the mile or so between the door and the desk, and shook Robert's hand. "Thanks for sparing me a few minutes," he said. "I know you're busy."

Robert gestured toward one of the ergonomically curved chairs facing him across the desk. Liam sat, and so did Robert. To his credit, he didn't give Liam's casual attire the once-over the way the receptionist had. "I'm sorry you had to wait. I've been out of town, and I'm still trying to catch up." He gestured toward his desk, which looked a hell of a lot neater than Liam's desk at home.

"That's all right."

"You're here about the ballet?"

Liam nodded. "I understand you're one of their benefactors."

"Well..." Robert smiled. His smile, thank goodness, wasn't impeccable. It was slightly crooked, lending his face a sly quality. "The San Francisco Ballet is more my fiancée's hobby than mine."

Liam nodded, struggling to keep his face from giving anything away. "Perhaps I ought to get in touch with her, then."

"What exactly is your involvement with the ballet, Mr. O'Neill?"

"I'm writing a book about a ballet company. I know how difficult it is to keep an artistic enterprise afloat in these days of tight budgets. Fund-raising is a big part of it. I wanted to meet with a few donors, to get a feel for things." That last sentence was the truth, at least.

"You're an author?"

Liam nodded again. "I've written a few horror novels. I have one out now, called *The Unborn*." He figured it was worth mentioning for credibility's sake. "I'd love it if I could dig up something horrible about the ballet."

Robert let loose with a laugh. "Everything about it is horrible. Mallory—that's my fiancée—seems to think we've got to participate in all these galas for the San Francisco Ballet because her family owes it to the city."

"That would be Mallory...?"

"Powell," Robert completed.

"As in Powell Enterprises?"

"This is her father's outfit," Robert confirmed. "Like me, he couldn't care less about the ballet. But there are social obligations. So, you've actually written novels?"

"I actually have."

"I've got to tell you, that sort of thing impresses me. *The Unborn,* you said?"

Liam nodded.

"I think I've heard of it. I'm afraid I don't have time to read much—other than reports and memos. But I'm impressed, Mr. O'Neill. I'm impressed."

Liam was immune to Robert Benedict's flattery, but he suspected Robert Benedict wouldn't be immune to his. "I'm impressed by this great big corner office. You must be running the show here."

Robert chuckled and shook his head. "Hardly. Leland Powell runs Powell Enterprises, and he will be until the day he retires."

"And then you could take over," Liam guessed. "Being married to the boss's daughter and all."

Robert chuckled, falsely modest. "I've been working with Leland for five years. I guess he thinks of me as a son—which is probably one reason he introduced me to his daughter. I suppose it will always be Mallory's and my job to go to assorted society balls, high-profile things, fundraising for acceptable charities and the like. Most recently, we attended a ball for the San Francisco Ballet."

"I read about it in the newspaper not too long ago. The woman in the photograph with you—that was Mallory

Powell, wasn't it." Liam sounded absurdly slow-witted even to himself.

"That was us," Robert said, then rolled his eyes. "It's what happens when you're engaged to a Powell. You put on a monkey suit, write a hefty check and get your picture taken for the newspapers."

"I gather it isn't much fun."

"Well, I've had more fun in my life than I had at that party. You want some information for your book? There were lots of dancers present at the gala. Most of the ballerinas looked anorexic, and the male dancers looked a little light in the pants." He smirked.

Liam dutifully smiled back. "It sounds like it's got horror-novel possibilities."

"It was one of the most frightening nights of my life," Robert joked, obviously enjoying the exaggeration. "All those skeletal ladies and swishy men. But with Mallory on my arm, I somehow got through it. One hefty check bought me a lot of appreciation from Mallory."

Liam resisted the urge to ask Robert exactly how much appreciation Mallory had given him that night. The gala had taken place less than two months after Mallory had given Liam everything—for free.

No, it hadn't been for free. It had cost him his soul. Which was why he was here now, trying to figure out how to regain his soul—and the woman who had found it after it had been lost for so long, and had run off with it.

"If you marry your boss's daughter," he ventured, bleaching each word of incriminating emotion, "you may get stuck going to a lot more parties with skinny women and swishy men."

Robert groaned, evidently sensing sympathy from Liam. "Oh, please—the ballet is just the start of it. If you want to write a horror novel, write about AIDS fund-raising parties."

"Mallory Powell drags you to those, too?"

"When you're a Powell, it's expected. It comes with the territory."

"You must love her very much," Liam remarked, wondering yet again if Robert Benedict could hear his skepticism.

Robert smiled. "Mallory is a special woman. I consider myself very lucky to have her in my life." An intercom on his desk buzzed. "Excuse me," he said, then lifted the receiver and connected the call. "Robert Benedict here—oh, hi, Leland!" He grinned at Liam.

Leland Powell was the boss. The head of the company. Mallory's father. Liam shifted in his seat and stared out the window to camouflage his eavesdropping.

"Tonight? You're going to her house?" Robert spoke into the phone. "No, I didn't know. Oh, your sister's going. Well, Mallory's so close to Grace.... If Mallory wanted me there, she would have invited me. Did she invite you...? Yes, I did pick it up. It's—I don't know if you'd say it's gorgeous. If the price is anything to judge by, it was the most gorgeous one in the store. I hope it fits.... Tonight? If she doesn't want me there... Okay. If you think it's best..." He sighed. "Five-thirty? That's early.... Oh, okay. If that's when your sister is going, five-thirty it is. I'll see you then." He hung up and shook his head.

Liam turned back to him, his face perfectly blank.

"It appears I'm attending a dinner party at Mallory's tonight."

"You know, I'd love to talk to your fiancée about the ballet, too," Liam said. "She's probably more on top of the fund-raising stuff than I am. As an author, I like to get my information straight. You've offered me some really good insights...." *Not necessarily about the ballet, but about your relationship with Mallory,* he added silently. "I'd think Mallory could supply me with some useful information, too."

"You *should* talk to her," Robert agreed. "She owns a restaurant on Union Square—named Mallory's, of all things." He grinned at his own humor. "She won't be there tonight—obviously, she's hosting this spur-of-the-moment dinner party. But tomorrow—"

"I'd hate to have to bother her at work," Liam demurred. "If she's running a restaurant, she isn't going to have time to talk to me."

"Well, I wouldn't want to give out her address, but I suppose you could phone her."

"That'd be great," Liam said.

Robert pulled a business card from a carved mahogany box on his desk, flipped it over and scribbled Mallory's name and a phone number on the back. "Tell her you spoke with me," he suggested. "I'm sure she'll have something to contribute to your book."

Smiling, Liam pocketed the card and stood. If he tracked Mallory down at her home, he suspected she would have something to contribute, all right—and it wouldn't be printable. But now, armed with her phone number, he had improved his odds of finding where she lived. If she was one of the hundred or so Powells listed in the city telephone directory, he could match the number and appear on her doorstep.

Maybe even tonight. With her dinner guests as witnesses, she would have to act civilly toward him, wouldn't she? She would at the very least have to answer her door on the chance that he was another guest.

After thanking Robert Benedict for his time and shaking the man's hand, Liam sauntered out of the office and headed downstairs to the bank of public phones in the building lobby. There were directories there, directories listing Powells. He would look her up and crash her charming, elegant dinner party.

Just thinking about it made him hungry.

CHAPTER EIGHT

BY FIVE O'CLOCK, the Bonnie Raitt CD had been replaced by Vivaldi. The table in the dining area had been spread with a burgundy red cloth and set with white china, silver flatware and rose-hued napkins rolled inside silver rings. The champagne Alex had brought was thoroughly chilled, the 1988 Riserva Salice Salentino was breathing, the bruschetta was ready for the oven and the kitchen smelled like heaven, Italian style. Alex, worn out from his heavy labor cutting dough as it emerged from the pasta-maker in flat, narrow strips, had retired to the terrace with a Campari while Mallory changed into a simple sack-dress of navy velvet and contemplated whether Aunt Grace would hate her forever for having included Alex in the evening.

It was so wonderful not to be thinking about her own problems that she didn't mind risking her aunt's wrath. And anyway, what about Alex Stowe could possibly inspire anyone's wrath? Compared to a certain man Mallory had recently had dealings with, Alex was a pussycat.

Liam was a jungle cat. But Mallory wasn't going to think about him, ever again—or at least not for the next few hours.

The doorbell sounded. She gave her reflection in the mirror above her dresser one final check, adjusting the jewel neckline of her dress and noting the way her teardrop-shaped earrings glinted through her loose black hair. Then she left the bedroom, heading down the hall to let Grace in.

"Hi!" she said as she swung open the door. Her mouth went dry and her smile disintegrated as she discovered her father on the other side of the threshold. "Dad!"

"Hello, Mallory." Tall and graceful, his face weathered into an expression of vaguely patriarchal wisdom, Leland Powell stepped into the foyer and pecked her cheek with a kiss. "I hope you don't mind my inviting myself over like this."

She *did* mind. But before she could ask him to disinvite himself, Alex appeared in the foyer entry, his glass still nearly full and his expression quizzical. Mallory's gaze shuttled between the two men, one easy and comfortable in his casual apparel, the other stiff and rigid in his expensively tailored business suit. Both men had silver hair, but Alex's fell in loose waves while Leland's was short and severely groomed. Alex smiled. Leland scowled.

"Oh, God, it's worse than I thought," Leland muttered.

"What's worse than you thought?"

Still taking Alex's measure, Leland answered her. "I've been talking to Robert about what he perceives to be a growing rift between the two of you. I had hoped pushing up the wedding date might have remedied the situation, but you rebelled against that. In fact, Robert told me you wanted to postpone the wedding indefinitely."

"I'm so glad he shares everything with you." Mallory didn't bother to hide her irritation.

"He was nursing an intuition that there might be someone else in your life. And now this—you've got a strange man here at your house—"

"I'm not that strange," Alex joked, extending his right hand. "Alex Stowe. I'm Mal's upstairs neighbor."

"Be that as it may..." Leland gave Alex's hand a perfunctory shake. "Mallory is already spoken for—"

"Oh, please!" she groaned. Why, at the ripe old age of thirty, did she still feel like a clumsy teenager when her fa-

ther was around? "Dad, I invited Alex to join me for dinner—"

"Because she wants to set me up with your sister," Alex
said, completing the sentence for her. "I may be guilty of
many things, but dating women young enough to be my
daughter isn't one of them. I'm afraid I didn't catch your
name."

"Leland Powell," Mallory mumbled, all too aware that
she was never going to be able to get her father to leave. "I
wish you'd phoned first, Dad."

"I wish you'd phoned, too. You invited Grace to dinner, but it didn't occur to you to invite me. When was the
last time you and I had dinner together?"

Mallory couldn't remember. But that wasn't news. Even
as a child, she had rarely spent the dinner hour in her father's company. Most nights, she would eat in the kitchen
with Emma, the housekeeper. Fridays, her father would
make an effort to get home from his office by six, and he
and Mallory would eat in the formal dining room. Their
conversations would be stilted, but that hadn't mattered to
her. She had adored her father, and he'd tried his best to
show some interest in her. "What did you learn in school
this week?" he would ask. "Have you had any playmates
over lately? Are you still playing soccer?"

Saturdays, he'd never eaten at home; in retrospect, Mallory realized that he'd probably been out on dates. Sundays after church, he would take her to the Top of the
Mark, where they would eat a huge midday meal. Like their
Friday dinners, they strove hard to talk to each other during those meals, and to make their stop-and-start discus-
sions feel natural. They'd really put a great deal of effort
into trying to make their relationship work.

She still loved her father, but she had long ago given up
on trying to talk to him. Thank heavens for Robert. He got
along well with both Mallory and her father, and when the
three of them were together, he served as the translator, fa-

cilitating communication between two people who seemed incapable of understanding each other.

Tonight, she supposed, Grace would have to be the translator—which meant Grace would have less time to become acquainted with Alex. Then again, if it turned out that the chemistry between Grace and Alex was all wrong, Leland's presence could dilute things, preventing a debacle. Mallory had already figured out that this evening wasn't going to focus on her. If her father wanted to be a part of it, he would provide yet another distraction.

"Loosen your tie," she suggested, wishing he looked just a bit less uptight. "Make yourself comfortable. I'll get you a drink."

Her father tugged gingerly at the knot of his tie as he followed her down the short hall to the kitchen. "Is anyone else here yet?"

"Who? Aunt Grace?" As if on cue, the doorbell rang again. Mallory halted a step from the kitchen doorway, sighed and about-faced. "There she is now," she said, edging past her father and returning to the foyer, where Alex was opening the door.

A small gasp escaped her as she saw Robert filling her doorway, beaming his picture-perfect smile and bearing a dozen long-stemmed red roses. Like her father, he must have come straight from work, since he was clad in a neat gray suit and a silk tie with a muted paisley print.

Robert was here. Robert Benedict. Her fiancé, who didn't yet know she was pregnant with another man's baby. Robert, who had gone off to Los Angeles without even having the courtesy to inform her that he would be out of town for several days, and whose answering machine held a day-old message from Mallory to which he hadn't bothered to respond.

Dizziness briefly swamped her, and she stared at the roses until she had regained her balance. She considered all the emotions available to her and decided that the most appropriate one for the moment was anger. "What are you doing here?" she blurted out, not even remotely polite.

Robert seemed oblivious to her rage. "Surprise," he declared, handing over the flowers. "Are you going to let me come in? I heard a rumor that you were hosting a dinner party tonight."

"*I* didn't hear that rumor," she retorted, taking the roses begrudgingly. "But if I *were* hosting a dinner party, I would have issued invitations. Which I didn't."

Robert tuned out her indignation and turned to Alex, offering his right hand. Alex looked as if he'd just swallowed a feather and it was tickling his innards. "I'm Robert Benedict," Robert introduced himself. "Mallory's fiancé. And you're . . . ?"

"Alex Stowe. I live upstairs. Mallory's mentioned you."

Mallory swore under her breath. She didn't like Alex's treating Robert so nicely when he'd just barged in on what had once been intended as an intimate, chatty ladies' night. All of a sudden, Mallory was surrounded by unbidden men, one of whom had just presented her with the sort of bouquet reserved for apologies and grand claims of passion. Robert owed her the former for disappearing to Los Angeles and not returning her call. As for the latter, she would prefer not to receive any grand claims of passion from him.

She scowled at the fragrant bouquet weighing down her arms and turned to shut the door. Footsteps in the outer hall caught her attention, and she peeked around the doorway, hoping those footsteps belonged to her aunt. If ever Mallory needed Grace to lend poise to bedlam, it was now.

But the footsteps didn't belong to Grace DeWilde. They belonged, Mallory saw with wrenching dread, to someone destined to make the bedlam a thousand times worse than it already was.

Glaring at the too-familiar man approaching her door, she swallowed a curse and leaned hard against the door, determined to slam it on him. He was faster than she was, though—or more purposeful, more committed to destroying her fragile equilibrium. He managed to step onto the threshold, not enough so that she could have the satisfaction of breaking his toes, but enough so she couldn't shut the door.

"Ms. Powell," he said, his apparent calm the direct opposite of her own agitation. "Could I have a few minutes of your time?"

"Who's there, Mal?" Robert asked.

"No one."

But Robert was already easing her away from the door and opening it. "Liam O'Neill! Don't tell me Mallory's agreed to let you interview her now."

Mallory sucked in a sharp breath. Perfume from the roses filled her lungs and she suppressed a choking cough. How on earth did Robert know Liam? Had they met? Had Liam already told Robert about his entanglement with Mallory at the retreat? Was that why Robert had brought this absurd bouquet of roses?

"Mal," Robert was saying, "this is Liam O'Neill. He's an author. A novelist. He and I met just hours ago."

"Aren't you lucky."

"He's writing a book on the ballet, and he mentioned he wanted to talk to you about your fund-raising activities. You set this up with Mallory, didn't you?" he belatedly asked Liam.

Liam stepped inside the foyer. "I tried to call her and couldn't get through. But I got her address, and I was in the neighborhood, so I thought..." He concluded with a shrug.

He was in the neighborhood? What a joke! The only reason anyone would be in this exclusive, hilly residential neighborhood would be to visit someone who lived there. Her, for instance.

And there Liam O'Neill was, visiting her, standing in her home, a vision of black-clad virility, his eyes dangerously seductive, his smile defiant, his dark-blond hair framing his face like a lion's mane. Once again, the image of a jungle cat filled her mind.

That image provoked as much fear as if he actually had been a feral beast. Liam O'Neill was at her home, in the flesh. In some way, thanks to Robert—may the man rot in hell, she silently prayed—Liam O'Neill now knew where she lived. She was no longer safe from him.

Well, she hadn't been safe from him since the instant her eyes had met his at the retreat in December. But now...now he had tracked her down. He could force his way into her life. He could interfere with her decisions. He could demand that she get rid of the baby—or he could take the baby from her, once it was born.

No, he couldn't—not easily, anyway. She vowed, right then and there, that if he tried to meddle in her life she would fight him with every ounce of strength in her.

"I hope you don't mind," Liam said quietly, attempting to fend off her hostility with a quirky smile.

"Keep hoping," she muttered. Aware that she had an audience, she tried to subdue her panic.

"You two didn't work this out, then," Robert deduced, his perplexed gaze shifting back and forth between them.

"No," Mallory snapped.

Robert had the dignity to look contrite. "Well. Liam is a—a novelist, and he and I have had a nice chat, and I suggested that he get in touch with you. Which he has. Obviously. Liam, this is my fiancée, Mallory Powell."

"It's a pleasure," Liam said with such spurious innocence she almost laughed. What humor she found in the situation vanished as soon as he closed his hand around hers. God, just a simple, cordial handshake from him was enough to shoot heat through her body. Just a knowing look from him reminded her precisely of the sort of pleasure it had been—and could be again, if she was willing to relapse into insanity with him. Her thoughts and memories were painfully vivid. She hoped she wasn't blushing.

As soon as she could, she slid her hand from his.

"Forgive me for not welcoming you with open arms," she muttered. "It's just that long ago, in a mist-shrouded past, I invited my aunt to have dinner with me. Now, all of a sudden, I'm stuck feeding four big men."

"You're not stuck," Alex consoled her, the only one of the foursome she herself had invited. "We can leave."

"I'm not leaving," Leland objected.

"Or we can send out for Chinese," Alex suggested, meeting Mallory's gaze and giving her a reassuring smile.

She answered with a scowl. At the moment, she would have liked nothing more than to ship the lot of them across the city to Chinatown, where they could feed themselves at someone else's table.

Of course, she was fuming at her four unwanted guests only because it was easier than confronting the one guest who had already thrown her world into turmoil, the one big man whom she'd thought she had successfully escaped, only to learn that he had ingratiated himself with her fiancé. How on earth was she supposed to sit through a meal with her father, Robert and the father of her baby gathered around her table? Add to that odd group her aunt—the only other person who knew Mallory was pregnant—and her neighbor Alex, and it was no wonder she was just this side of hysterical.

Behind Liam, the elevator door slid open in the hall, and Grace DeWilde stepped out. It took all Mallory's willpower not to bolt into the hallway, grab her aunt's arm and dive with her back into the elevator, abandoning the men. But she wrapped herself in self-control and stood stoically as her aunt sauntered up the hall to the door, a perplexed frown deepening the lines in her forehead as she noticed the mass of humanity crowded into Mallory's foyer.

"Oh, my," Grace said as Mallory drew her inside. Her gaze circled the crowded entry. "Whatever have we here?"

A catastrophe in the making, Mallory almost answered.
"Apparently, a dinner party."

"I do hope you've enough shrimp to go around. I had
intended to eat like a fiend tonight. Leland, what are you
doing here?"

"Visiting my daughter," Mallory's father said stiffly.

"Good heavens, look at these roses." Grace cast a dubious glance at the American Beauties cradled in Mallory's arms. She lifted her eyes to Robert. "A man doesn't
give flowers like that to a woman unless he has something
to atone for."

"Or unless he plans to present her with an engagement
ring," Robert said, pulling a small velvet box from his
jacket pocket and handing it to Mallory with a flourish.

She wanted to scream. Or maybe faint. Kicking something would be good. Punching a few people in the nose
would be better.

Instead, she fingered the box and steadied her breath. "I
thought we were going to pick out a ring together," she
said. She also thought she'd asked him to consider post-
poning their wedding—which was probably why he'd decided to jump the gun with this ring.

He shrugged off her admonition. "Open the box."

She didn't want to open it. Opening it would force her to
acknowledge that she was actually supposed to marry him.
Then again, it might force Liam to accept that there was no
chance of a relationship developing between the two of
them.

"Go ahead," her father goaded her. "Open it."

She raised her eyes to Leland, who smiled proudly, and
then took in Aunt Grace's wary frown, and Robert's exuberant grin, and Alex's curious perusal of Grace. And
lastly, Liam, whose gaze was as hard as steel and as blinding as the sun at midday. "Open it," he murmured.

Her heart pounded like a mallet against stone, leaving
cracks in her soul. She opened the box and bit back a curse.

The diamond solitaire was huge and glittery, almost as hard and blinding as Liam's eyes.

She didn't want this ring. She didn't want anything but to be left alone with her beloved aunt.

"Put it on," Robert urged her, then took the box from her and plucked the ring from its velvet bed. She opened her mouth to protest, but a glimpse of Liam silenced her. He was watching, gauging her reaction, registering each subtle change in her expression.

"Yes, put it on, Mallory," Liam echoed.

Damn him. She would wear the ring, if only for tonight, just to show him. She took the ring from Robert.

It felt like a lug nut around her finger. She didn't want to guess how many carats the gem weighed; it protruded a good quarter of an inch from her knuckle, and it was flanked by smaller diamond baguettes. She could just imagine trying to cook while she was wearing it. Within minutes, the facets would be caked with crusts of dried sauce and crumbs of dough. The bevels would tear through endive. Maybe she could tenderize meat with it.

That image gave her something to smile about. "Aunt Grace," she said, snapping the box shut and setting it on the mail table, "this is my neighbor, Alex Stowe. He's the only person besides you who's actually welcome here. Alex, this is my aunt, Grace DeWilde."

Grace nodded graciously. "I believe Mallory told me you're an architect," she half asked.

Alex's smile deepened. Seeing Mallory's hands still full of flowers, he helped Grace take off her taupe trench coat. "And you are the city's empress of bridal accoutrements."

Grace gave a musical laugh. "I should hire you for our advertising staff. Empress, indeed!" Her gaze came to rest on Liam, and her smile grew quizzical.

Reluctantly, Mallory introduced them. "This is Liam O'Neill. He's an acquaintance of Robert's. He's writing a book about the ballet." She glared pointedly at him, and he sent her a private, disturbingly intimate smile that awakened a memory of the warmth and taste of his lips upon hers. She hastily looked away. "I've got to get these flowers into water," she mumbled. "Alex, be a doll and take drink orders."

Hurrying down the hall to the kitchen, she heard Grace declare in a chipper voice, "Well, it would seem we've got quite a party tonight."

Quite a party, indeed, Mallory fumed, dumping the flowers in the sink and wishing she had a rear exit from her condominium. Lacking a means of escape, she was simply going to have to tough out the evening. She would cook dinner—the pasta and shrimp would probably stretch to feed at least five, and since she was feeling more than a little queasy about the evening's prospects, five appetites were all she had to satisfy. She would pour vast quantities of wine until everyone was so lubricated no one would care what anybody did or said. By nine o'clock, she would kick them all out.

And then, assuming she had any energy left, she would tear the roses to shreds.

LIAM KNEW HOW TO DETACH himself from his environment. He'd mastered the skill five years ago, when detachment was the only way he could get through each day without being crushed by the pain. By the time he'd regained his strength, he'd found detachment a good way to protect himself. Plus, it helped him in his writing.

From his detached perspective, he observed this environment, Mallory's world. Her condominium was clean and uncluttered, the decor as attractive in its simplicity as she was. Just as she eschewed heavy makeup, distracting earrings and elaborate hairdos, the living room lacked dust-collectors and knickknacks, busy carpeting and fussy furniture. A wall of glass encompassed the dining area and opened onto a terrace that offered a vista of the western slope of the city and the ocean beyond.

His cabin stood near the western edge of California, too. The same ocean visible through her windows extended north to his remote property.

He wanted to believe she would love his cabin, but he doubted she would. She was a city woman, wealthy and accomplished. Just because her apartment overlooked the same ocean that surged below the bluff on which his cabin stood didn't mean the rustic, hand-constructed dwelling would hold any appeal for her.

"Ballet, huh," Alex Stowe remarked to him.

Liam wrenched his thoughts back to the dinner gathering. It had been so long since he'd found himself at anything resembling a party that he almost couldn't remember how to make small talk. Even before the accident, he'd never been adept at it. But if he didn't put forth an effort, Mallory might kick him out. He'd seen the fury in her eyes when he'd invaded her home. He was here only because if she'd thrown a fit, she would have had to explain her behavior to too many onlookers.

He sipped the well-aged Scotch Alex had pressed into his hand ten minutes ago, then said, "I'm researching ballet fund-raising for a horror novel I'm writing."

"I've read some of your earlier work. Not the latest book, yet. *The Unborn*. I bought it a couple of days ago, after Mallory raved about it."

"She's read it?"

Alex grinned. "She said it kept her up at night. She doesn't usually read that kind of stuff."

Liam took another sip, rolled the mellow liquor over his tongue and savored the way its heat slid down his throat. "If she's read my book, then I guess she knows who I am." He realized that Alex Stowe was the only person in the living room worth talking to. Mallory's father looked as if someone had shoved a broom handle up one of his ori-

fices, and Robert . . . Jeez. The guy was worse than a mannequin—he was a mannequin who talked and acted as if he
had sawdust where real people had brains, and he shamelessly kissed up to Leland Powell. Grateful though Liam
was for Robert's having inadvertently led him to this soi-
ree, Liam couldn't imagine a man of such blithe insensitiv-
ity marrying Mallory. If Liam succeeded in breaking them
up, he would be doing her a big favor.

He liked her aunt, though. She reminded him of one of
his English department colleagues back at Berkeley.
Mildred had been about twenty years his senior, strong and
centered, exuding a mature, no-nonsense confidence that
he'd found oddly sexy. Men were supposed to go all silly
over nubile blond sophomores, but Liam had found
Mildred much more exciting in her earthy, intelligent way.

He'd never had more than a friendship with Mildred, of
course. He'd been madly in love with Jennifer, and he
doubted Mildred had thought of him as anything other
than an ambitious junior colleague. She used to laugh at his
interest in "those macho dharma-bum books," as she
called his area of expertise. "When you want to discuss a
real writer, like Kate Chopin or Virginia Woolf, let me
know," she would tease.

Grace DeWilde struck Liam as the sort of woman who
would waste no time putting him in his place. For that
matter, so did Grace DeWilde's niece. The only problem
was, Liam and Mallory had vastly differing ideas of exactly where his place was.

Grace emerged from the kitchen, untying her apron and
using it to dab a sheen of perspiration from her brow.
"Mallory has asked me to summon you to the table. Dinner is ready."

"Now, there's a woman," Alex murmured under his
breath.

Liam wasn't sure whether Alex was talking to himself,
but he saw no harm in responding. "She talks like a Brit."

"She's been living in England for the past thirty years. But she's a native of San Francisco, I think."

"Then I'll forgive her," Liam joked, blowing off his reflexive Irish dander.

"Mallory thinks the sun rises and sets with her aunt."

"What do you think?"

"I think she could exert a gravitational pull on me. I've got Mallory in my corner. Maybe she'll talk Grace into letting me help her get over the breakup of her marriage."

"Is Mallory a matchmaker?"

Alex shrugged. "The only match I've ever seen her make so far is her own, to Robert." His sour expression implied that he shared Liam's opinion of the young executive. "What do you think, Liam? Is it a good match?"

"If she's interested in big diamonds, it is."

"Trust me—Mallory isn't the big-diamonds type. That just proves how little Benedict knows her."

"She's wearing the ring," Liam commented.

"Well, what was she going to do, with everyone yelling at her to put it on?"

She hadn't put it on until *he* had asked her to, Liam recalled. And he still wasn't sure why he'd asked. Maybe he'd wanted to see if she would stand up to him. Or maybe he'd just felt like making the situation more complicated.

She might be wearing Robert Benedict's ring, but Liam sensed no great warmth between the two. As he ambled over to the table, its surface now crowded with hastily added place settings, he wondered whether Robert would sit next to Mallory or across from her, whether he would secretly nudge her with his toe under the table or send goo-goo eye messages to her between the candlesticks. He wondered, for that matter, whether Mallory would even be joining them. Ever since her aunt had arrived, she had remained holed up in the kitchen, avoiding her guests.

Grace took charge of the seating arrangements. "Leland, you sit at the head of the table—and for heaven's sake, don't add salt to everything. Mallory has seasoned each dish to perfection. Robert, you may take the foot of the table. Mallory will want to sit here, closest to the kitchen. Mr. O'Neill, perhaps you might sit across from her. And, Mr. Stowe, if you'd sit beside Mallory... Yes, that will do." With that, she swept back into the kitchen.

"My sister can be bossy," Leland said, a halfhearted apology to no one in particular.

"If you put salt on one of Mallory's masterpieces, I'll boss you, too," said Alex. "Mallory's culinary creations are the work of an artist. You don't adjust the colors on a Monet."

"My palate isn't subtle enough for Mallory's cooking," Leland complained. "She does delicate things with her seasoning, and I'm not a delicate sort of man." He eyed Liam superciliously. "You probably love delicate cooking. You said you were writing a book on ballet?"

Liam swallowed a laugh. He had expected his white lie to come back to haunt him, but he hadn't expected Mallory's father to cast aspersions on his manhood. "I'm sure I'll love Mallory's cooking," he agreed.

Grace DeWilde swept into the dining area carrying a platter of marinated tomatoes and cheese. Mallory followed her in, moving with all the verve of an aging tortoise. She bore a platter of sliced Italian bread layered in steaming eggplant, pepper, tomatoes, cheese and olive oil.

"Bruschetta!" Alex exclaimed. "Oh, God. I'm in love. Mallory, forget about Robert. Marry me."

Mallory sent him a sickly smile, then leaned forward to light the two white tapers at the center of the table. Liam saw the shadow of her throat, the hollows etching her collarbone. Her dress was stylishly shapeless, but he knew that beneath those folds of dark velvet lurked a slim, sleek body, a body that quivered when he touched her, that shimmered with an inner radiance, as if she were burning from the inside out.

When he touched her, he sure burned from the inside out.

And if he had any hope of getting through dinner, he'd better not think about it.

Opened bottles of red wine and icy champagne were produced. "The champagne is in honor of Alex's new commission," Mallory announced. "His architectural firm will be designing the new Carlisle Forrest Hotel in Atlanta."

"Bravo!" Robert cheered.

Grace eyed Alex with fascination. "How very thrilling! We Powells are related to the Forrests, did you know that? Do tell us about your design, Alex. Will it be soaring? Will it have suites and a rooftop health club? Best of all, will it have retail boutiques on the ground floor?"

"Only for bridal shops," he said. "No souvenir shops, no drugstores. Just bridal shops."

Grace seemed to know he was joking, but she played along. "As it should be. People will be getting married at the hotel. They should have everything they need, right at hand."

She chattered away, opinionated yet charming, as cheerful as Mallory was grim. Platters and bottles were passed around the table. Liam declined the champagne and filled the crystal goblet beside his plate with the red wine. He helped himself to a slice of the vegetable-topped bread and tasted it. It was anything but delicate in flavor, and it sure as hell didn't need salt.

Across the table from him, Mallory nibbled on a chunk of tomato. She had poured herself a dainty quantity of champagne, but after toasting Alex with a small sip, she seemed more interested in staring at it than drinking it. Or else she was staring at it to avoid staring at Liam.

He had no hesitancy about staring at her. In the candlelight her face took on a golden sheen, and her dress looked as dark as her hair. Her eyelashes were as thick and dense as the velvet, as if they were artificial.

But they were hers, natural, unpainted. He'd been close enough to her to know that every stunning feature, every striking hue, the creamy skin, the hollow cheeks, the startlingly clear eyes and black lashes were Mother Nature's gift to her.

His gaze shifted briefly to Alex, who seemed transfixed by the loquacious woman next to Liam. If it weren't for Grace, the dinner might have turned into a wake. Robert was too busy devouring every crumb of food in sight to talk, and Leland picked sullenly at his unsalted salad.

"Speaking of weddings," Leland said when Grace paused to catch her breath, "why can't you move yours forward, Mallory?"

"My wedding is my business," she said laconically. Liam didn't know why she chose to punctuate her statement by looking at him, but something in her piercing gaze jolted him. Was she trying to warn him that the wedding was going to take place sooner or later? Was she trying to scare him away?

"Isn't it a coincidence, Mal," Alex interjected, "that you just finished reading Liam's new novel a few days ago, and now here he is, eating dinner at your table?"

"It *is* a coincidence," she agreed feebly.

Robert sat straighter and swallowed the last slice of bruschetta. "You've read Liam's novel?" he asked. "You don't read that stuff, Mallory."

"Obviously, I do."

"What did you think of it?" Liam asked, testing her.

She met his gaze bravely. "I thought that whoever wrote it must be sick."

Uneasy laughter scattered around the table. Liam grinned, refusing to break his gaze from her. He felt as i an invisible bond connected her eyes to his, forged in th flame of the candle and heated further by the unspoke emotions passing from Mallory to him, from him to her. "Did you like anything about it?" he asked.

"The revenge plot. There's something satisfying in revenge."

"Are you a vengeful person?"

"No. To me it's just a fantasy, not the sort of thing civilized people do."

"Maybe that's why I like to write about it."

"I thought you wrote about ballet," Leland broke in, short-circuiting their exclusive exchange.

"Yes, Mr. O'Neill. Do tell us about your book on the ballet," Mallory's aunt encouraged him.

Reluctantly, he turned from Mallory. "It's just in the research stage right now."

"That's how Liam came to me," Robert said, sounding boastful. "He saw a photo of us in the paper, Mal—at that godawful fund-raiser you dragged me to."

"I remember that photo," Mallory murmured, firing a quick look at Liam before she stood. "I'll bring in the main course."

"You'll need help," Liam said, jumping to his feet before she could refuse his generous offer. She shot him another dagger-sharp look but said nothing as he followed her into the kitchen.

The door swung shut behind him, enclosing them in her bright, fragrant kitchen. Mallory headed straight for the microwave oven, the upper half of a two-oven wall unit. Liam observed her majestic posture, her lush hair, the slender curves of her legs below the above-the-knee hem of her dress.

It had been a long, interesting, occasionally trying day—and it wasn't nearly over yet. He had accomplished a great deal: tracking Mallory down, evaluating his competition, seeing her in an entirely new context as daughter, niece, fiancée, friend. Before tonight, he'd known her only as a lover. Now... he wanted her as a lover even more.

In silent strides, he crossed the kitchen to join her by the oven. He gathered a lock of her hair in his hands and let the heavy black silk spill between his fingers.

"Don't," she scolded.

"You look beautiful." Unable to resist, he brushed her hair back from her cheek and touched his lips to her temple.

She sucked in a breath and turned her back to him. "I'm not kidding, Liam. Back off. I don't want you here."

"But you do want me."

"Not in a million years." Yet when he cupped his fingers around her shoulder, she leaned back into him, her resistance no stronger than a light spring breeze.

"I want to make love to you," he whispered.

"Don't even think about it."

"It's all I ever think about."

"Robert is out there. He gave me this ring. Doesn't that mean anything to you?"

"It means he's rich and has bad taste. I still want to make love to you."

"It's not going to happen, Liam." But her hips defied her, pressing back into him, letting him feel the soft, tantalizing curves of her bottom.

God. How could she expect him to resist her when she moved like that? How could she expect him not to respond, when her body was speaking as eloquently now as it had at the retreat? "You can't get rid of me, Mallory. One way or another, you're going to have to deal with me."

"You're just like your books," she muttered, forcing herself to step away from him. "My worst nightmares, come to life. You're right—I have to deal with you this evening. So grab those pot holders and carry this bowl of pasta out to the table. Make sure you place it on the trivet. It's very hot."

"I'll bet it is," he murmured.

She glanced anxiously at him, but she must have seen the amusement in his eyes, because a reluctant smile curved her lips. "You're obnoxious, Liam."

"No. Just crazed with lust."

Before she could issue any more warnings or tag him with any more insults, he strolled out of the room, handling the very hot serving dish of linguine with a great deal more caution than he'd been handling Mallory.

CHAPTER NINE

MALLORY STARED at the clutter of her kitchen. Dirty dishes jammed the sink; pots and pans littered the surrounding counters. Crystal goblets stood in a fragile cluster on the center island. The stove top was spattered with sauce; the floor was littered with bread crumbs. A dozen red roses peeked out over the edge of her trash can.

She let out a long breath. Messy kitchens were her milieu. As long as all her guests were gone, she could handle the physical upheaval they'd left behind. The emotional upheaval was something else—something much more difficult to deal with than sauce-caked pots and stained linen napkins.

She wasn't quite sure how she'd gotten through the dinner. Fortunately, the meal had met with everyone's approval. And since her appetite never revived, there had been enough food to go around. Even Aunt Grace hadn't complained of not having enough shrimp.

Thank God for Grace, Mallory thought with a sigh. Thirty years of hobnobbing in the upper echelons of London society had taught her everything she needed to know about how to bail out a waterlogged party and make it sail. She'd been scintillating when scintillation was called for; she'd been brisk when Robert had become overbearing; and she'd scolded her brother Leland whenever he said anything Mallory might possibly construe as critical. She had interrogated Liam shamelessly, and he'd willingly answered her questions, revealing that he lived by himself in

orthern Marin County, that he'd retired from his teach-
ng job at U.C., Berkeley to write full-time, that he rarely
isited San Francisco, that he felt no ties to his old em-
loyer, that he had a Ph.D. but found it embarrassing to be
alled Dr. O'Neill.

Mostly, though, Aunt Grace had charmed Alex. Mal-
ory had watched the stars gather in Alex's eyes as her aunt
edazzled him and everyone else at the table with her
harm, her verve, her dignity and beauty. Grace had let slip
hat she'd taken a cab to Mallory's home, and before any-
ne could blink, Alex had offered to drive her home.
hey'd left as soon as the dessert glasses of zabaglione were
mpty and the last drop of espresso was consumed.

The instantaneous rapport between Grace and Alex had
lmost given Mallory a reason to believe romance was pos-
ible. Perhaps, for some people, it was. Perhaps romance
ame to those who had already suffered through failed love
ffairs. Survivors of broken marriages might be more de-
erving of happiness, somehow.

Certainly Aunt Grace was deserving. Mallory still
ouldn't understand what had come between Grace and
effrey DeWilde, but whatever it was, it couldn't possibly
ave been Grace's fault. Maybe Mallory was just a touch
iased, maybe she sided with Grace because her aunt was
er blood relation ... but she simply refused to believe that
Grace could have done anything terrible enough to destroy
er marriage. It had to be Jeffrey's doing.

Mallory would have protested her aunt's abrupt depar-
ure that evening, except that setting Grace up with Alex
ad been her goal. Unfortunately, her reward for having
layed cupid successfully was to wind up stuck with three
nwanted guests: her father, Robert and Liam. Robert had
uggested that they open another bottle of wine, but to her
reat relief, Liam had vetoed that idea, pointing out that it
vas getting late and reminding Robert that he had to drive
ome. Maybe the reminder had been Liam's way of hint-

ing that Robert had better not consider spending the night with her.

With or without Liam's comment, Robert would not have spent the night. The part of Mallory that advocated marrying Robert—the pragmatic part, the part that ached for her father's approval, the part that figured true love was a fantasy beyond her reach—was being drowned out by other voices inside her, voices crooning to the fetus developing in her womb, voices pleading with fate for the chance to make a man's eyes sparkle the way her aunt had made Alex's eyes sparkle. Voices arguing that no marriage was better than a bad marriage, and that a father who could not accept her as she was wasn't going to accept her just because she'd married his trusted lieutenant.

None of which had anything to do with Liam, she cautioned herself. Liam might have been the catalyst, forcing her to reevaluate her plans, but he wasn't going to be the man whose eyes sparkled for her. He couldn't possibly fit into her life. He lived in a remote cabin. He didn't like to visit San Francisco. He had nothing in common with her—nothing but a baby he didn't even know about.

She gave her kitchen a final assessment as she rolled up the sleeves of her cozy cashmere robe. As soon as everyone had departed, she'd pulled off the damned diamond ring Robert had forced on her and then her clothing. She'd taken a quick shower and donned a silk nightie and then the robe for warmth. As soon as she was done cleaning up, she intended to go straight to bed.

She moved to the sink and adjusted the faucet to a hot spray. She had just submerged her hands in the steamy water when the doorbell rang. A glance at her wall clock told her it was after ten. The only person who would stop by at this hour was Alex. No doubt he had returned from driving Grace home, and he wanted to express his boundless gratitude to Mallory for having introduced them.

She dried her hands on a dish towel, adjusted the knotted belt of her robe on her way to the foyer and opened the door.

"Hello, Mallory," Liam said.

She wasn't really surprised. Not the way she'd been surprised a few hours ago, when his appearance on her doorstep had proved to her that she hadn't gotten rid of him. She must have known subconsciously that he would be back sooner or later—although she would have hoped it would be later. He had gone to a lot of trouble, wheedling his way into Robert's life and lying about his new project—a horror novel with ballet fund-raising, of all things, as its theme—just to find out where Mallory lived.

So now he was back. But without witnesses to protect him, Mallory didn't have to pretend she'd never met him before. She didn't have to be polite.

She started to close the door, but he easily pushed it back open. She might have been alarmed—she certainly wouldn't have expected him to muscle his way in. But Liam didn't have to use force to reach her, and he knew it as well as she did. All he had to do was gaze at her, his mouth curved in a mysterious half smile, his tall, solid presence permeating her consciousness, and her resistance softened.

"What do you want?" she asked, knowing damned well what he wanted. He'd been uncomfortably honest about his wants earlier that evening.

He must have read her mind. "I didn't come here for that."

"You didn't come here for *what?*" she goaded him.

He said nothing for a minute, then asked, "Can we talk?"

She should have said no. She should have recognized that he was a smooth character who had already proved his flair for lies in the way he'd finessed Robert into revealing her home telephone number.

But his eyes were too hypnotic, his smile too wistful, his body too virile. She couldn't bring herself to slam the door on him. "What do you want to talk about?" she asked suspiciously, pinching the lapels of her robe together when his gaze strayed below her chin.

He raised his eyes, and she saw wry amusement in them. "We could talk about the state of the world. What do you think of the ozone layer? Or the health care crisis? And how about those 49ers?"

It occurred to Mallory that she had no idea where Liam O'Neill stood on the environment, or health care—or, for that matter, San Francisco's football team. It occurred to her that she didn't care. What she cared about was his understated wit, his laughter-filled eyes contradicting his deadpan words.

"Are you sure you wouldn't rather hear my views about fund-raising for the ballet?" she shot back.

"Oh, yes, the ballet. There's nothing I'd rather talk about than how to raise bucks for the ballet."

She considered all the reasons she shouldn't invite Liam in. She was dressed for bed. The hour was late. He could wreak havoc with her life. He could find out about her pregnancy. He could ruin everything. And her kitchen was a disaster.

The last reason was the only one that seemed to penetrate her dazed pleasure that, for once in their very odd acquaintance, she and Liam were actually joking with each other. "If I let you in," she warned, "you're going to have to help me with the dishes."

"If there's anything I like more than talking about the ballet, it's doing dishes," he said.

If only he would stop smiling, stop teasing and get serious, she could resist him. But whatever defenses he hadn't broken down with his quiet sex appeal, he'd swept away with his sense of humor. She stepped back from the door, allowing him to enter.

As soon as he closed the door behind him, she realized she was in trouble. He could haul her into his arms and kiss her. Even when they were kidding around, a sensual current flowed swift and deep between them. She hadn't been able to swim against it in the alley behind Mallory's, or in the greenroom at the television station. How was she going to swim against it here, when she was alone with him in her home?

She braced herself, issuing a silent lecture that she would have to push him away if he made an overture. But he didn't touch her. He gave her an expectant look, as if he really intended to help her with the dishes.

Cleaning up from dinner would keep them too busy to think about sex. Adjusting the lapels of her robe to reveal as narrow a wedge of her upper chest as possible, she led the way down the hall to the kitchen. Liam followed her into the brightly lit room and whistled softly. "Wow. Even my kitchen never looks this bad."

"This doesn't look bad," she corrected him. "It looks *used*. Kitchens are made to be messed up and then cleaned. I do have a dishwasher," she added, crossing to the sink. "If you want to rinse the dishes and hand them to me, I can fit them into the racks."

Like her, he rolled up his sleeves and turned on the water. His clothes—black cotton shirt, black denim jeans—looked sleek and sexy on him, and his forearms were an extension of that sleekness, taut and graceful, covered by a light webbing of golden hair.

The water steamed as it gushed from the spout. Evidently, he could handle a hotter temperature than she could. She watched as he plunged his hands into the scalding flow. Large, strong, hard with calluses, they glistened wet as he raised a plate to the spray, rotated it, and then shook off the excess moisture before handing it to her.

She was so transfixed by the sight of him working in her kitchen, she almost forgot to take the plate from him. She was going to have to occupy her mind with something other than the agile power of his hands. "What do you want to know about the ballet?" she asked as he handed her a second plate.

He laughed. "Not a damned thing."

"Then why did you tell Robert you were writing a book about the ballet?"

"I saw that photo of you and him in the newspaper," he explained. "The one taken at the ballet fund-raiser. It was all I had to go on. I couldn't think of any other way to get in to see the guy."

"Why did you want to see him?" No doubt she could come up with the answer if she thought about it, but thinking seemed particularly difficult when Liam was standing less than two feet away from her.

He tossed her a quick look, then held a bread plate under the spout. "He was a route back to you," Liam said.

"If you wanted to find me, you could have gone back to the restaurant. You already found me there."

Liam shook his head. "He was a route to who you are. The last time I saw you, you made it very clear that you wanted me to go away." He handed her the bread plate and turned back to the sink. "I thought, maybe if I met the love of your life, I would realize why you were so eager to shut me out."

She heard the irony in his voice and saw it in the quirk of his eyebrows. "You know Robert isn't the love of my life."

"But you're marrying him, anyway."

"I . . . I'm not sure."

Liam passed her a fistful of dripping silverware. His gaze lingered for a moment on her left hand. "How many minutes after he left did you take off the ring?"

Less than a full minute, she admitted silently. Right now, the engagement ring was sitting in its box on her bedroom dresser. As soon as she'd taken it off, her hand—and her heart—had felt measurably lighter.

She was still angry with Robert for so many things, the most recent his arrogant decision to present her with a ring—a ring he'd selected by himself, although they had planned to pick one out together—in front of so many other people. But once he knew the truth about her current physical condition, he would have as much reason to be angry with her. If the marriage didn't happen, it would be as much her fault as his. Probably more her fault.

She eyed the man beside her, the man she would have blamed for her pregnancy if she were given to disclaiming responsibility for her own actions. But she didn't blame Liam. What had happened at the retreat was her doing, her mistake—her choice. That she was pregnant as a result was also her choice.

"I don't want to talk about Robert," she said abruptly.

Liam handed her a stack of plates. Bending over the dishwasher to arrange them on the rack, she felt his gaze on her. But he didn't press her, and she was grateful. "I guess that leaves ballet, doesn't it," he said.

Actually, it left many other subjects—most of them revolving around Liam O'Neill. He had met her father, her aunt, her fiancé and her neighbor. He had consumed beer in her restaurant and shrimp and pasta in her home. And all she knew about him—other than the fact that making love with him had been an experience almost otherworldly in its intensity—was that he used to teach at Berkeley and now he wrote scary novels.

She listened to the rush of water in the sink, the percussive hiss as the spray glanced off the plates. The dishes hardly needed to go through the dishwasher now, but Mallory was reluctant to tell him that in case it broke the comfortable rhythm they had established working together. "Tell me about yourself," she said instead.

He eyed her warily, then turned back to the sink. "Can we narrow that down a little?"

"Tell me about your childhood."

Apparently he found her bluntness amusing, if his laugh was anything to judge by. "I grew up in South Boston, working-class Irish. My parents still live in Boston. I've got two younger sisters, both married, both living in the Boston area. They're good people, my family."

"What do they think of your books?"

He grinned. "My sisters like them. My mother prays for my soul. My father..." His smile faded. "My father is the silent type. If he's read them, he's never mentioned it to me." He traced the edge of the plate with his thumb, considering. "I think he *has* read them. I hope so."

"You must miss them all, living so far away."

"Not really," he said, then shrugged. "I need solitude."

"For your writing, you mean?"

He passed her the plate. He seemed to be grappling with his thoughts. "Until I met you, solitude suited me just fine."

His words unnerved her. He was sharing something essential with her—only she didn't know what it was. "What do I have to do with it?"

"You're warm. You're open."

He was leading them into treacherous terrain, and she felt obligated to stop him. "Look, Liam—what happened at the retreat—"

"Took us both by surprise," he acknowledged. "Me as much as you. I didn't go up there looking to have a fling. But I just felt...comfortable with you."

"It's not hard to be comfortable with a stranger when you don't have to stumble through awkward conversation," she joked, trying to ward off the intimacy of his words, the vulnerability they exposed.

"It had nothing to do with conversation," he argued. "We fit together. We meshed. I haven't felt that way about another person in years."

She couldn't dispute what he said anymore. It felt true to her. From the moment she'd seen him at the retreat, she'd sensed the fit, the meshing, the comfort of being in his company. The sex had been one thing, but the days leading up to it had been something else. With Liam, even before she'd known his name, she'd had a sense of belonging.

Yet to admit to that meant admitting that Liam was important to her now, that she couldn't easily dismiss him from her life. She wanted to go back to the light banter, the easy chatter. "You must have felt comfortable with your students," she pointed out.

"My students?"

"When you were teaching at U.C., Berkeley."

"Oh." For some reason, he didn't seem to think this qualified as light banter. His brow furrowed, and he got busy with a sauce-encrusted plate. "Yes," he answered.

"Did you enjoy teaching?" she asked.

He mulled over the question. "For a while," he answered. His tone carried a hard edge, an unspoken warning that this subject was as perilous as the last.

But so what? She already knew that curiosity was a risky impulse. "So why did you quit and move to the sticks?"

"I like the sticks," he said simply.

"You didn't like Berkeley?"

He didn't answer immediately, and when he did, it was a curt "No."

"What town do you live in? I know southern Marin, but not the northern part of the county."

"I live outside town," he said. "I'm up in the woods, near the ocean."

"It must be beautiful."

He shrugged.

"Why do you live alone? Is the solitude really that important to you?" She was a city person; solitude must be nice, but she wasn't sure she could stand a daily diet of it.

He sent her another swift look. She noticed that the humorous glow had faded from his eyes. "I'm not good company most of the time," he said, running his thumb over a stubborn bit of pasta that clung to the plate he was rinsing.

"You're good company now."

"Maybe you bring out the best in me." Heavy sarcasm layered his words.

At the moment, his best was borderline. He seemed only inches away from losing his temper. But she wasn't going to back down. She was enough of a risk-taker to reject her father's goals for her and attend the American Culinary Institute instead of a good liberal arts college, to become a caterer, to amass financing and open a restaurant, to develop a cooking segment for a daytime television talk show. She was enough of a risk-taker to give herself to a stranger, miles from home, without a word. She wasn't going to run for cover now, just because Liam seemed vexed by her questions. "So, you've never been married?"

His eyes had grown as dark as bullets, his gaze as deadly. "I've been married," he said.

"Then you're divorced?"

"No."

The word was so sharp it stung like a bullet fired into her soul. Without looking at her, he handed her the last of the silverware and reached for a pot. Adjusting the plug in the drain, he squirted a stream of liquid soap into the sink, and bubbles foamed up, white and heady, much too playful for the dark mood that had settled over the room.

"Your wife died?" Mallory asked. His terse responses to her questions implied as much, but she needed to hear him say it. She needed to know. That was the hazard of curiosity in full bloom.

"Yes," he said. "My wife died."

"I'm sorry, Liam." A quick mental calculation added up the evidence. "She died in Berkeley, didn't she."

He stared at her. Pain shaded his eyes, pain and resentment and regret. Yet he didn't refuse her the answers she needed to hear. "Yes. My wife died in Berkeley. So I left."

"I don't blame you." She drifted to the center island to gather more pots and mixing bowls—and also to put a little distance between Liam and herself. She hadn't realized that a conversation could be as intimate as the kisses they'd shared, the love they'd made. "How did she die?"

"You don't want to know."

Maybe she didn't—but her heart told her she *had* to know. "Please tell me."

"She was killed," he said, then fell silent, leaving Mallory to wonder just where the source of his horror novels lay, what dark place spawned his perverse concepts of violence, revenge and bitterness. In his wife's death? Or in his wife's life?

Liam could be right: it might be better if she didn't know.

But now that she'd gotten him started, he was going to tell her. "She was standing on the sidewalk," he said. Mallory heard the rasp of a scouring pad rubbing against the aluminum surface of a pot. "She was minding her own business, waiting on the corner until it was safe to cross." The water from the tap echoed against the inside of the pot. "A nice young man—a student at the law school, in fact—was driving back to campus after a brunch that had included so many mimosas that his blood-alcohol level was more than twice the legal limit. It must have been quite a brunch."

"Oh, Liam." Mallory could guess what was coming. She wanted to tell him she'd heard enough, but he continued relentlessly.

"This fine young law student's car jumped the curb. It just leaped right up onto the sidewalk where my wife was standing. It rolled over her, pinned her to the concrete and crushed her. It was a sunny spring day, just before noon."

Mallory let go of the pots, unable to think about something as mundane as cleaning her kitchen after what he had just told her. All she could do was reach around him from behind, circling his waist with her arms and hugging him.

She felt the arch of his back against her cheek, the hollow at the base of his spine as he gazed up at the ceiling. He turned off the faucets and stood motionless, letting Mallory hold him, letting her absorb the tension in his posture, the stiffness that conveyed how much it hurt him to remember.

Then his hands, still hot and damp from the water, closed around her wrists. He separated her hands from each other and curled his fingers around hers, letting his thumbs rest against her palms. "After the accident, I couldn't feel anything except pain and rage." His voice was low, husky, straining against the raw emotion in him. "It went on for five years. Five years, Mallory. I was so full of hate, I couldn't let anything else touch me. A friend told me I had to get away or the rage would kill me. So I went to the retreat. And I met you. And for the first time in five years, I was able to feel good again. I was able to let something good touch me."

"Why, Liam? Why me?"

"Because you're you." He released her hands and turned in her arms until he could peer down into her face. "Because I didn't have to tell you who I was or where I came from for you to read me. Because when I looked into your eyes I saw love in them," he said, bowing to kiss her.

The dishes went forgotten. The bizarre dinner party, the unwanted roses, the obnoxious engagement ring, the matchmaking, even the reason she'd originally asked her aunt for dinner—all of it fell away, leaving behind only a man whom Mallory had somehow touched, a man she had given the gift of goodness after so many years. Never in her life had Mallory been so necessary to another person. Never had she done so much, simply by being herself and trusting her instincts.

Never, she had to admit, had a man made her feel as good as Liam O'Neill had made her feel that night at the retreat. Never had a man made her feel as vital as he made her feel right now.

His kiss unfurled tendrils of heat inside her, springs that relaxed as the tension drained from her and then coiled again with excitement. Tonight Liam was not a stranger kissing her, not a mysterious lover who had crossed paths with her somewhere outside reality and awakened a passion she wasn't sure she could cope with in the normal everyday world of her existence. Tonight he was a man who had been wounded and had found in her arms the strength to heal. Tonight he was a man willing to show her who he was, willing to let her touch him once more.

She kissed him deeply, hungrily, with an understanding of why he hadn't left her last week, why he couldn't leave her. She would straighten out her kitchen and her life later. For now, strengthening the bond between Liam and her was the most important thing she could do.

His hands moved on her, slowly, gently, skimming the soft fabric of her robe down to her waist. Without breaking the kiss, he brought his hands forward, tracing the sash to her belly and untying the knot. The robe's flaps fell open to reveal the cream-colored silk of her nightgown, falling from narrow straps in a translucent drape over her breasts, down to her thighs. Through the fabric she felt the warmth of his hands on her waist. In her mouth she felt his broken sigh as his fingers followed the feminine contours of her torso.

He pulled his mouth from hers; the effort seemed to cost him. He gazed down at her barely clothed body, at the lush curves of her breasts straining the silk, at his hands caressing her, at her long, exposed legs. Then he lifted his eyes to hers again. "Tell me you want me as much as I want you," he whispered.

"I want you, Liam." She wanted him, not for what he'd been to her two months ago, not for what he'd done to her, but for now, for who he was and who she was and the goodness they made each other feel.

In one easy, graceful motion he lifted her into his arms. Without her having to direct him, he strode down the hall to her bedroom. She clasped her hands around his neck and gazed up at his face, his determined jaw, his sexy mouth. His eyes no longer radiated pain or rage. Only desire.

He carried her directly to her bed and laid her across the mattress. She heard the muffled thud of first one of his shoes and then the other hitting the carpet, and then he stretched out beside her and covered her mouth with his.

His kiss sparked tiny fires inside her, in her breasts, in her hips and in places she wouldn't have expected—her inner wrists, the creases behind her knees, her temples. He propped himself up on his elbows and forearms, but she would have accepted his crushing weight on her. She would have welcomed it.

She stroked down his back, gathering handfuls of shirt as she went, tugging the garment free from the waistband of his jeans. He lifted himself higher so she could reach the buttons. While she unfastened them from the bottom, he worked his way down from the collar. Their hands met at the center of his chest, and he slipped off the shirt.

She remembered his chest, remembered every rippling muscle, every ridge of bone and sinew. She remembered the bronze undertone of his skin, the indentation of his collarbone, the brown circles of his nipples, already tight with arousal. She remembered Liam's body better than she had realized.

It was as magnificent now as it had been then—only now it was warm, not glazed with a midnight chill. Now when she skimmed her hand over the surface of his chest, he groaned aloud. She had not just his body but his voice, his words.

"Your hand is so soft," he murmured, covering her hand with his and lifting it to his lips. "How can a grown woman have such baby-soft hands?"

"I get other people to do my dishes for me," she joked.

He laughed, a loud, joy-filled hoot that resonated within her. Still smiling, he eased her robe out from under her. Her lingerie seemed to astonish him. He traced the narrow straps of the gown, the scooped neckline, the piped edging under her arms.

Her legs moved restlessly against his. Why his touching her shoulders should stimulate reflexes in her thighs was beyond her, unless it was similar to the way his smile caressed her solar plexus, or his gaze charged her pulse, or his sigh brushing against her throat sent flutters of sensation the entire length of her, making her toes curl.

He grazed downward, pressing his lips to her shoulder, her collarbone, the rise of her breast, kissing her through the silk. She moaned in glorious discomfort. Her breasts were overly sensitive; just the moist heat of his breath caused her nipples to swell, and when he closed his lips around one tight bud and then the other, she moaned again, fighting the tide of heat that surged through her. When he lifted his head he had a vaguely intoxicated look, as if his kisses were driving him as mad as they were driving her.

"I want you naked," he murmured.

"Yes." She wanted herself naked, too. And him. She wanted to feel him against her, inside her, unleashing all the goodness they could share, all the healing love.

He took the hem of her gown in his hands and lifted it up, baring the curve of her hips, her stomach, her midriff, her breasts. He pulled it over her head and tossed it aside, then reached down for her panties and stripped them off. It took him a matter of seconds to shuck his jeans and shorts, and then he was just as she wanted him, naked to her eyes and her hands.

They touched each other everywhere. Hands glided over skin, climbing rises, floating into hollows, discovering, conquering. Liam kneaded her derriere; he threaded his fingers through her hair; he caressed the surface of her abdomen and the dampness between her thighs. He rolled her onto her stomach so he could kiss her shoulder blades, so he could nibble the slender column of her spine. His body pressed warm against her, his legs tangling with hers, his lips savoring every inch of her.

She explored him as he explored her. She nipped the hard ridge of his shoulder with her teeth. She twirled her tongue over his nipples and felt the tremor of his groans against her lips. She splayed her fingers over his abdomen, scraped her nails lightly over his thighs and smiled as his arousal built, as his body grew tense and hard with need. When at last she closed her hands around him, he gasped and shut his eyes, his muscles primed, his heart drumming wildly against her cheek as she rested her head on his chest.

He permitted her to touch him for only a few precious seconds before peeling her hands away and rolling her onto her back. He took her mouth with a fierce kiss and then rose above her. He was breathing heavily, his eyes bright with longing. He drew a long line with his hand from the base of her throat down between her breasts, across her belly and lower, into the thatch of curls between her legs and lower still. She was wet, aching as he pressed and circled and slid his fingers inside her. "Do you have anything?" he asked, his tone hushed but urgent. "Do you have protection here?"

She might have told him that it was a little too late to be worrying about birth control. But she wasn't prepared to stop everything and tell him what had happened the last time, when they hadn't been protected. As a healthy single woman she kept certain items on hand, even though she rarely had an opportunity to use them. "In the drawer," she said, then lost her voice to a sigh as he probed deeper, finding sensitive places she hadn't known about, tiny fuses that ignited and burned inside her.

"Talk to me, Mallory," he said, deftly reaching to open the drawer of her night table. "I want your voice this time. I want you to tell me."

"Tell you what?" Her words were more a whimper than a question.

"Everything." He found a condom and stopped stroking her only long enough to ready himself. "Tell me everything," he murmured, poising himself above her, brushing against her so provocatively her hips lifted off the bed to meet him. "Let me hear you."

"Yes," she promised, a faint hint of sound in the quiet room.

He thrust deep into her. Her body tightened around him, desperate to hold him inside her. She wanted to tell him, but she could barely think, let alone articulate her thoughts.

Liam spoke instead. "It's like coming home," he whispered, holding himself still. "You feel like home to me."

Her hips writhed, her hands clung to his back. She wanted him deeper, wanted him to fill her, not just her body but her spirit. "Love me, Liam," she pleaded.

He surged, steel-hard and possessive. A low moan tore from her throat as the heat built, spreading its shimmering glow through her. He surged again, sending the fever deeper into her, into the deepest recesses of her heart, the lonely, quiet places where no one had ever touched her before.

She clutched his shoulders as if he—the man who had set her on fire—could save her from the conflagration. He thrust again and she sighed, her flesh contracting around him. A sheen of perspiration glistened on his skin. Flames nipped at the edges of her soul. She murmured an incoherent plea; his thrusts grew harder and faster until she was blazing, all heat and light and energy, her body convulsing in sweet surrender.

He shuddered in her arms, and she heard him speak her name, his voice less than a whisper. He was so big, so strong and muscular, yet as he sank down onto her he seemed helpless, holding her tightly, as if afraid of losing her. "I'm here, Liam," she vowed. "I'm here."

He barely had the energy to kiss her. His mouth opened gently over hers, absorbing her words. Then he eased off her and onto his side, bringing her with him. His arms closed around her, his legs wrapped around her, and he cushioned her head with his shoulder.

"You're here," he murmured, his lips ruffling her hair as he pressed another kiss to the crown of her head. Something in his tone, something in his embrace, told her he intended her to stay that way forever.

Something in her heart told her that forever would be just fine.

CHAPTER TEN

THE PHONE RANG.

Mallory swore under her breath, but she wasn't really angry. Her bedroom extension sat on her night table, just inches from her hand. She wouldn't have to leave Liam's arms to answer.

She did have to lean over him, though. He accommodated her, shifting onto his back and allowing her to sprawl across his chest. Her hair spilled over his chin, and he lifted it away from his face and tucked it out of the way, behind her shoulder. His fingers brushed lightly across her skin, sending a flicker of heat down her back.

She wanted nothing more than to align her body completely with his, chest to chest and hip to hip, so he could touch her all over. She wanted the shimmer of his caresses to spread completely through her, to reach her soul and illuminate it. As the phone rang a fourth time, she considered unplugging the extension. But she wasn't one of those people who could ignore a ringing phone.

Reluctantly, she lifted the receiver. "Hello?"

"Mallory? It's Aunt Grace."

"Oh," she said, then cleared the sensual thickness from her throat. Thank God it was Grace and not Robert. In a brighter voice, she said, "Hi!"

"I didn't catch you in bed, did I?"

Mallory felt her cheeks burn with color. She knew her aunt had meant something entirely different from what she was thinking, though, and she managed to reply, "No,

Aunt Grace, you didn't wake me. I was just...um... cleaning up."

Eavesdropping on her half of the conversation, Liam chuckled. His chest vibrated beneath her, making her blush all over again—and making her want to hang up and concentrate on the taut, lusciously male body beneath her. Instead she signaled him to be quiet and turned her attention back to the phone.

"It was quite a dinner party, Mal. The food was superb, as always."

"I'm just glad I had enough to go around," she said. Her scalp tingled and her toes curled as Liam skimmed his hand down the slope of her back and molded his palm to the soft curve of her bottom. She struggled to keep her voice from giving her away. "I was afraid I'd bought too many shrimps this morning—"

"There's no such thing as too much shrimp," Grace argued. "Nonetheless, I did want to apologize. It's my fault a quiet supper for two turned into a full-fledged dinner party."

"Oh, Aunt Grace, you don't have to apologize."

"Yes, I do. I should have realized what a boor Leland can be. He rang me up this morning, and I mentioned that you and I were planning to dine together. The next thing I knew, he was whining about how you never invite him for dinner. I told him I was willing to bet he never invited you for dinner, either. But he wouldn't be consoled. He ran on about how much closer you and I are than you and he— which, I suppose, is true—and he said he hears about you mostly through Robert, but now he feared something was amiss between the two of you. He was worried, Mallory. I suspect that tonight's dinner did nothing to reassure him."

Mallory pursed her lips. Liam's hand, roving in a maddening path from her derriere up to her waist and then back again, was just one very strong indication of how amiss things were between her and her fiancé. She wanted to demand that Liam stop, but her body defied her, her hips squirming and her legs shifting apart.

He took what she offered, drawing his hand down to her thigh. She suppressed a sigh and commanded her brain to stay focused on her aunt's voice rippling through the receiver. "My brother may be dense, Mal," she was saying, "but he isn't stupid. You and I both know he has a legitimate right to be worried."

"Yes," Mallory murmured, wondering if she sounded as breathless to Grace as she did to herself.

"I would never betray your confidence, of course. I didn't invite Leland to join us for dinner, and I certainly didn't tell him the rest. I do wish you and I could have had tonight to discuss your situation, though."

"We'll talk about it another time," Mallory said, then flinched as Liam's fingers detoured to the inner skin of her thigh, urging her legs farther apart.

"You will have to do something, and soon," Grace lectured. "Even if you've made up your mind, you'll have to see a doctor. If you don't want to go to your regular doctor, perhaps you could talk to Kate. I'm sure she would know some doctors who could be discreet about your situation."

"I'll talk to her," Mallory promised, then swallowed hard as Liam's wicked hand inched higher.

"But we can discuss this some other time. It's late and you must be exhausted."

"Exhausted," Mallory echoed. "Yes."

"Before I go, though, I simply had to tell you... Alex Stowe is charming."

"Yes, he is," Mallory agreed. She bit back a cry as Liam glided upward, reaching his goal. Her hips rocked in rhythm with his fingers.

Grace's voice sounded as electrified as Mallory felt. "He drove me home, and—oh, Mal, he's smart, and handsome, and... really, absolutely charming."

"Yes."

"He's asked me to accompany him to some avant-garde theater thing by a playwright I've never heard of. It's playing at the American Conservatory Theater, and it's bound to be awful."

"Yes."

"This Saturday night. We'll have dinner first. Would you be a dear and make a reservation for us at your restaurant?"

"Yes."

"Thank you." Her aunt paused, and Mallory panicked. Did she have any idea what state her niece was in? Any idea what Liam O'Neill was doing to her? "Did you plan this?"

"Plan what?" Her voice barely had enough breath to be audible.

"Plan for me to meet Alex."

"Well, I..." Liam's thumb drew a circle against her most sensitive skin as he slid a finger deep into her. Her back arched and she moved the mouthpiece away from her lips until she was sure she wasn't going to groan. "I did, Aunt Grace," she managed to say weakly. "He invited himself in...." She heard Liam chuckle again, evidently applying her words to himself. Closing her eyes, she continued, "I thought you and he might—" she stifled another incipient moan "—enjoy each other."

"Oh, my. You're very sly, Mallory. You should have warned me. I'm really—well, anxious. This would be my first actual date in ages. I haven't been on a date with someone new in more than thirty years."

"Yes." Mallory's body was melting against Liam, turning liquid from the increasing heat. He moved his hand in a devastating rhythm, and her hips stayed with him, her mind straying dangerously.

"I'm very excited."

"I'm—excited, too."

"But nervous. If you speak to Kate, Mallory, please don't mention this date to her. I want to tell her myself. I know she won't be thrilled to hear that I'm going out with a man. I would like to break the news properly. It's only a date, of course, but even so... oh, heavens, Mallory, Alex *is* terribly charming."

"Yes. Aunt Grace—" Her voice broke, and she pulled the phone back from her chin again, at last permitting herself a small, blissful moan. "I really can't talk anymore," she mumbled, aware of how true that was.

"I won't keep you any longer, then. Thank you for being so understanding about my having botched dinner tonight. I'm sorry the evening didn't go as you would have hoped."

"Sometimes things work out for the best," Mallory assured her, then choked on another moan as Liam lifted his free hand to her breast. "Good night, Aunt Grace."

"Good night, dear. I'll speak with you soon."

The receiver slipped from her numb fingers. Liam released her breast long enough to hang up the phone for her, then guided her onto her back and kissed her lips. He skimmed his lips down to her breast and took her nipple gently between his teeth.

Her body shook, and seized, and imploded. A torrent of sensation rushed down from her breast to her womb and then spread from there, pulsing to her extremities, rising to flood her mind with dark sensation.

She let out a slow, tremulous breath. She couldn't believe what Liam had just done to her—while she was on the phone with her aunt, no less. What little heat wasn't inundating her body had risen into her cheeks as she realized how close she'd come to losing control while talking to Grace. If she hadn't been feeling so utterly sublime, she would have been mortified.

"That was terrible," she scolded Liam, glaring up at him through barely open eyes.

He appeared vastly amused. "You seemed to enjoy it all right."

"You're an evil man."

"Guilty as charged." His shameless grin contradicted his words.

"And besides, I feel very selfish. You didn't get to...well, you know."

"I'm still recovering from a few minutes ago," he told her, his smile losing its teasing edge. "I'll have another turn soon."

She glanced down the length of his body. "You look pretty recovered to me," she remarked, reaching down to stroke him.

He pulled her hand away and pinned it to the mattress. "Are you going to marry him?" he asked.

He didn't have to explain whom he meant, or why he'd abruptly introduced the subject. His expression conveyed an odd mixture of determination and tenderness, seasoned with a pinch of fear—fear that if he didn't fight for her he might lose her, fear that if he fought too hard he might scare her away.

She wished she could reassure him, but the truth was, she had no idea what she was going to do—with Robert or with Liam, or with herself. All she knew was that whatever direction her life took, her destination was going to include a baby. "Liam, I..." She sighed, wishing she could explain her doubts and her certainties. She wished she could tell him she was pregnant, but she couldn't, not until she felt as sure of him as she did of herself. "I don't know what I'm going to do about Robert," she conceded.

"I told you before, I didn't seek him out as a way to get to you. I wanted to meet him for myself. I wanted to know what I was up against."

She attempted a smile. "Gee. It sounds as if you're ready to challenge him to a duel."

Liam shook his head. His thumb moved lightly against her wrist; his eyes shed a silver glow down onto her face. "If I met him and saw that he was the man for you, I would have backed off. It would have broken my heart, but I would have done that. I care about you, Mallory. I want you happy."

His words warmed her as much as his lovemaking had. She cared about him, too. More than she had realized. More than she had ever cared about a man before.

"Robert's not the man for you," Liam said. "We both know he isn't."

"I'm not sure I know that."

"He doesn't love you, Mallory."

"Oh?" Liam's audacity amused her. "Did he tell you that?"

"He didn't have to tell me." Liam propped a couple of pillows against the headboard and leaned back, pulling Mallory up so she could recline in the curve of his arm. "If he loved you," he went on, toying with a lock of her hair, "he wouldn't have forced that engagement ring on you in front of your family without giving a thought to how you might feel. If he loved you, he wouldn't have embarrassed you like that."

"I see." She eyed him askance. "But making love to me while I'm on the phone with my aunt isn't embarrassing."

Liam could easily argue that he didn't love her, either— and maybe she'd left that implication dangling between them because she wanted to hear him say again how much he cared about her.

"I'm not sure how that happened," he confessed, a trace of self-deprecating humor filtering through his voice. "I had only meant to hold you. But then you started to move. And you seemed to want me to keep going. If you'd made any sign that you wanted me to stop, I would have." He twined her hair through his fingers and chuckled. "Did I really embarrass you?"

"Just a little." She laughed, too. "Aunt Grace was so giddy about Alex Stowe, I don't think she noticed that I was a bit...distracted."

"I like your aunt," Liam said. "She seems very cultured and poised."

"Not like what you'd expect after reading the tabloids, huh."

"The tabloids?" He twisted so he could peer into Mallory's face. "I don't read the tabloids. What did they say about your aunt?"

Mallory reminded herself that he lived all alone in a rural outpost, miles from the city, and that for the past five years he'd been in solitary confinement, locked in a prison of grief over his wife's death. Apparently, celebrity gossip of the previous year had passed him by. "She's been one-half of a messy divorce. Her husband was Jeffrey De-Wilde, of the international bridal store chain. You've heard of DeWilde's, haven't you?"

"No."

This, too, wasn't surprising, given that Liam was a widower with no apparent interest in weddings. "It's an exclusive family-owned chain of bridal shops, with branches in London, New York, Monaco, Paris and Sydney. Aunt Grace married Jeffrey and they built the chain into a major high-end retailer. When their marriage broke up, it was big news in the society pages. She came home to San Francisco and opened a bridal shop of her own. The tabloids made a major to-do about it for a while, but things have finally calmed down."

"I'm glad." He wove his fingers through her hair, lulling her. "The public eye is a nasty thing. My publisher is always pushing me to do book tours and TV interviews, but I don't like it."

"Then how come you agreed to appear on 'What's Up?'"

"Because I knew you were in San Francisco. And I wanted to find you. If I hadn't been able to find you, maybe you would have seen me on TV and found me."

Or maybe I would have gone into hiding, Mallory thought. When she'd first realized who Liam was, she had been petrified at the possibility of his finding her, because she knew how easily he could turn her life upside down. But he *had* found her, and he *had* turned her life upside down, and she couldn't shake the belief that he'd actually done her an enormous favor.

"So, why do you want to marry Robert Benedict?" he asked, bringing the discussion back to where it had started.

"It's complicated."

He smiled wryly. "I'm not an idiot. Perhaps if you explain it slowly, I'll understand."

She returned his smile. "I've dated on and off in my life. No one special ever came along, no one who could sweep me off my feet. It's probably my own fault—"

"Fault?"

"I don't know. Maybe I just wasn't going about it in the right way." She sighed. "It just never happened. Meanwhile, my father adores Robert. Robert is like a son to him. And—I mean, Robert likes me, and we get along, and we stay out of each other's way."

"It doesn't sound like much of a marriage," Liam observed.

"If I married Robert, I wouldn't be disappointed. I'd know what I was getting into, and I'd know what I was getting out of it. And... I want my father to adore me as much as he adores Robert. I figured if I married Robert, maybe that could happen." A shudder seized her as she realized what she'd just admitted. She had never declared her feelings so baldly before.

He twirled his fingers against her scalp, still soothing, still thoughtful. "You can't think of a better way to win your father's approval?"

"All my life I've been trying to get my father to love me."
She didn't discuss her insecurities with anyone, not even
Aunt Grace or her cousins. Mallory suspected they had
some idea about her uneasy relationship with her father—
Grace's phone call of a few minutes ago implied as much.
But it was a private matter, something between her father
and herself—or something within herself alone. It was
something she didn't feel comfortable sharing with others.

Until now.

"I think my father *does* love me," she allowed. "He just
doesn't talk to me—unless it's about his business. He
doesn't listen to me. He doesn't understand me. He treats
me as if I were a fascinating alien who fell into his lap from
a distant galaxy, and he keeps his distance."

"What about your mother?"

"She died when I was four."

"Ah." Liam pulled her more firmly into his arms. "Your
father is pushing this marriage, then."

"He and Robert work together. They understand each
other. Robert is a bridge that can connect us. My father and
I both want that bridge, Liam. We just could never seem to
figure out how to build it ourselves."

"Doesn't it bother you to think of your future husband
as a bridge instead of as your one true love?"

She snorted. "Frankly, I don't know if there really is such
a thing as true love. Infatuation, sure—lust, friendship,
fondness . . . But true love? Lasting love? I haven't seen it
in my life."

Liam stiffened almost imperceptibly. She eased out of his
embrace and gazed at him, searching his face. He looked
solemn but unflinching as she scrutinized him.

"You did have that love, didn't you," she said, wishing
she hadn't brought his sorrow out into the open, even
though she knew that they were going to have to address it
sooner or later. "You had that kind of love with your
wife."

For a long moment he was silent. Then he said, "It was a good marriage."

She wasn't jealous—not of his wife, anyway. What she was jealous of was all the people in the world who had known true love. "Maybe that kind of love is possible for some people," she observed wistfully.

"There are many different kinds of love, Mallory." He gathered her back into his arms and urged her against his shoulder. His cryptic statement hung in the air, tantalizing her. Did he love her? Was his love for her different from his love for his wife?

Wherever Mallory was headed in her life, could she dare to hope that Liam wanted to make the journey with her? With her and their child?

"How did you meet your wife?" she asked, astonished at how little she knew about this man to whom she felt so intimately connected. Before she could begin to assess where she stood with him, or what she wanted, or how much she could trust him, she needed to learn who he was.

He seemed to recognize that she had a right to ask personal questions—as much a right as he'd had to search out Robert. His fingers resumed their aimless wandering through her hair as he contemplated his answer. "Jennifer and I met in college. I wasn't much of an intellectual. I was a working-class kid, an immigrant's son from South Boston. But I played football and soccer, and Cornell gave me a scholarship." He shrugged, as if he considered his education a whim of good fortune. Mallory knew that even the finest football and soccer players didn't get accepted into Ivy League schools without having the academics down solid, but if Liam wanted to pretend he wasn't an egghead, that was his prerogative.

"So you met her at Cornell?"

He nodded. "After we graduated, she was heading off to graduate school in Ann Arbor, and as far as I could see, there was nothing going on in Ann Arbor but the University of Michigan. So I followed her there and wound up getting a Ph.D. And then we got married."

"I'm sorry you lost her," Mallory said, meaning it. She really couldn't feel jealous of what he'd had with his wife. She cared too much about him to feel anything but sympathy for his suffering.

His hand moved deeper into her hair, as if he were afraid his honesty might cost him her affection. She eased back to face him, then straddled his lap and pressed a kiss to his mouth.

"Thank you for telling me."

"It feels strange to talk about her."

"Do you feel disloyal, being here with me?"

"No," he murmured, pulling her down to kiss him. "God, no." He kissed her again, a long, thirsty kiss, then broke away from her. "Do you feel cheated?"

"That you loved her? No."

"She's been a memory for five years, Mallory," he said, cupping his hands around her face and holding her steady, his gaze locked onto hers. "A memory that used to be encrusted in bitterness. The crust is falling away, but she's still just a memory. Can you understand that?"

"Yes."

"When I see you, when I talk to you, when I touch you—" his gaze penetrated her, searing through her body to graze her soul "—I forget what it was like to feel that bitter. I feel . . . *joy*. I never dreamed I could experience joy again, but I do. With you. That's what you do to me, Mallory."

His lips met hers, and they said nothing more. This time they didn't need words. Only their bodies. Only the fierceness of his desire and hers, the hot, aching hunger they nourished within each other, the yearning they satisfied, the emptiness they filled with their passion. This time, all they needed was the deep, luminous emotion that neither of them had yet labeled love.

BESIDE HIM SHE SLEPT. The room was silent except for the soothing rhythm of her respiration. All he could make out in the dark was the shape of her arm slung over the edge of the blanket and her face, the skin almost translucent, framed in a tumble of black hair.

Restless, he eased out from under the cover and spread it smoothly around her. Stealing through the shadows, he found his jeans and tugged them on, then grabbed his shirt. He padded barefoot out of the bedroom, slinging his arms through the sleeves as he went.

He needed to think. To breathe. To evaluate what was going on, to come to terms with it.

Light slanted through the hallway from the kitchen. He followed the light into that room, which was still cluttered with pots and stemware in need of washing. He considered gathering the remaining items and dumping them into the sink to soak, but decided he wasn't feeling that altruistic. If Mallory were awake to help him, he would be willing to scrub the room from top to bottom. But solo? No way.

He continued through the kitchen, turning the light off behind him and letting his eyes grow accustomed to the gloom. Actually, the dining area wasn't as dark as her bedroom. She had left open the drapes, and faint moonlight seeped in through the sliding glass door.

He released the lock, opened the door and stepped outside onto the terrace, ignoring the slap of cold against the bare soles of his feet from the whitewashed stucco. Patches of fog herded across the sky. The cool air caressed his chest, but he didn't feel moved to button his shirt. In truth, he needed to cool off.

He leaned against the railing and gazed out in the direction of the Pacific, even though he couldn't see it. Closing his eyes, he tried to conjure Jennifer's image. Like the ocean, she lay hidden from his view.

All he could see was Mallory.

He wouldn't call what he was feeling love. He couldn't. But the promise of love shimmered inside him, the promise that the woman sleeping inside, the woman who aroused his emotions as much as she aroused his flesh, could be his lover. *Should* be his lover.

He wanted her. If she married that twit Benedict, Liam would go insane—but he was wise enough not to pressure her. She seemed to be gravitating to him on her own. If she needed to work things out with her father, Liam would help. He would be a bridge builder, too, if he could. And if he couldn't, he would try to offer Mallory enough to compensate for what she lost by losing her father. He would do whatever it took to keep her with him. He simply couldn't bear to consider living the rest of his life without her in it.

"Liam?"

He spun around. She stood in the open doorway, her robe wrapped around her, her hair tousled and her cheeks flushed. Her eyes were round with concern.

"I'm sorry, I didn't mean to wake you."

She stepped out onto the terrace, hugging her robe more snugly around her as the midnight chill struck her. He opened his arms, and she quickly moved into them. He could warm her more effectively than her robe could.

"Are you all right?" she asked. Her voice was muted, as if the fog had softened its edges the way it softened the moonlight.

"Yes," he assured her, then touched his lips to the crown of her head. "I'm better than all right."

He couldn't see her smile, but he could imagine it. "Then why are you out here?"

"I couldn't sleep." He rubbed his hand gently up and down her arm. "We left the kitchen in a mess."

"Well, I'm sure not going to do anything about it now," she said. "Do you know what time it is?"

"It's late," he murmured.

She nodded, letting her head come to rest against his shoulder. Together they gazed out over the silhouetted houses and apartment buildings that spread down the hill toward the western edge of the city.

Their silence was thoughtful, yet companionable. Liam was brimming with things he needed to say, but he wasn't sure how to say them. Writing horror, he had no difficulty coming up with the right phrasings, the right idioms. Speaking his heart, though, was altogether different. It had been so long since he'd exposed his deepest emotions, and he was no longer certain how to put them into words.

For better or worse, she spoke first. "You haven't asked anything of me, Liam."

Confused, he frowned. "What do you mean?"

"You haven't..." She sighed, evidently struggling for words, too. "You haven't made any grand statements. You haven't talked about commitments, or the future. You haven't asked me any of that. Maybe you *won't* ask."

He knew now what she meant. Her candor amazed him—and touched him, too. How could he not love a woman who confronted the truth so unflinchingly, who demanded the same degree of honesty from him? "Mallory—"

"But if I even allowed myself to consider what you haven't even asked—" he definitely felt her smile now, sensing the lift of her cheek against his chest "—it would mean putting an end to a whole lot of my plans. Before I take any steps that can't be reversed, I need..." She sighed, and he knew she was no longer smiling. "I need to know what's going on with us."

"What do you need to know?" He would tell her anything, anything she asked. He would tell her he loved her, if she had to hear it. Even if he wasn't exactly sure it was love, even if he believed it was too soon to call what he was feeling love, even if he feared that he would never be able to make himself vulnerable to love again... he would tell her.

"I'm thirty years old," she said, her voice as clear and pure as the crystal glasses in her kitchen. "I'm ready to settle down. I want to know where I belong. I want to know who I can count on. I want..." She sighed again, but refused to retreat. "I want a family."

Was she asking him to marry her? Demanding a proposal from him? It wasn't as if he were stubbornly opposed to such an idea. In this day and age, making love with a woman shouldn't require a man to fall to his knees and propose, yet Mallory... Maybe he wanted her that much. Maybe the thought of losing her was scarier than the thought of getting married again.

If she could just give him—give them *both*—some time. They needed it. If only she could give them the chance to get used to each other...

"I want to have a child, Liam," she said.

"No." The word shot out of him before he could stop himself. He felt his spine jerk, felt the back of his eyes explode with pain. No, no children. He couldn't give her that.

She drew back and gazed up at him, her face pale and her eyes wide. "What do you mean, no?"

He scrambled to rescue the moment. But what she was asking... a child, *his* child...

It didn't matter that he was probably already in love with her. This was the one thing he could never yield on. "I can't have children," he said, his voice brittle from the effort not to scream.

"You *can't*? Physically, you mean?" She appeared stunned.

"I just can't. I'm sorry, Mallory. I can't."

She seemed to struggle to get her breath. She put more distance between them, inching along the railing until she had reached the corner of the balcony, as far as she could be from him without leaping over the railing or fleeing indoors. She stared at him, looking horrified. "Why can't you have a child?"

Because there was one kind of love that hurt too much, he wanted to tell her. Because there was one kind of grief he would never recover from, and he would never, never open himself to such blinding pain again. Because, while he could get over the loss of his wife, he could never get over the loss of his son.

Merely thinking about his child staggered him. He turned away, afraid to let her see him shatter under the agony of it.

"Liam?"

He shook his head, furious to discover that there was, indeed, something he couldn't tell her. Even at the risk of losing her, he couldn't say it.

"Is it...something physical?"

"No." The word rasped against his throat, aggravating the pain in his heart, in his gut.

"Then what? You had a terrible childhood? You're afraid you can't handle it? What?"

He shook his head again, breathing deeply, praying not to snap.

"You already have a child," she guessed, her voice a pale whisper.

Her words were like a stiletto running through him, so sharp he barely felt the cut. All he felt was his life spilling through the wound and draining away.

He fought to keep his shoulders steady, his feet firm, his voice even. "I *had* a child," he corrected her.

She gasped. "Oh, no. Liam...? Did you lose a child, too? Oh, God—in the accident—"

"Mallory." He sensed her nearing him, and he steeled himself against her touch. He couldn't bear for her to touch him now. Her urge to console him only made him feel worse. "I don't want to talk about it."

"Tell me," she insisted. She must have read his body language, because she fell back a step. But she refused to back off in her questioning. "Was it in the accident that killed your wife?"

"Yes."

"How old?"

He swallowed. If he had any chance of salvaging his relationship with Mallory, he had to answer. "He was nearly two." Old enough to say *Daddy*. Old enough to race into Liam's arms the instant Liam entered a room. Old enough to kiss Liam and giggle with him and shriek in outrage when Liam gave him a bath. Old enough to snuggle up in Liam's embrace, on his lap, and murmur every night, as he drifted off to sleep, "I love you, Daddy."

"What was his name?"

"John."

"I'm sorry, Liam. I'm so sorry."

Her sympathy couldn't erase the pain. Nothing could erase it. Nothing ever would. "I will never have another child, Mallory. I'm sorry, too—but I can't. It hurt too much to lose him. I don't know how I survived. I'm still not sure I *did* survive. I won't risk it again."

"Not all children die, Liam. Not all children are victims of terrible accidents."

"It wasn't an accident. It was a drunk driver, someone who deliberately broke a law, drank too much and took the wheel. This wasn't some chance happening. It was a criminal act. My son was murdered." He swore under his breath. The rage was back, swamping him, roaring through him, just when he thought he had finally triumphed over it. Just when he thought Mallory had saved him.

"Most children live long and healthy lives," she said.

"My son didn't. He died, Mallory. The one time he needed to be saved, I wasn't there for him. A father lives to protect his child from harm, and I . . ." His voice faltered. "I failed him."

He lapsed into silence. If he said anything more, only bitterness would erupt. The wound was still bleeding, hemorrhaging. He was still too full of hatred to find room in his life for love.

He couldn't give Mallory what she longed for: a real family, complete with children. But he cared for her too much to keep her from achieving her dreams. If she wanted children, she would have to have them with another man.

If Liam loved her, he had to let her go. He had to free her to make her commitment to a man who could give her what she wanted.

That man could never be Liam.

With a bleak, despairing sigh, he stalked into the apartment, abandoning her to the night and the fog and the anguish he'd left in his wake.

CHAPTER ELEVEN

"THERE'S A WOMAN HERE who says she's your cousin," Burt murmured.

Mallory peered up from the scallops she was marinating in sauterne and herbs. Her back felt stiff and her starched white toque sat heavily on her head. Around her the kitchen bustled as it always did on Saturday night, the staff moving with frenetic efficiency to accommodate the crowds in the dining room. There was no time to revel in the scents of ingredients being blended and cooked, no time to beam with pride at the esthetically garnished arrangements of food on bone china dishes before the waiters scooped them up and rushed out of the kitchen to deliver them to waiting patrons in the dining room.

The boom box on the shelf blasted a Jimi Hendrix cassette, a feast of chugging rhythms and flamboyant guitar licks. Burt had chosen the evening's background music and it clashed vibrantly with Mallory's mood. But she didn't care.

She didn't care about much of anything, lately. Ever since Liam had walked out of her apartment and her life, she had been in a trance, the external world obliterated by her own spiritual fog, her thoughts and dreams directed inward to the fetus inside her, nearly a week further along now, with an infinitely stronger hold on her.

She had fallen in love with Liam O'Neill, and she was still reeling from the irony that the only way she could pursue a relationship with him was to give up the most precious gift he had given her: his child. She had dialed Dr. Gilman's office number twice in the past week, and twice had changed her mind and hung up before the call was connected. She wasn't going to end the pregnancy. Even though it meant losing Liam forever, she wasn't going to do it.

"Mallory?" Burt leaned closer to her and spoke directly into her ear. The music—Hendrix's guitar gliding through "The Wind Cries Mary"—and the conversations of the cooks and waiters weren't so loud that Mallory hadn't heard him. It was just that his words hadn't registered because her senses were dulled, her receptors out of kilter. All she could think of was Liam's pain and his children, plural: the child he'd lost, and the child he would never know. All that mattered was that Mallory's heart had shattered the night Liam had walked away, and it would never heal.

"Mallory, there's some lady outside who says she's your cousin Kate."

Mallory grimaced. "Oh, swell. The least she could have done was call first. That would have been courteous, don't you think?"

Taken aback by her uncharacteristic crankiness, Burt eyed her doubtfully. "I guess," he said, too smart to disagree with his boss.

"I don't suppose we've got an available table," she muttered. "Did anyone cancel a reservation?"

"I'm pretty sure she didn't come to eat. She's at the back door. In the alley." He watched Mallory cautiously, as if braced for a major outbreak of fury.

It took a full minute for his statement to register fully with her. She turned from the scallops and studied his cherubic face, her brow tugged into a frown. "Kate's in the alley?"

"She doesn't want dinner. She just wants to talk to you."

"Oh. Okay." Mallory lifted a linen towel from one of the racks, dried off her hands and gestured toward the marinating seafood. "Stir those for me, would you?"

Not bothering to wait for his answer, she moved woodenly through the kitchen and down the hall. Through the screen door, she spotted Kate standing in the bright glare of the outdoor light. Kate wore chinos, a thick sweater and a down vest. Her breath emerged from her mouth in little puffs of vapor. The chilly air drifting in through the screen helped to ventilate the kitchen and keep it from becoming unbearably hot with all the burners and ovens running. But Kate wasn't in the hot, hectic kitchen. She was literally cooling her heels in the wintry evening air.

The sight of her outside in the alley, hugging her arms around herself for warmth, jolted Mallory. She hurried down the hall, unlatched the screen door and swung it inward.

"Kate! Come in! Why didn't you use the street entry?"

"I was afraid they'd see me. Are they here?" she asked, stepping inside and rubbing her hands briskly together. "Did they get here yet?"

"Who?"

"My mother and her—her *date*." Kate clearly had difficulty speaking the word.

"I don't know if they're here or not," Mallory admitted, glancing at her watch. "Garth—my maître d'—takes care of the dining room. But your mother and Alex probably are here by now. I made them an early reservation so they wouldn't be late for the theater."

Kate swore under her breath and started down the hallway. Mallory grabbed her arm, restraining her. "I'm not going to bother them," Kate insisted. "I just want to take a peek."

"You can't go marching through the kitchen."

"If I use the front door, they'll see me. Mother would die if she knew I was spying on her. Or maybe she'd kill me first and *then* die."

"Don't be silly, Kate. You aren't going to spy on her." Mallory relaxed her hold on Kate's sleeve slightly, but not enough for her cousin to slip free.

Kate glared at Mallory, her eyes glassy with anger. "I can't believe Mother did this. I can't believe *you* did this, Mal. Setting her up on a date! The whole thing is—"

"Let's go in my office," Mallory suggested, ushering Kate into the cramped room off the hallway. "Would you like something to drink?"

Kate mumbled a syllable that bore a passing resemblance to *yes.* Once she was sure her cousin wouldn't try to make a break for the kitchen, Mallory set off in search of an open bottle of wine. In less than a minute, one of the waiters had brought her a half-full bottle of cabernet sauvignon from a Napa winery. Armed with the bottle and a single glass, Mallory returned to her office, where Kate was attempting to pace but discovering that the room's dimensions were too confining. Three steps and she reached a wall. Three steps in the opposite direction and she collided with Mallory's desk.

In spite of everything that was currently fouled up in her own life, Mallory found herself smiling at her cousin. Unlike her older siblings, Megan and Gabriel, Kate was intense and, on occasion, insufferably self-righteous. Mallory had a feeling this was going to be one of those occasions.

"Here," she said, filling the glass with wine and pressing it into Kate's hands. "It's a good vintage. I think you'll like it."

"Aren't you having any?" Kate asked before taking a small sip.

Mallory shook her head. "I'm working." That was simpler than telling her cousin why she had no intention of drinking anything alcoholic for the next seven months.

Reluctantly, Kate dropped into a chair. Mallory circled the desk and took her own seat, facing Kate. "I haven't seen you in a while," she observed with a smile. Maybe some casual chitchat would help Kate to unwind. "How have you been? How are things at the clinic?"

"Things are fine at the clinic," Kate snapped. "It's everything else that's a disaster. Why did you set my mother up on a date, Mallory?"

"What's wrong with her going on a date? Alex Stowe is a very nice man."

"So is my father."

Mallory frowned. Kate's father was no blood relation of hers—which had never meant anything to Mallory as long as Jeffrey made her beloved aunt happy. But he had hurt Grace, and Mallory was a loyal Powell who felt no compunction about taking Grace's side in the DeWildes' breakup. "Your father has been gallivanting around the world, taking care of the family business," she argued, not bothering to hide her disapproval. "I haven't seen him in San Francisco, being nice to your mother."

"Mal...." Kate took another drink of wine. When she spoke again, she seemed to be choosing her words carefully. "My father has a lot to worry about with the business, you know that. And other worries, too. Family stuff about some decades-old burglary. And of course he's terribly worried about my mother—"

Mallory perked up. "What decades-old burglary?"

"It doesn't matter. Just some old jewels—"

Mallory grinned, bristling with interest. The notion of an old jewel heist was enough to distract her from her own dreary problems. "What old jewels?"

"Really, Mallory, it doesn't matter."

"I'm curious. Did they steal something from one of the DeWilde stores? Sheesh. That gaudy tiara in the London store—"

"Mallory, please, it's not important. Father's hired a detective to take care of it." Kate glanced away for a moment, as if captivated by Mallory's framed certificates on the wall. Her cheeks bloomed with color.

"What detective?" Mallory pressed her, even more intrigued by Kate's sudden discomfort than she was by thoughts of a robbery.

"He's..." Kate's cheeks grew darker. "He's just a detective. Nick Santos. He seems very competent, and I'm sure he'll solve everything. The point is, everybody's been under a lot of stress. It's just been one thing after another. And now this—Mother on a date. She phoned me this morning and told me some man was bringing her here for dinner, and then to an avant-garde theater production. You know what avant-garde means, don't you? The actors are probably going to be romping around the stage naked."

"Well, I should hope so," Mallory said with mock solemnity. "Why bother sitting in a theater for two hours if you aren't going to see naked actors?"

Kate ignored her teasing. "Mother told me the man is a friend of yours. You introduced them."

"That's right." Realizing how distraught Kate was, Mallory put her joking aside. "Trust me, Kate, he's a gentleman."

"Have you ever heard the expression 'gold digger'?"

"He's got plenty of his own gold to dig. He's a successful architect. He isn't after your mother's money."

"Then what is he after? Her body?"

Mallory shrugged, succumbing to another smile. "Would that be the end of the world? She's a beautiful woman. Why shouldn't he be attracted to her?"

A strangled shriek escaped Kate. She took a long swig of wine. "Forgive me, Mal, but maybe somewhere in the back of my mind I had this wild fantasy that my parents might someday be able to reconcile. But that's not likely to happen with you getting in the way."

Mallory refused to let Kate's accusation bother her. "I wish your parents hadn't split up," she said gently, "but they did. It's not my fault. It's not your fault, either. It happened. All you can do is love them both and wish them well."

"Thanks for those pearls of wisdom. As if you were in any position to comment on marriage."

Mallory blew off her anger. She had never been as close to Kate as she'd been to Gabriel and Megan, but she loved Kate. Right now, Kate was so upset about her mother's date with Alex she couldn't possibly have meant to insult Mallory. "What is that supposed to mean?" she asked mildly.

Kate looked sheepish. "I'm sorry, Mal. It's just... Mother said this morning that she thinks your marriage plans are in limbo."

Mallory sighed. Whether or not Grace had told Kate why her marriage plans were in limbo, Kate was going to find out sooner or later. Mallory had considered and reconsidered contacting Dr. Gilman often enough this past week to know where she stood and what she was going to do. She wasn't going to be able to keep her pregnancy a secret for much longer.

She would have been perfectly content with her decision if only Liam could have known about it and embraced it. But she couldn't tell him. If he learned about the baby, he would demand that she get rid of it. He'd made it quite clear that he didn't ever want to have a child again—and he'd made it just as clear that if Mallory wanted to have a child, he didn't want her.

Remembering their last few minutes together caused a deep, searing pain to stab through the center of her chest, so fierce she gasped. "What?" Kate asked, leaning forward, bristling with concern. "What's wrong?"

"Oh, everything," Mallory said, attempting a blithe laugh. "You may as well know, Kate—I'm pregnant."

"You're pregnant?" Kate lowered her wineglass onto the desk and leaned even closer, staring into Mallory's eyes as if she could diagnose a pregnancy by examining a patient's pupils. Kate was a doctor, after all. Maybe she saw physical changes in Mallory's face. Maybe she detected the heartbreak sucking all the joy from what should have been a blessing.

Abruptly, she cut loose with a hoot of raucous laughter. "I can't believe it!"

"What can't you believe?" Mallory muttered, finding Kate's amusement less than flattering.

"Robert! I can't believe he'd lose control like that! He's so...so..."

"Passionless," Mallory supplied.

"Organized," Kate overruled her. "He's so goal-oriented. I can't imagine him getting so carried away he lost track of the consequences." She must have sensed that she was the only one in the office who found Mallory's pregnancy hilarious, because she politely coughed to cover her giggles. "What are you going to do?"

"I'd like to punch you in the nose for laughing at me," Mallory snapped, although she succumbed to a faint chuckle. "But what I'm going to do is see a doctor."

"You haven't seen anyone yet?" Kate immediately shifted into her professional persona. "How far along are you?"

"Almost twelve weeks."

"Quit stalling, then! If you're going to do something, it's now or never."

"I'm going to have the baby," Mallory told her. No matter what her choice ultimately entailed, she felt good when she said the words. She felt settled, centered—as happy as she could feel, given that her decision had cost her the man she loved.

"In that case, you'd better make an appointment with an ob-gyn right away. Get a complete physical, make sure your blood pressure and blood sugar are in line. And start taking some prenatal nutritional supplements. It's very important, Mallory.''

"I know." Mallory nodded obediently. "And I will. See a doctor, I mean."

"What about the wedding? If you're almost twelve weeks now...let's see, the baby would be born in September, right? So it would be a good three months old by the wedding. If it's a girl, it can be your flower girl. As one of your bridesmaids, I'd be honored to push the stroller down the aisle.''

"Kate, stop." Kate had thoroughly wrung every last drop of humor from Mallory's predicament. "I haven't even discussed the situation with Robert."

"He doesn't know?"

Mallory shook her head. He also didn't know by *whom* she was pregnant. "I was going to discuss it with him, but he really ticked me off—"

"The ring." Kate nodded knowingly. "Mother told me. That was truly tasteless, his foisting it on you that way."

"That was only part of it. He took off for four days without even mentioning that he would be out of town. I left him a message to phone me, and he never did. Half the time he forgets I exist. Then he panics and does something like shoving a huge, ugly diamond ring at me to prove that he *is* aware of my existence. He has no idea how I might feel. He's insensitive."

"He's always been insensitive. It never bothered you before."

"Yes, well, now I'm pregnant. I'm entitled to be bothered by things that didn't used to bother me." She groaned and forced a smile. "I don't know what I'm going to do, Kate. My life is a mess. All I know is, I want the baby."

"Well, congratulations, then." Kate eyed her quizzically. "It's changed you."

"I know. For the first time in my life, I'm bigger than a B-cup."

"No, it's changed you in some other way. You seem . . ." She briefly scrutinized Mallory. "I don't mean to imply you've turned into an earth mother, but you seem more grounded. The way your eyes glowed when you said you wanted the baby—it's the first time I've ever heard you say you want something. I mean, something real, something that really matters. Not just a restaurant, or a career as a chef—but something *real*. Something personal."

"There are lots of other personal things I want," Mallory argued. Like her father's respect, for instance. And her aunt's happiness. And Liam. Oh, God, how she wanted Liam!

"Maybe—" Kate continued to assess her "—it's that you want something and it's within your reach. Something vitally important, something you don't have to work for or pay for . . . and it's yours." Tears flashed unexpectedly in her eyes. "I envy you, Mal. You've got one hell of a road ahead of you, but I envy you." She blinked, then rose to her feet. "I know you're busy, so I won't take up any more of your time. Please, do me a favor and don't set my mother up with anyone else."

"I wouldn't dare," Mallory promised, touched by her cousin's sentiments but discreet enough not to comment on them. "I want to maintain a good relationship with Alex. He lives upstairs from me—he could make my life miserable if I introduced Aunt Grace to other men."

"Not funny," Kate said, once again brisk with indignation. "Take care of yourself, Mal. Get some vitamins. And if you see anything tonight in the dining room—if Mother throws her drink in your neighbor's face—call me."

Mallory grinned. "You'll be the first to know." Moving out from behind her desk, she gave her cousin a genuine hug. "Your mother will be fine," she said.

"She'd better be, or I'll blame you." Kate returned her hug. She and Mallory walked arm in arm down the hall to the back door, and Mallory remained just inside the screen door, watching until her cousin was safely locked inside her car. The headlights erupted into twin high beams, the engine purred, and she steered out of the alley.

Mallory felt herself deflate. She no longer had to be bright and cheerful; she no longer had to pretend that, despite her unplanned pregnancy, everything was all right with her.

The only thing that was all right with her was her baby. Everything else was all wrong. The man she loved was too wounded to return her love. The man she loved was gone. And the only thing she could possibly do to get him back was the one thing she would never, never do.

HOW MANY ACRES OF TREES would he have to chop into toothpicks before he stopped hurting?

He set down the ax and kicked aside the chunks of wood he'd been about to hack into unnecessarily smaller wedges. He'd been in and out of the house half a dozen times a day, picking up the ax, reminding himself that using it wasn't going to make his life better, and putting it back down again.

Nothing was going to make his life better. Not writing: his current manuscript-in-progress had detoured down such a dark path he could scarcely stand to read his own words as they scrolled across the monitor of his word processor. Not drinking coffee: he'd guzzled so much his kidneys had all but sent him a telegram begging him to cut back on his consumption. Not reading the newspaper: he was afraid to skim a San Francisco daily on the chance that he might see a photograph of her, standing beside her fiancé and flashing that obscene diamond ring. Not hiking through the mist-shrouded woods around his house, not tossing back beer after beer at Smitty's, not fleeing to a retreat where talking wasn't permitted.

Nothing was going to make him stop wanting Mallory Powell.

He'd done the only honorable thing, leaving her to her dreams of children. He couldn't possibly be a father ever again. The fear, the agony, the constant, gnawing expectation of tragedy would destroy him. He couldn't give the woman he loved the one thing she wanted, and if he couldn't do that, he had to give her the freedom to find someone who could.

He cursed. He'd been doing a lot of that lately. He'd heard himself uttering oaths he hadn't even known were in his vocabulary. He'd spewed colorful, bitter expletives describing anatomically impossible acts. He'd cast aspersions on mothers, sons and assorted deities. He was a novelist; he could be creative. When it came to profanity, the muse hadn't left his side.

But cursing didn't help. It barely reduced the simmering tension inside him.

Maybe...just maybe for Mallory he could open his heart to another child. A baby, a piece of his soul torn from him, mixed with a piece of Mallory's soul and molded into a creature who would batter down every last defense he had, who would love him and trust him, who would extract from him the deepest, most essential promise a father could give his child: *I will protect you. I will never let anybody hurt you.*

Liam had broken that promise to John. Objectively, he knew he wasn't to blame, but in his heart, in his gut, in the lightless corners of his mind, he knew that he had sworn, at the moment of John's birth, that he would keep this child from harm. And that child, his son, had been killed.

He couldn't go through it again. Not even for Mallory.

He trudged toward the house, stomped up the porch steps and shoved open the door. The phone was ringing, but he was in no hurry to answer.

Midway through the fourth ring, his answering machine clicked on. He strode through the kitchen to his office and listened as a familiar voice recorded a message onto the tape: "Liam, this is Hazel Dupree. If you're there, please pick up. I've got important things to discuss with you."

He exhaled and sank into a chair. Hazel worked so hard to keep him functioning. He supposed he could listen to whatever important things she wanted to discuss.

He picked up the receiver. "Hello, Hazel."

"Ah, see? You *are* there, after all!" she exclaimed. "Do I know you, or what?"

"What," he grunted, half an answer to her rhetorical question and half an attempt to get her to state her business.

"Grouchy, aren't we."

"It's been a lousy few days."

"Well, here's some news that will cheer you up," Hazel said briskly. She was the only person Liam knew who could announce cheering news in a tone of voice that implied he should brace himself for a calamity. "Creighton and the rest of the brass were impressed with the television interview you did in San Francisco. I'm not just talking about your performance, although everyone who's seen the videotape is very pleased with the way you acquitted yourself. But beyond that, Liam, your sales really spiked in the Bay Area this week. The books are flying off the shelves."

"They were flying off the shelves before I did the interview," he reminded her. "Those were your exact words, I think."

"They were flying like prop planes. Now they're flying like the space shuttle. Creighton wants you to do a little more promotion—"

"No," Liam said automatically.

Hazel laughed. "You always say no first. Now, be a good boy and hear me out. New York. You could fly in, do some print interviews, one TV show, and give Creighton a chance to fete you."

"No."

"The publisher wants to take you to the Four Seasons or else Elaine's. They want to give you a legitimate writer's experience."

"I have a legitimate writer's experience every time I sit down at my desk," he argued, tapping a key on his computer to shut off his screen saver. A page of text winked onto the screen. That was his legitimate writer's experience—page after page of text, composed by him.

"If you came to New York, you could see me," she wheedled.

That brought him up short. He liked Hazel. He wasn't going to insult her by blurting out another unthinking *no*.

"I'd take you out to dinner in Chinatown, if you'd like. Or we could go to Brighton Beach and eat kosher Russian food. Or Little Italy for Italian. Or Second Avenue for Ukrainian. I'd give you a legitimate *New York* experience."

"Did it ever occur to you that we people in California do know how to feed ourselves?" Especially when Mallory was cooking. Especially when he was seated at her table, in her home, gazing at her through flickering amber candlelight. Especially when the only thing more delicious than her cooking was her smile.

"But you don't have to worry about earthquakes interfering with your digestion. Consider it, Liam. You could even take a side trip up to Boston and say hello to your folks."

He groaned. He hadn't seen them in a while. They knew how touchy he was, how deep his pain ran. They knew enough to give him the space he desperately needed.

His parents had last been out to visit him a little over a year ago, for Christmas. His mother had fussed and fretted, complaining that he was too skinny, too pale, too withdrawn. His father had sat on the porch with him, drinking beer and allowing him his silence.

They loved him. Damn it, he loved them, too.

"All right," he heard himself say. "Maybe I ought to get away for a few days and see the folks. This book I'm writing sucks, anyway."

"I'm going to pretend I didn't hear you say that," Hazel told him. "I'm sure the book is terrific. But if you need a break, take one. When do you want to fly in?"

"Tomorrow," he said, a sense of grim resolution stealing over him. Why not get the hell out of California, as far from Mallory as he could go? Why not put as much distance as he could between himself and his misery? "I'll book a flight. Tell Creighton to set something up."

"Liam?" Hazel sounded dubious. "Are you sure? I'm not used to you being so cooperative."

"I'm not doing it for you," he said. "I'm not doing it for Creighton, either. You can tell him I said so."

Hazel laughed, apparently reassured. "I'll convey the message. Give me a call once you've got your arrival time worked out." She hung up before Liam could retract his promise to come.

Sighing, he hung up the phone. The words on his monitor floated before his eyes, a meaningless jumble of shapes, and he turned off the computer. Lying beside it on his desk was the month-old photograph of Mallory from the San Francisco newspaper's society page.

He didn't want to look at it, but he couldn't help himself. Not that he needed the clipping to see her. He could see her just by closing his eyes. She was there, permanently etched into his memory. Her velvet-soft skin. Her sensuous voice. Her black, black hair. Her lips. The heat of her body taking him in, drawing him deep, throbbing around him. Her tremulous cry of ecstasy singing in his brain, casting a spell over him.

Damn. It wasn't just her body, it wasn't just her soft, sweet moans of pleasure he missed. It was her tenderness, her generosity, her laughter, her surprising lustiness. Her lack of pretense or pretentiousness. Her vulnerability. Her quiet longing to be loved the way she deserved to be loved.

Liam wanted to give her his love. He *had* given it. If he hadn't loved her, he would have stayed with her, enjoyed himself with her, taken up as much of her time and her life as she would allow. Selfishly, he would have won her heart and labored to convince her that she didn't really want babies. He would have deprived her of her most significant dream.

But he *did* love her, enough to leave her alone, enough to give her a chance to find a man who could make her dream come true. Liam loved her enough to stay away.

He would survive. It hurt, but he was used to hurt. He knew how to live with pain, to endure it. And he was probably right to believe that the pain of living the rest of his life without Mallory wasn't anywhere near as bad as the pain of opening his heart to a child, a child he and Mallory would create in love, a child he would never be strong enough to save from the cruel whims of fate.

CHAPTER TWELVE

MONDAY MORNING, after a visit to her doctor and a stop at the drugstore to fill a prescription for nutritional supplements, Mallory parked in the alley behind her restaurant and walked downtown to the office building that housed Powell Enterprises. The sun had burned off the fog, leaving the air unseasonably clear and mild. Even if the morning had been damp and clammy, though, she would have chosen to walk rather than drive. She needed to burn off her nervous energy before she saw Robert.

Today was the day she would tell him. So far, breaking the news of her pregnancy to Kate had proved no harder than breaking the news to Aunt Grace. Informing her gynecologist had been even easier. Mallory harbored no illusions about how the morning with Robert would go, though. *Easy* was not what she was expecting.

A crisp breeze tugged at her hair, which she was wearing loose. The wind carried an undertone of warmth, hinting at spring. In just a few weeks, the trees would be budding, the green spikes of daffodils and tulips breaking through the soil. The bay would lose its gray tinge and spread its turquoise shimmer outward from the city's eastern shore. Mallory would fold down the roof of her car. She would rediscover her appetite. She would start thickening around the waist as the life inside her grew.

Tears stung her eyes and a lump filled her throat, but she kept walking, kept pumping her sneaker-clad feet against the pavement, kept her face forward and her arms swinging. It didn't seem fair that the most joyous event of her life should cast so dark a shadow over her. It didn't seem fair that the most important thing she had ever shared with Liam was the one thing she could never share with him.

Fairness was irrelevant. This was her life, and she was going to have to make the most of it.

A city bus roared past her, drowning out her thoughts. Soon enough she would have a squalling baby to drown out her thoughts. By the time her existence was once again peaceful enough for her to hear herself think, maybe those thoughts would have something worthwhile to teach her.

She reached the office tower on Montgomery Street without having come up with a strategy for approaching Robert. She had no idea what she was going to say or how she was going to say it. Lacking a better idea, she resigned herself to speaking the truth.

She shoved her hands into the pockets of her red wool blazer. Inside the left pocket she felt a velvet cube—the box containing her engagement ring. Returning the garish ring to Robert would probably express her feelings better than any speech she might have prepared.

She rode the elevator up and emerged into the plush decor of Powell Enterprises' reception area. Ellen glanced up from the reception desk and smiled. "Mallory! Hi!"

Mallory smiled back, well aware that the company's entire staff, from the cute young receptionist on up, was going to know soon enough that Leland Powell's daughter didn't have much to smile about. Leland Powell's firm had expanded significantly over the years, but despite its size it still maintained the atmosphere of a family enterprise. Everyone knew everyone; everyone talked about everyone. And when the Boss-Man's daughter was pregnant—and *not* thanks to her fiancé, the Boss-Man's first lieutenant—everyone was sure to be talking about it for quite some time.

"Is Robert in?" Mallory asked.

Ellen nodded. "Let me just buzz him and make sure he isn't in a meeting." She lifted the receiver of her console and pushed a button. Mallory tried to keep smiling, but her cheeks cramped and her fingers felt icy around the box in her pocket. The waistband of her jeans pinched slightly. She had just barely gained back the pounds she'd lost a couple of weeks ago, she had no appetite, and yet she was already feeling fat.

And she still had no idea what she was going to say to Robert.

Ellen lowered the receiver. "He's free," she reported. "You can go right in."

"Thanks." Mallory turned and stalked down the hall, directing her thoughts away from herself and her predicament and focusing them on Robert. She didn't want to hurt him, but she wasn't sure how she could drop her bombshell without inflicting pain. How could a woman tell the man she had publicly declared she was going to marry that she was pregnant with the child of another man, who had deserted her because he didn't want to be a father? Robert wasn't perfect, but he didn't deserve the indignity of losing his fiancée to a man who had already vacated the premises.

Still, the truth remained her best—her only—recourse. She would shoulder all the blame, of course. She would cushion the blow as best she could. She would hope that Robert would accept the situation calmly. Much as she hated what she was about to do, *not* doing it would only prolong everyone's anguish, including Robert's.

When she reached the heavy oak door with Robert's name affixed to it on a small brass plaque, she paused and took a few deep breaths. She felt queasy, but she suspected that had less to do with her pregnancy than with dread. She had no talent for hurting people. She had no stomach for it.

Reminding herself that not telling Robert would hurt him more in the long run, she mustered her courage and knocked on the heavy oak door, then nudged it open. Robert was already on his feet, a vision of meticulous grooming in gray pinstripes and a burgundy silk tie, striding across the acre of carpet to greet her.

He gave her a perfunctory kiss, then hurried back to his desk as if pressing matters awaited him there. "What brings you downtown today, Mallory?" he asked.

He seemed preoccupied. Well, she was about to snare his attention. With a deep sigh, she followed him across the spacious office, removing the box from her pocket. When she reached his desk, she set the box on it, directly in front of him.

He had been studying a spread sheet on his blotter, but sure enough, the sight of the box hit him with all the subtlety of a wrecking ball. He lifted his gaze cautiously to meet hers and offered a placating smile. "You're angry."

"Not anymore," she said. She had forgotten how furious she'd been when he had sprung the ring on her. She was too busy feeling guilty for how furious she was going to make him.

"I know, we had discussed picking out a ring together," he admitted. "I jumped the gun. I don't blame you for being upset. I guess I had sort of figured the roses would counteract that."

"You heard what my aunt said that night," Mallory reminded him. "When a woman gets a bouquet like that, she assumes the guy has done something to atone for. But—"

"I preempted you with the ring for a reason," he said, cutting her off. "I felt our paths were drifting apart. We just weren't connecting the way we should have been. I thought this would help. Actually, I thought it was kind of romantic. I spent a fortune on it, you know."

"I can believe that," she muttered.

They were both still standing, with Robert's massive desk between them. He didn't motion for her to take a seat, and although her hike from Union Square had tired her out, she was too tense to sit. As for him, he looked as if he were about to depart for a meeting or some other professional duty. Surely he could find something more exciting to do just down the hall, in another office, if only Mallory would state her business and leave.

"Anyway, the ring wasn't entirely my idea," Robert elaborated. "I asked your father what he thought about it—not just the ring, but my surprising you with it. He thought it would be effective."

Mallory sighed again, more weary than annoyed. Even if she married Robert, he would still be wedded to her father rather than her. It boggled her mind that the two of them could have discussed the pros and cons of Robert's presenting the ring to her while he was crashing what had never been intended as a dinner party in the first place. Sex aside, she couldn't help wondering whether Robert loved her father more than he loved her.

"I don't want the ring," she announced.

"That's all right," he said smoothly. "It can be returned. We'll pick out something else. When are you free to go shopping with me?" He began flipping through his desk calendar. "Does it have to be a Monday? Maybe you could take an hour off from the restaurant, and—"

"Robert." She spoke sharply, afraid that if she didn't he would just keep babbling, talking more to himself than to her. "Robert, please, look at me."

He did. His gaze grew speculative, his eyes narrowing on her. "What?"

"I'm pregnant."

"You're what?" His voice actually squeaked.

"Pregnant."

At last he sat, as if his legs had suddenly gone pudding soft. Reluctantly, Mallory took a seat, too. He gaped at her for a lengthy minute, then asked, "How?"

"The usual way."

"But we haven't..."

"You aren't," she said, as gently as she could.

Robert opened his mouth and then shut it. He drummed his smooth, callus-free fingers against the surface of his desk; he swallowed repeatedly, causing the knot in his tie to quiver. He opened his mouth and shut it again, like a fish lying on the dock, choking in the air.

"Robert, I'm so sorry." She heard a sob in her voice but refused to give in to it. "I really wish—"

"No, wait a minute. Wait a minute." He spoke in a staccato voice, like a business executive trying to figure a route through a sticky negotiation. He took a deep breath, twitched his tie with a few more gulps and stopped drumming the desk. "Cripes. What a mess."

"It's *my* mess, Robert. You had nothing to do with it and I—"

"Of course I had something to do with it. I was supposed to be your...what? Your boyfriend? Your lover? Your sweetheart? I mean, for God's sake, we were *engaged!*"

"I know, but—"

"And where was I? Miles away from you, God knows. We didn't do this well, did we."

She shrugged. His reaction bewildered her—and yet it didn't. This was the way Robert was: pragmatic to a fault. Analytical. And usually a bit unfathomable.

"Okay," he said, apparently having collected his thoughts. "Who's the father?"

His composure confused her. She should have known better than to think he would rail at her. His cool demeanor and his refusal to take anything personally were what made him indispensable to her father. Those partic-

ular traits were what had convinced Mallory that he would
be the ideal husband for her. Like her, he didn't seem to
expect or want high-flown emotion in his life. She should
have assumed he would chalk the problem up to his and her
failure to "do this well." Robert was dispassionate in every
sense of the word.

Until she met Liam O'Neill, Mallory had believed she
was, too. But Liam had taught her otherwise. Liam and the
silence of the retreat. For once in her life, she'd been
wrenched from the world of logic and dispassion. She'd
been forced to listen to her heart, to trust her instincts—instincts that had led her directly into Liam's arms.

"The father..." It was her turn to swallow. "The father
doesn't matter. He doesn't want the child. He doesn't want
anything to do with it."

"You sure picked a winner, didn't you," Robert observed bluntly.

She wasn't about to defend Liam, to explain that the father was a man who had been so devastated by love and loss
that he couldn't bear to expose himself to such intense
feelings again. She wasn't about to explain to Robert that
Liam was no more to blame for her situation than she was,
that they had reached for each other in need and found
something rare and magnificent with each other, and if
Liam couldn't accept something so rare and magnificent,
then she would understand why and forgive him, even if she
grieved for him in his self-imposed exile from love. None
of it was Robert's business.

Besides, if she told Robert who the father was, he would
feel even worse than he already did. He would not take
kindly to the news that he'd been conned by the man who
had made Mallory pregnant. Robert had fallen for Liam's
ridiculous story about writing a horror novel about the
ballet, and as a result he'd led Liam straight to Mallory's
front door.

Robert continued to assess her, his mind clicking, his hands steepled and his fingertips tapping against each other. "I'm not pleased by this," he said.

"I didn't think you would be pleased. I'm really sorry, Robert—"

"I just never guessed you were that kind of person."

"What kind of person?" she asked defensively.

"The kind who sleeps around."

"I *don't* sleep around!"

"You slept around with *someone,*" he pointed out with sneering logic. His gaze dropped to her abdomen, and when he lifted it back to her face, she saw disdain burning in his eyes.

"I made love to a man," she asserted, her pride rearing up and giving her strength. "*One* man. And to tell you the truth, even though my life is a complete fiasco at the moment, I don't have a single regret." So much for sparing Robert's feelings!

Her blunt words glanced off him, leaving him unscathed. "This isn't the end of the world, Mallory. Women make mistakes. There are legal ways to fix those mistakes. There are doctors—"

She cut him off. "I'm keeping the baby."

He scowled, evidently peeved that Mallory wasn't viewing things as unemotionally as he was. His fingers tapped. The knot of his tie bobbed. His eyes zeroed in on her. "What exactly is going on here? Are you in love with the man who did this to you?"

She'd been honest so far. She wasn't going to start lying now. "Yes."

He snorted. He stared out the window, meditating, looking extremely irritated by her failure to do the sensible thing. After a long minute, he turned back to her, scrutinizing her with a calculating eye. "All right. We can work with what we've got. I'm not opposed to an open marriage. If that's what you'd like, no problem. We've probably been headed in that direction all along."

"We have?" This surprised her. Robert wasn't just *dispassionate*—he was *passionless*. If she couldn't picture him engaging in extramarital affairs, it was simply because he had never seemed to be overloaded with libido. But given his statement, he might have been having affairs all along. Perhaps his trip to Los Angeles last week had been to see a girlfriend. Why else would he have stayed in L.A. through the weekend? Financiers didn't transact business on Saturdays and Sundays.

"The problem is," he went on, breaking into her dizzying ruminations, "you haven't been discreet. You're a smart woman—or so I mistakenly thought."

"I *am* smart!"

"But you did a stupid thing. You were careless. You screwed up."

"Maybe it looks that way," she argued. "But the fact of the matter is, I *want* this baby. So maybe it wasn't so stupid, after all."

"Well, what are we supposed to tell people? That the baby is mine? Do you think that will play?"

"It's not going to look like you," she predicted.

He snorted again, shaking his head. "This is what I mean by stupid. Why couldn't you have gotten knocked up by someone who looks like me?"

A bubble of laughter escaped her. The conversation had taken an absurd turn somewhere along the way. "Robert, what difference does it make who the baby looks like? You don't want to marry me at this point. You sure don't want to try to convince the world that the baby is yours."

"Who says I don't want to marry you?"

His pigheadedness would have been hilarious if it weren't so exasperating. "How could you possibly want to marry me?"

"I *like* you," he said. "You've fallen a bit in my esteem, but I like you. I've always thought we could make a go of it. We were both looking for the same things in this marriage."

"And what were they?"

"Stability. Security. Companionship. Maybe children." He gestured in the direction of her abdomen.

"I thought you were mainly interested in cementing your relationship with my father," she charged.

Robert's eyebrows fluttered up and down. "And I thought you were hoping that marrying me would win you a few points with him."

Mallory studied Robert with new insight. They'd never talked this way before, as friends, confidants, conspirators. She really did like Robert, she realized. "I'm not sure anything could make my father happy. I used to think our getting married would do it, but I don't know. I can't remember him *ever* being happy. Not since my mother died."

"He must have loved her very much."

Without having to think, Mallory nodded. Although she'd been too young to have any clear memories of her parents together, deep in her soul she knew that her parents had been devoted to each other, and that her father's emotional isolation had been the result of having lost his one truelove. The insight stunned her, like a needle pricking her heart. True love *was* possible. If her father had experienced it, why shouldn't she believe she deserved to experience it, too?

And why didn't Liam deserve to experience it again? He might be afraid, and she couldn't blame him. But to hide from love, to turn his back on the fruit of that love... That was exactly what her father had done to her.

She wasn't going to let Liam do that to her child—his own child. At least, she wasn't going to let him do it without acknowledging the damage he would be inflicting on the people who needed his love.

"Robert," she said, reaching across the desk to take his hand. "I'm convinced my father will stand by you, even if we don't get married. This isn't going to hurt your relationship with him, either professionally or personally. You know that."

"I don't know that at all," Robert argued, looking apprehensive.

It occurred to Mallory that Robert's attachment to her father wasn't mere opportunism. He was fond of her father; he doted on Leland. And why shouldn't he? He was the son her father had never had, being groomed to run the family business.

"I promise you, my father isn't going to turn on you. He'll turn on *me*, probably, but not you."

"He won't turn on you. Absolutely not," Robert insisted.

"But—you said it yourself. I was indiscreet. I was careless and stupid, and—"

"You met a man and fell in love," Robert said, simplifying it for her. "Who would have predicted that you'd do such a thing? I really thought we were on the same wavelength."

"We were," Mallory swore.

"Until you went and fell in love." Robert shrugged and gave her an ingratiating smile. "I'm still willing to be flexible, if you want to go ahead with the wedding. We could go the open route, each pursuing our own private pleasures. We could pull this off, Mal."

She shook her head. "I have a different idea of marriage now than I did when we first agreed to get married. Call me a sentimental fool, but...you're right. I met a guy and fell in love. And if I can't marry him, I don't see marriage as an answer to anything."

Robert weighed her reply and decided to make one final push. "Why don't you think about it a little more, before you make up your mind?"

"It's all I've been thinking about for weeks." For months, really. She'd been thinking about it even before she'd left for the retreat. She had needed those few days of silence and contemplation because she'd been troubled by her decision to marry Robert, because a part of her had believed that, just maybe, a marriage ought to be built on something more than practicality and loyalty. And she had turned to Liam, a total stranger, because she hadn't found what she was looking for with Robert—because she hadn't even known what she was looking for until Liam had entered her life.

She'd been questioning this marriage since Robert had first proposed. The only problem was, she'd had no answer for her questions until one wordless night beneath the moon, when she'd discovered love.

"I'm sorry, Robert, but my mind *is* made up."

He leaned back in his hinged leather chair. "Does this mean I don't have to go to any more ballet fund-raisers with you?"

She smiled sadly. "I think you're off the hook."

"Who's going to tell your father?"

"I am."

"And your aunt? And the St. Francis Hotel?"

"I'll take care of it."

He gestured toward the box she'd placed on his desk. "I guess it's lucky I didn't have the ring engraved," he remarked. "Once they carve initials into the band, you can't return it."

Mallory pushed herself to her feet. She felt uncommonly lucky right now—lucky that Robert wasn't demolished, or angry. Lucky that she'd called off the wedding before it was too late.

Lucky that she'd known true love once.

She didn't know whether her luck would hold enough for her to convince Liam that her love could sustain him through all of life's hardships. But as long as luck was with her, she would try.

"WHAT ARE YOU DOING HERE?" Cassie exclaimed.

Mallory had run into her in the hallway outside the production offices for "What's Up?" The young production assistant looked utterly floored that Mallory should have shown up at the studio on a day she wasn't taping her segment.

Unlike her visit with Robert, she had mapped out her strategy before coming to the studio. She hadn't had a chance to talk to her father; he'd been in a meeting with someone obviously more important than Mallory—an investment banker, or a mortgage lender, or someone equally exalted. She wasn't exactly eager to face her father, anyway—certainly not eager enough to sit around in the reception area until he could squeeze her into his hectic schedule. So she'd left Powell Enterprises, determined to spend some time trying to locate Liam.

She knew he lived somewhere in northern Marin County, but she hoped the TV talk show would have records with more specific contact information on its guests. Liam had appeared on the show; somewhere there must be a file containing information on how to reach him.

"The restaurant's closed today," she told Cassie, trotting out her fib. "I was in the neighborhood on some other business, and since I had an hour to spare, I figured I could stop by and play around with my script. Is that a problem?"

"No. No problem at all," Cassie assured her. "Do you need a place to work?"

Mallory nodded. "I could use a word processor, too, if you've got one."

"Um...sure. Let's see whose desk you can use." She escorted Mallory into the production office. A secretary sat at the front desk, playing her computer keyboard with as much virtuosity as Vladimir Horowitz used to play his Steinway. The secretary didn't even spare a glance at Cassie and Mallory.

Cassie beckoned Mallory to follow her into an unoccupied inner office. "Here," she said, switching on the computer at the unused desk. "This is Sheila's desk. She's doing a location spot with the mayor. She won't be back for at least an hour."

"Great." Mallory gave Cassie a big smile as she settled into the chair.

"What's this week's show going to be about?"

"High-quality protein," Mallory said, that morning's appointment with her gynecologist still fresh in her mind. "Creative ways to use egg whites and skim milk."

"Yuck. I still think you ought to do a piece on peanut butter."

"I will," Mallory promised, then sent Cassie another smile, dismissing her.

Cassie backed out of the office, closing the door to give Mallory privacy. Mallory counted to three—just in case Cassie returned—and then used the mouse to press the file-search icon. She wasn't the most adept person in the world when it came to computers, but she did know how to do a file search.

It didn't take long to locate a directory of interview subjects. She scanned the list of files, hit the scroll button and scanned some more until she found Liam O'Neill's name.

She lifted her gaze to the door. Not a sign of movement, not a sound. No intrusion seemed imminent.

She clicked the button to open Liam's file.

The screen filled with data on the interview itself—its length, its subject matter, the number and date of the show and a code to identify the library's videotape of that show. Mallory scrolled down the screen, skimming the information about his publisher—address, phone number, name of contact person. She jotted down the contact's name and phone number on a notepad, then resumed reading.

The name Hazel Dupree appeared, identified as Liam's literary agent. Mallory noted the name and phone number on her pad.

She scanned the rest of the text. At the very end of the file she found what she was looking for: Liam's address. Or at least *an* address—a post office box number in Fallon, California. No phone number was listed for him.

She wrote down the address, then quickly closed the file and stuffed her notepad into her purse. She would prefer not to have to get in touch with his agent or his publisher, but she was glad to have their phone numbers, in case this post office box in Fallon didn't pan out.

She switched to a new word processing screen and tried to think of what on earth she could say about egg white omelets and tofu. As an expectant mother—dear Lord, she hoped that phrase would start feeling more natural to her soon—she was going to have to increase her consumption of calcium and protein. She had never been a fan of milk, but she was going to have to start drinking it. Perhaps she could discuss some recipes for fruit-flavored skim milk shakes. Banana, skim milk, crushed ice...

She typed a few ideas onto the screen, labeled the file and sent it through the printer. She couldn't concentrate on nutrition. All she could think of was Fallon. Fallon, California. Liam's home.

Perhaps if she called directory assistance she could get his phone number. But if the producers of "What's Up?" didn't have it, it was probably unlisted. He was so reserved, so self-protective. He wouldn't want people telephoning him unexpectedly.

What if she telephoned him and he told her not to come? What if he told her to leave him alone? What if he told her, in no uncertain terms, that he didn't want this baby?

He already *had* told her that, more or less.

But he'd spoken in ignorance. Maybe, if he knew there actually was a baby on the way...

Dream on, Mallory muttered silently. What was the point in chasing Liam down like a bounty hunter on the trail of a fugitive? If she found him and told him the truth, she would only make him miserable—which, in turn, would make *her* miserable. Which wouldn't do the baby any good.

And she was doing this for the sake of the baby, wasn't she? For herself, too—and for Liam, if he could find the courage to admit that he needed love in his life. But primarily for the baby.

If Liam wasn't the man she thought he was, if he turned on her and turned her out, she vowed to herself that she alone would give her baby all the love it needed. She would not be a single parent like her father, too busy licking her own wounds to recognize that her baby needed her.

But still she sent a prayer heavenward that, no matter where he'd been or what he'd endured, Liam would find a little more love in his heart. If not for Mallory, then at least for his child.

HER DOORBELL RANG Monday evening while she was studying her road map of California. According to the map, Fallon was a nearly microscopic dot of a town riding the northern border of Marin County. She could make the drive tomorrow morning, locate Liam, announce her news and return in time to oversee dinner preparations at the restaurant.

But she didn't want to have to find Liam on a tight schedule. For one thing, locating his house might pose a greater challenge than merely locating the town. For another, she couldn't very well knock on his door, say, "Hi! I'm pregnant and you're the father, I've got to run...." and then make a U-turn and drive back to San Francisco. Liam might want to talk about it. For hours.

Or he might want to do something else for hours. And if he did, Mallory knew there was no way in hell she would want to drive home.

The trip would have to wait until next Monday, when she could set out early, spend the day with him and still get home in time to meet Reuben Cortes's vegetable truck in the alley behind the restaurant Tuesday morning.

Maybe it was just as well that she was forced to wait a week. The delay would give her a little more time to get used to her new life as a pregnant, no-longer-engaged woman. And the delay might feed Liam's loneliness. Perhaps by the time she found him, he would be so crazy from missing her that he would embrace her—and the news of their baby—with enthusiasm and love. Perhaps by the time Monday rolled around, he would have grown so desperate to see her, he would come to San Francisco after her, and she wouldn't even have to track him down.

It was a nice fantasy, anyway. But she was too much of a realist to believe Liam was the person ringing her doorbell. It was probably Alex, scrounging for food—unless, of course, he was having dinner with Aunt Grace. Maybe both of them were on her doorstep now, holding a bottle of champagne and proposing to toast their fine new relationship with Mallory.

She headed for the foyer, folding her map along its creases as she went. A glance through the peephole in the door revealed Aunt Grace, accompanied by someone else. The shadow of a taller person—a man—sloped across Aunt Grace's shoulder.

Yes, true love was possible, Mallory thought with a flush of warm sentiment. Fantasies came true. Aunt Grace and Alex had arrived to celebrate with her.

She swung open the door to discover that the man Aunt Grace had brought with her was her father.

"May we come in?" Grace asked, forging past Mallory without waiting for permission.

Leland stepped into the foyer after Grace and drew to a halt in front of Mallory. He looked grimmer than usual, his lips pressed together, his brow pinched into a frown. Mallory eyed him dubiously as she closed the door behind him. "Can I take your coats?" she asked.

"Mallory, are you all right?" Her father's voice was rough with emotion, more emotion than she'd ever heard in it before.

"Yes, I'm fine." Did he know? Had Robert told him? Or Aunt Grace? Honestly, Mallory had wanted the privilege—or the burden—of announcing to her father that he was about to become a grandfather. She didn't need anyone, no matter how well intentioned, to run interference for her.

"I got a message that you'd stopped by to see me at my office today. Ellen didn't want to interrupt me during my meeting. If I had known—"

"That's all right, Dad." She wasn't used to such solicitousness from him. "Can I take your coat?"

"But Robert said I really ought to see you. The way he said it worried me. So I called Grace—"

"And I gave him a rather large piece of my mind," Grace explained, removing her own coat and then easing Leland's off his shoulders. She waved off Mallory's assistance and hung the coats in the closet, leaving Mallory to deal with her father.

"She did," he admitted sheepishly. "She told me I was too wrapped up in myself to see my own daughter. She told me I never paid enough attention to you. That's not true, is it?"

Mallory hesitated. That her father was paying attention to her now was so gratifying she didn't want to discourage him by criticizing his past behavior. "I'm sure you meant to, Dad. You're so busy, though—"

"We're all busy. And I *do* pay attention," he added, shooting a dark look at his sister. "Perhaps I just don't communicate my interest as much as I should. Grace lectured me—"

"Let's not turn this into a discussion of you and me, Leland," Grace gently reproached. "You came here to talk to Mallory. And I came," she went on, with a smile to her niece, "because he was afraid to come alone."

"I'm not afraid," he protested.

"You begged me to accompany you," Grace reminded him.

"Because Robert made it sound urgent," Leland said. "He wouldn't tell me what's going on. All he said was that I'd better get in touch with you immediately."

"You could have telephoned me," Mallory said, although she was secretly glad he had come. What she had to tell him was better said face-to-face.

He obviously shared that opinion. "I didn't want to. If it was as bad as I feared, I wanted to be able to see you with my own eyes." He took a step back from Mallory and appraised her with a long, sweeping gaze. "You look all right. Have you gained weight?"

She smiled, strangely disoriented by her father's sudden interest in her appearance. The changes in her body were so slight, only someone who did indeed pay close attention could have detected them. "I haven't gained weight, but I've added a couple of inches here and there," Mallory said, taking his hand and leading him into the living room. "Can I get you a drink?"

He looked aghast. "You've added inches? Don't tell me you got some of those silicone implants!"

Following them into the living room, Aunt Grace laughed. Mallory sat beside her father on the sofa. She would get him a drink later—he would probably need one, once he knew what was going on—but now that she was holding his hand, she didn't want to let go of it. "I didn't have breast augmentation surgery," she assured him.

"Then what? You look different, Mal."

"I'm pregnant."

Her father blanched. His hand tensed against hers. He let out a long, slow breath. "Robert isn't the father, is he," he guessed.

"No. Robert and I broke up. It's not his fault, Dad, so please don't get on his case. It was my doing, my decision."

"Oh, God." Leland shuddered. He looked stricken. Mallory wondered whether she ought to get him that drink now, or just dial 911 and start administering CPR until the ambulance arrived.

He refused to let go of her hand. After a moment, she realized he was no longer squeezing it in panic. He was simply holding it, tightly, protectively. "How is your health?" he asked.

Not: *Who's the father?* Not: *How could you be such an idiot?* She was so touched by his concern, she wanted to weep. "My health is fine," she assured him. "I saw my doctor today—Kate ordered me to," she added for Grace's sake. "And the doctor says I'm in terrific shape."

"Is it a boy or a girl?" her father asked.

She felt tears beading along her lashes. Where was his condemnation? Where was his disappointment? "I don't know," she replied. "I don't need to have any screening at this point. Assuming there are no problems, I guess we'll just wait and find out when the baby is born."

"And I'm going to be a grandfather?" Her father sounded almost dazed. "I was a terrible father. Grace says so. Ask her."

"What I said," Grace clarified, "was that it's never too late to make things right."

"You said I was self-involved, and—"

"You *are* self-involved. But now you're going to be a grandfather, and you have the chance to give your grandchild priority over your business."

"Do I?" Leland gazed at Mallory, his expression equal parts fear and hope. "Do I still have a chance to be a better father?"

Now it was Mallory's turn to squeeze his hand, in comfort and reassurance. Forgiveness overflowed her heart as tears overflowed her eyes. "You know Aunt Grace. She's always right. If she says you can do it, you can."

"It's a pity things didn't go right for you and Robert," her father said. "Will you marry the baby's father?"

"I'd like to," Mallory admitted. "I love him. I don't know if we can work things out, though."

"Well, you must. It's better for a child to have two parents. No one knows that better than you."

"I had Aunt Grace," Mallory pointed out. "And I had you. I had people who loved me—"

"Even if some of us weren't very good at showing it." He sandwiched her hand in both of his. "I've always wanted to be a grandfather. I began to fear that your restaurant was the only baby you would ever have. You'd grow up like me, buried in your work, losing track of what was most important in life."

"Oh, Dad—"

"And I thought, well, if you married Robert, maybe someday you'd have a family, and you'd arrange your life with a better balance. Grace had her career with De-Wilde's, but she also had her children. I wanted you to have it all, the way she did."

"I have more now than I ever had before," Mallory murmured, leaning over and kissing her father's cheek, then smiling at her aunt, who stood respectfully out of their way near the window, watching them with a teary smile of her own.

"I'd like to meet the father of your child," her father said.

"I hope to work things out with him," Mallory murmured. "He's a good man, Dad. He's been through so much hell, he's afraid to believe in heaven. But I hope I can persuade him to take a chance on happiness.''

''Whatever happens, Mal, we'll always love you.'' He looked up at Grace, as if to include her in that *we*.

Mallory looked up, too. Her aunt appeared wistful. ''I guess I'll simply have to accept that not everyone wants the wedding of my dreams,'' she conceded. ''You have our support, Mallory. Do what you must do, for your baby and yourself.''

What Mallory had to do was find Liam, and touch him, and love him so much he could no longer deny the power of love. For her baby and herself—and for Liam, too—she had to reach him, and heal him, and persuade him to take a chance on joy.

CHAPTER THIRTEEN

NEW YORK WAS COLD. Liam obediently endured the author routine, dining at literary hangouts, engaging in minimally surly exchanges with reporters, signing books and wishing he were somewhere else—either home, battling his nightmares, or else with Mallory, indulging in his dreams. The three thousand miles between them hadn't miraculously erased her from his thoughts. The distance hadn't convinced him that he could live without her—and it also hadn't convinced him that he could give her the kind of life she wanted.

So he went through the motions. He played the role of successful novelist with all the artistry of an amateur thespian in the throes of terminal stage fright. Then he escaped to Boston.

Playing the role of son wasn't much easier. His mother fussed over him, force-fed him, fumed that here he was, this famous author, and he seemed unable to enjoy his success. His father rescued him by getting some tickets to a Celtics game. Seated beside his father, Liam watched the basketball players tear up and down the floor in their new arena and found himself grieving for the old Boston Garden, which had been torn down a few years ago.

It was easier to grieve for a sports arena than for Mallory.

That was the oddest part of it. He wasn't grieving for Jennifer, or for John. He wasn't grieving for the people he'd loved and lost. He was grieving for a woman he had deliberately pushed away, a woman he'd cut loose so she wouldn't grow to hate him. He had lost her because he loved her.

The Garden was gone, and Liam no longer felt as if Boston was his home. When he left Monday morning to fly back to California, he was ready to put winter weather behind him, as well as his mother's doting concern, and his father's brooding silence, and his memories of what life had been like when he'd been a happy, scrappy kid, burning with energy and inquisitiveness and utterly certain that he could avoid the world's booby traps.

It was a half hour to noon, Pacific time, when he retrieved his Jeep from the long-term lot at the San Francisco airport. He headed north on the highway, ignoring the tension that gripped his body as he circumvented the city. Not until he'd crossed the Golden Gate Bridge, leaving Mallory's hometown behind, did his lungs return to normal function, his palms stop sweating, his heart resume its regular tempo.

By denying himself Mallory, he was torturing himself—but he was also doing her a big favor. Noble gestures weren't his habit. But by being noble, by clearing out of her way, he was allowing her to marry Robert Benedict, to have her big society wedding, to attend fund-raising galas for the ballet . . . and have children. Strong, healthy children who, if destiny permitted, would grow up to be adults. She would make a good mother if fate chose not to play evil tricks on her.

Thinking of fate and healthy children and Mallory caused the tension to return, shaping a fist in the center of Liam's chest. He pictured Mallory sprawled out beside him in her bed, her skin soft and smooth, her eyes luminous as she watched him love her. He pictured her lips parting for him, and her arms opening, and her body absorbing him, and the fist in his chest began to pummel him from within.

If only he'd loved her a little less, he could have held on to her. He could have been with her right now, knowing an ecstasy he'd never known with any other woman. If only he'd put his own desires ahead of hers, if only he'd been a little less honorable...

The road grew steeper and more rugged as he ascended into the hills above Marin County's ocean coast. Towns thinned out, yielding to sequoia forestland. He drove through tunnels of trees, around bluffs and cliffs, into the small village that served as his postal address and then out of it, onto a narrow country road that veered west to his driveway. The box at the mouth of the driveway held the morning newspapers of the past several days, but he didn't bother to get them. God knew, there could be a photograph of Mallory in one of them, doing some charitable deed in a sexy black dress, with Robert Benedict hanging from her arm.

The Jeep bounced along the unpaved driveway, kicking up stones and twigs, splashing in and out of a puddle left over from a recent rain. Up ahead, a swath of light filtered through the trees, announcing the clearing where his cabin stood. He downshifted, slowing the Jeep. He almost didn't want to be home. Once he was there, he would be all alone with his thoughts.

Well, there was always wood to chop. Always a novel to write. Always the long nights to lie awake, wrestling with his memories, warding off his nightmares, wondering how he'd managed to make his life even worse than it had been before.

As he took the last turn and coasted into the clearing, he saw a car parked at the top of the driveway, near the shed. He didn't immediately recognize the dark green late-model Saab, but the fear that swept over him wasn't caused by the assumption that burglars were ransacking his house. Burglars didn't drive expensive Saab convertibles.

This was a different kind of fear, bubbling up from a spring deep inside him. It was a fear that his best intentions were about to get trashed, a fear that he was about to face a challenge he would not be able to surmount. It was a fear that his most stubborn, frustrating nightmare was about to assail him at the brightest hour of the day, because gradually he remembered where he'd seen the Saab before: in the alley behind Mallory's.

He rolled his Jeep to a halt, turned off the engine and looked around. The shed was locked shut. His house looked undisturbed. And then he saw her, walking around from the rear of the house.

Her shoulders were squared, her back straight, her head held high and proud. Her thick black hair blew back from her face in the light breeze, a touch of midnight in the noontime sun. She wore a suede jacket over a sweater and a pair of blue jeans; her hands were buried in her pockets. Her large green-and-grey eyes were riveted to him.

If he were a wiser man, he would have ignited the engine, turned the Jeep around and fled. But he wasn't that wise, so he shoved open the door and climbed out.

After five days of inhaling the frigid, sooty atmosphere of New York and Boston, the air of home bathed his lungs with the tart fragrance of pine and cedar and decaying needles. As Mallory took another step toward him, and another, he smelled the suede of her jacket and the jasmine scent of her shampoo. He wanted to reach into the back seat of the Jeep to pull out his bag, but to do that would require turning from her, and he seemed physically unable to do that.

"How long have you been here?" he asked.

"About an hour."

It could have been worse. He'd been gone for days; she could have been camping out on his back porch since he'd departed for the East Coast.

She took another step toward him, and he tried to ward her off with his words. "How did you find my house?"

"I learned your town by poking through the computer files at 'What's Up?' Then I drove to Fallon. I asked a store clerk and the lady behind the counter at the post office, but they refused to tell me where you lived. So I went to a tavern named Smitty's. Some people start hitting the bottle early, and I asked the drunkest-looking guy I could find. He told me."

Liam nodded. Fallon was a small town, and most people protected his privacy, just as he would protect theirs. But drunks didn't always know enough to shut up.

Mallory moved closer yet. So close that if he shifted his foot, he would step on her toes. So close that if he lifted his hand, his fingers would brush her cheek. So close that if he tilted his head, he could kiss her.

"Why did you come here?" he asked, exerting himself not to tilt his head.

"I came because I love you," she said, lancing right through his defenses.

He felt the fist release his chest, felt his blood rush hot through his veins, felt his soul compel his hands upward, his mouth downward. He caught her in his arms and covered her lips with his, and nothing else mattered, not her future, not his past, nothing but this instant, this kiss.

Her mouth softened against his for a moment, then withdrew. She curled her hands around his upper arms, both holding him and blocking him. "We need to talk," she insisted.

He wasn't going to argue with this woman. She was strong enough, brave enough to breach the very real obstacles he had erected between them, and for that alone she deserved to call the shots. "I've just flown in from the East Coast," he told her, then shook his head and laughed at the realization that Mallory Powell was here at his home, like a loyal wife awaiting the return of her husband at the end of an arduous business trip. "You can talk while I un-pack."

"The East Coast?"

He reached into the Jeep for his heavy leather duffel bag, then shut and locked the door. "New York, to meet with my publisher," he told her, starting across the grass to the house. "Boston, to see my folks."

"You couldn't have been gone long."

"Five days." Not long enough to get over her.

Her laughter was tinged with amazement. "I guess I'm lucky that you came back today."

She wasn't lucky enough to have chosen a steadier man to love. As the effects of kissing her wore off and he collected his wits, he resolved to explain that to her. No matter that she'd sounded so earnest when she'd said she loved him, no matter that the words had resonated inside him like a drug, the one potent drug that could cure him of everything that was wrong in his life ... If she were truly lucky, she would be loving a man who could make her happy.

"I would have come up earlier, but with the restaurant, I can't always get away," she said. "Mallory's is closed on Mondays, so I was able to get out of town today. Lucky for me you decided to fly home Monday."

Her insistence that she was blessed with good luck vexed him. "I flew home Monday because I was done back East," he retorted. "If I'd had more to do, I would have stayed."

She shot him a curious look but didn't respond to his gruff tone. He jiggled the key into the front door lock, then pushed the door open and let her enter ahead of him.

"Oh, Liam!" She waltzed into the small living room, her face glowing. He would have thought she would be turned off by the snug proportions of the room, the solid, grace-less furniture, the absence of curtains to brighten the windows, the lack of knickknacks and paintings on the walls. But she only swept around the room in a cheerful circle. "This is wonderful! It's so cozy! It's almost like living inside one of those beautiful redwood trees outside your window." She spun toward him, beaming. "It's exactly how I'd picture the perfect writer's lair."

"It's not a lair," he muttered. "It's my home."

"And it's perfect," she repeated, undeterred by his curtness. "I'll bet you knew, the minute you saw it, that it was the ideal house for you."

"I didn't see it," he said, crossing the living room with his duffel bag. "I built it."

Mallory followed him down the hall, past the room he used as his office and into his bedroom. "You *built* it?"

Why did she find that so hard to believe? "Yes, I built it."

"You have talents I haven't even discovered," she murmured. The whispery cadence of her voice made him want to help her discover those talents, in his bed, right now. Desire lapped at him like flames licking firewood. He refused to look at her, but that left him looking at his bed, broad and inviting, all made up with fresh sheets and thick feather pillows.

"Mallory." He dropped his bag to the floor with a thud and turned. Once again, she was standing too close to him, testing his resistance. He smelled her; he felt the warmth of her seeping into him. Her eyes were too wide, too radiant. Her lips were too soft.

In desperation, he threw another obstacle into her path, cruel and blunt. "I built this house when I was in mourning. I built it in anger. I wanted to hit things, so I hit nails with a hammer, and I wound up with this cabin. It's not a perfect house, Mallory—unless you think it's perfect that my family got wiped out and I went insane."

She refused to back off. "I think it's a miracle that you were able to create something so sturdy and lovely out of your grief. Like your books—"

"My books aren't lovely."

"Your books come from your heart. Just like this house does. You have a good heart, Liam. It's strong enough to heal. I know it is."

Liam didn't know that. But when she gazed up at him with such trust, such certainty, such yearning . . .

Heat gathered in his groin and higher, in the heart he believed was strong enough to heal. He wanted to trust her the way she trusted him. He *could* trust her—but he couldn't trust himself.

Maybe it was enough that she trusted him.

He reached for her and she practically flew into his embrace. Wrapping her arms around him, she peppered his face with kisses. Her body pressed along his, moving sinuously, seductively. Closing his eyes, he heard her voice resonate inside him: *I came because I love you.*

He skimmed his hands down the narrow length of her back to her hips and guided her against him. He was hard, but not just from her body, not just from her kisses. Her words aroused him, her sincerity, her willingness to make herself vulnerable, her fearlessness in the face of every hurt he could cause her.

Her body, too, he amended as she rocked against him. "You must be tired," she whispered. "The plane ride, and—"

"No." He tugged her jacket from her shoulders and let it drop to the floor. Then he slid his hands under her sweater to the silky skin of her back, tracing its inward curve at her waist and then wedging his fingers inside the waistband of her jeans. He wanted to feel her. He *needed* to. He needed to bare her fearlessness and absorb it, make it his. He needed her to teach him how to trust a world that could steal happiness from a man for no reason at all.

He needed Mallory more than he could imagine.

He felt her hands on his shirt, plucking open the buttons and then sliding inside to caress his chest. He heard himself moan, and then heard her sigh as he probed the sweetness of her mouth with his tongue. He brought his hands forward to the fly of her jeans and yanked down the zipper, then reached inside her panties.

She gasped. Her knees seemed to lose strength, and she swayed against him. He scooped her into his arms and carried her to his bed.

It took him less than a minute to strip naked, less than thirty seconds to remove her clothing. Her skin shimmered before him, gold-tinged and magnificent, her breasts swollen with passion even before he'd touched them. When he pressed his lips to first one and then the other, she cried out, as if all her nerves were centered on the tight round nipples, as if he could make her come simply by suckling her.

She tasted better than the mellowest wine, the most intoxicating liquor, the most exotic spice. Better than an aphrodisiac. Kissing her made him want to freeze time, to make this moment, this pleasure, last for all eternity.

But he couldn't stop the earth's rotation any more than he could stop her from stroking him, stoking his hunger for her. Her hands were everywhere, her lips everywhere else. Her hair billowed over his skin; her knees nudged his thighs in unspeakably erotic ways. When he skimmed his fingers between her legs, she closed her teeth on his shoulder to smother a groan.

She was so hot, so wet. Unable to stop kissing her, unwilling to stop arousing her, he reached blindly with his free hand into the drawer of the night table beside the bed, rummaging for a condom.

"No," she whispered.

"Mallory, I..." He cleared the hoarseness from his throat and labored to control his breathing. She curled her hand around him and rubbed him, making him harder, making him lose his mind from the dazzling tension. He pulled back, desperate to ready himself so he could take her. "I need to protect you—"

"It's too late for that," she said.

The earth did stop then. Like a beam of paralyzing light, her words held him motionless. He stared down at her; she lay beautiful and alluring, peering up at him, her expression unreadable.

He wasn't sure what she was talking about, but he could guess. "It's too late," he repeated, chills rippling through his body, undoing everything her kisses and caresses had done to him.

"I'm pregnant, Liam."

The fist was back in his chest, wrenching his heart. What the hell was she saying? Was this some sort of trick? A ghastly joke?

"At the retreat," she continued, her voice steady and velvet-soft, her eyes unwavering on him. "I'm three months along."

"No." He screamed the word, yet it emerged as less than a whisper. Slamming his eyes shut, he saw John, his son, his baby. He felt John's innocent little body curled up against his chest. He smelled John's baby-powder scent. He heard John's chirpy voice shrieking with laughter, giggling, crying, "Daddy! Daddy!"

No.

He begged God to make the images stop. He flung himself out of the bed, away from Mallory, the woman who would do this to him, put him through this horror, slice open his gut and watch the pain spill out until he was drowning in it.

No.

He forced himself to turn around and open his eyes. She sat in the center of his bed, naked, pale and troubled. Her breasts *were* swollen, he realized. Her belly was rounder than he remembered. And her eyes... Hurt, accusing, plaintive, glistening with unspent tears, they would haunt him forever.

"I considered ending the pregnancy," she told him, her lower lip trembling but her chin raised defiantly. "I won't do it. Not even for you."

Guilt sheered through him. This wasn't just her doing. Last December at the retreat, he'd been no more rational than she'd been. He hadn't protected her then. This was his fault, not hers.

Still, he felt cornered. Trapped. Not by Mallory, but by his own heedless passion—and by crippling fear.

"I made up my mind for sure last week," she told him. Her tears refused to fall. "I told Robert I was pregnant, and we ended our engagement. I told my father, and my aunt, and my cousin. I didn't tell them it's your child, because you swore to me..." Her voice threatened to crack, and she swallowed hard. "You swore you would never be a father. I won't force you, Liam. I won't force you to accept this new life and love it. I can't make you feel something you don't want to feel ever again."

"Mallory." The fist squeezed tighter, bruising his lungs and ribs, making the simple draw of a breath agony. He wished he could say what she needed to hear—that he was thrilled, that he wanted the baby, that he could imagine no greater satisfaction than to become a father again. But he couldn't push the words past the wall of pain rising inside him. Closing his eyes once more, he saw a final picture, John's small, broken body, lost within the white sheets of a hospital bed, his face battered, his skin discolored, his spirit snatched away. John. His baby.

He opened his eyes. Mallory was getting dressed. He watched as she struggled with the snap of her jeans. The denim strained around her waist, and he knew. Her breasts plumped above the edge of her bra, and he knew.

But the words wouldn't come. They couldn't pass through the barrier of ice that sealed his heart. He couldn't speak them.

And in another minute, she was gone.

SHE MADE IT ALL THE WAY back to San Francisco without weeping. She made it all the way to the garage in her condo, all the way to her apartment, all the way to her bed, before she collapsed in a welter of tears.

What had she thought? That declaring her love would transform a man who had endured wounds no amount of love could ever heal? That telling him she was carrying his child would turn him into Father of the Year?

Yes. That was exactly what she'd thought.

It hadn't worked. She was going to have to face this challenge alone. Her father and Aunt Grace would support her, but the bottom line was, she was going to have to raise the baby all by herself. It would be difficult, but not nearly as difficult as living the rest of her life without the man she loved.

"The hell with him," she fumed between sobs. She wiped her eyes, blew her nose, then shouted every ripe curse she could think of. "The hell with Liam O'Neill. He wants to wallow in his suffering—that's his choice. I'm not going to let him drag me down with him."

Slowly, shaking off a final hiccup, she pulled herself to her feet. She staggered into the bathroom and twisted the faucets above the tub. She was going to soak in a nice, hot bubble bath, she decided. And by the time the water had cooled off, she was going to be over Liam.

She watched the steam swirl up into the air, blurring the room like San Francisco fog. She watched the bubbles glint rainbows in their rounded surfaces. She inhaled the damp perfume of the bath oil. She listened to the hollow rush of water, echoing against the tile walls of the bathroom. When the tub was full, she turned off the faucets and got undressed.

She studied her naked body in the full-length mirror attached to the door. She looked...not quite fat, but altered. Had Liam noticed? Could anyone other than Mallory see the changes? Maybe she was just feeling them

from within. Her entire world had been turned inside out—
why not her perception of her appearance?

One thing she definitely felt from within was the ache of
unfulfilled desire. Maybe she should have let Liam make
love to her first, and then she could have told him about the
baby.

She discovered she knew a few more curses, and she gave
vent to them in the steamy room as she twisted her hair into
a knot on the top of her head and fastened it with a tor-
toiseshell clasp. If she'd made love with Liam, she would
only have loved him more. And then when he rejected his
child—and that child's mother—it would have hurt even
more.

As if anything could hurt more than this, she thought,
fighting off the fresh sobs that threatened her.

She sank down into the tub, praying for the hot, frothy
water to wash away every last trace of Liam's touch. She
hated him, loathed him, despised him. Abhorred him. Execrated him. A new list of curses filled her mouth, and she
howled them into the scented mist that hovered above the
bubbles. She hated, hated, hated Liam O'Neill, hated everything about him....

Except for his baby. *Her* baby.

She heard the sound of her telephone ringing, muffled by
the steam and the closed bathroom door. She lounged in the
tub, letting the machine answer for her.

The heat of the water seeped into her, soothing her.
Having grown up in a single-parent family, she knew the
drawbacks, but knowing them meant she could avoid them.
And unlike her father, she would have no interest in leaving her baby with a housekeeper on Saturday nights while
she went out for dinner. She wasn't going to date men for
the fun of it. And she wasn't going to date men in search of
a lover. She'd had a lover; she'd had Liam. She didn't need
to go through that again.

She heard the phone ring a second time. She closed her eyes, shutting out the noise.

The ringing stopped. In its wake, she heard the rustle of bubbles bursting on her shoulders and under her chin. She ran her hands gently over the curve of her belly, as if to reassure her baby. "I love you," she crooned, aware that she would never speak those words to Liam again. "I love you so much...."

The moisture on her cheeks wasn't from the bath. She let the tears come. This was it, her day to fall apart. Starting tomorrow, she would be as strong and sturdy as the house Liam had built. She would be as clear of clutter as his plain, homey rooms. She would be as strong and healthy as the redwoods bordering his land. She would give her baby everything that ought to have come from Liam.

The bath lulled her. She was exhausted. She'd arisen early and driven to Fallon, anticipating what would happen when she saw Liam. Then she'd arrived and *hadn't* seen him, because he hadn't been home. She'd spent an anxious hour prowling around his house, trying to decide whether to leave him a note or wait for him in town, or to put Burt in charge of the restaurant and return to Fallon on Tuesday. She'd spied through Liam's windows, trying to see if he'd marked his telephone with his number; she'd already learned that it was unlisted, so she couldn't call him. She'd just about given up hope of seeing him... and then he'd arrived.

And kissed her. And touched her, and aroused her, and made her feel things no other man had ever made her feel. And then turned his back on her, and his baby.

The drive home had taken a toll, and her weeping had taken an even greater toll. She felt a bone-deep fatigue, so profound she couldn't picture herself *not* being weary ever again.

The peal of her telephone shivered into her consciousness yet again. She pushed against the sides of the tub to raise herself out of the foam and realized that what she'd heard was not her phone but her doorbell.

She didn't have to answer. But the water had grown tepid, and she'd promised herself that once it did she would be cured of Liam. If this was cured, she wasn't impressed, but it might be the best she could hope for.

The doorbell rang again. She stood cautiously, lifted one leg and then the other over the side of the tub and reached for her robe. The tips of her hair dribbled water down her back. Her eyes were puffy and red-rimmed.

Opening the bathroom door, she was blasted with chilly, dry air—and besieged by the clamor of someone pounding on her door. She tied the sash of her robe tightly and tip-toed down the hall. Whoever was banging on her door sounded furious.

She hesitated at the kitchen doorway, considering whether she should get a knife. She decided she would look through the peephole first. And then phone the police. And *then* get a knife.

The sudden gong of the doorbell as she stepped into the foyer caused her to flinch. She squinted through the lens embedded in the door.

Liam.

She indulged in a brief, malicious fantasy of returning to the kitchen for the biggest carving knife she owned. But then his voice came through the door, pleading, "Mallory! Let me come in."

He didn't sound dangerous—at least, not in the obvious way. Of course he was dangerous. He had already destroyed all her plans, all her hopes. But then, he could be on another planet and still endanger her sanity and her soul. The danger he posed had no bearing on whether or not she opened her door to him now.

"Please," he implored. He must have known she was on the other side of the door, because he stopped punching the door chime. "Please, Mallory—if you don't let me in I'm going to make a fool of myself in the hall."

"I think I'd like that," she shouted through the door.

He lapsed into silence for a minute. Then he said, "I brought a teddy bear."

"What?"

"I brought a teddy bear. Look."

She peered through the peephole. Liam held up a fuzzy tan bear with stitched eyes and a mouth.

"No buttons," he said. "You're not supposed to give newborns stuffed animals with button eyes or a button nose, because the baby might suck the button into its mouth and choke."

Mallory hadn't known that. But Liam was experienced in the area of raising newborns. He knew about stuffed animals and buttons. She could use his knowledge once the baby was born.

But she hated him, and execrated him, and all the rest. She wasn't going to forgive him just because he happened to be an expert on teddy bears.

She glanced through the hole again. The bear had been replaced by Liam, who looked far more feral than the stuffed creature in his hands. His hair was mussed, his eyes wild with gray shadows and gold light. "I want our baby," he said quietly. She could see his lips move in the lens. "I tried to telephone you. I stopped twice to phone you on my way down here, but you wouldn't answer."

"How did you know I was home? I might have been flying to New York or something," she said.

"I hoped you'd be here. I prayed. Please let me in, Mallory."

She supposed she could hate him even if he was inside her apartment. Reluctantly, she edged open the door.

He swept inside, lugging the stuffed bear—which was much larger than she'd realized when she'd seen it through the distorting lens in her door. His clothing was disheveled, his jacket open. He looked in dire need of a hug, but Mallory must have appeared forbidding to him, because he wound up absentmindedly hugging the teddy bear, instead.

"Are you all right?" he asked.

"I've been better."

"I'm an ass," he said.

"No, Liam." If he was going to denounce himself, she couldn't, too. "You're not an ass."

"Then what am I?"

She gazed up at him. He looked truly lost, as if he no longer knew who or what he was.

Oh, God, she wanted to hug him. She wanted to so badly her arms ached from the restraint it took to keep them at her sides. "You're a man who's lived in pain for so long, you're afraid you won't know how to live without it."

He met her gaze unflinchingly. She noticed a muscle flexing in his jaw, a twitch in his shoulders as he wrestled with his emotions. "You're right," he conceded. "But I'm even more afraid I won't know how to live without you."

"This isn't about me," she insisted, his pain reaching out to her, reaching into her and holding fast. "It's about a baby."

"*Our* baby," he murmured. "Mine as much as yours." He set the teddy bear on the mail table and risked drawing Mallory into his arms. His hands trembled as they alighted on her shoulders. "I want the baby. I want..." He sighed, groping for the right words. "Being a father was the most important thing I ever did in my life. But I failed at it. I couldn't protect my baby when he needed me."

"It wasn't your fault," Mallory said. "You have to forgive yourself, Liam. You have to forgive yourself and let go."

"I won't let go of you," he promised, bowing and grazing her lips with a kiss. "I'm scared, but I won't let go."

"Just let go of the pain," she urged him.

Liam kissed her again, a slower, deeper kiss. "Did you mean it before, when you said you loved me?"

She lifted her head and met his steady gaze. She'd meant it before, but she loved him even more now. She loved him because he had chosen the future over the past, because he'd chosen a future that included her and their child. She loved him because he had the courage to let her see his fear. She loved him because, instead of bringing her an extravagant diamond ring, he had brought her a teddy bear.

"Oh, Liam," she murmured. "You can't begin to know how much I love you."

"I intend to find out," he promised. "If it takes me the next hundred years, Mallory, I intend to find out."

Mallory gathered up the teddy bear and clasped Liam's hand. "Come with me, then," she said. "A hundred years is a long time. We'd better get started."

Liam smiled. And if Mallory wasn't mistaken, the teddy bear seemed to be grinning too as she led the way down the hall to her bedroom.

turn itself Sometimes ... back, forget blue... Did you
mean it, then, when you said you loved me?" he said.

She lifted her head and met his steady gaze. She almost
it before, but she loved him even more now. She loved him
because he had changed, the future ... the past, because
he'd chosen a future that brought her and she'd ... she
loved him because he had the courage to ... her, see that ...

She heard him, heard her laughter and caught her in arms.

again ... him ... and back, in her a holly bear.

"Oh ... him," she murmured. "You could begin to ... love
how much I love you."

"I meant to find out," he promised. "It'll ... us twelve
more hundred years, while we spend in bed, eh."

"Mallory gathered up the empty tray and carried him ...
blood of Christ without him," she said. "A hundred years
is a long time. We'd better get started."

Laira replied. "And if that's her examination, the baby
has ... seems to be grinning too as she led the way down the
hall to the bedroom.

continues with

Terms of Surrender

by Kate Hoffmann

Merchandising manager Megan DeWilde had major plans for the expansion of DeWildes' Paris operation. But Philippe Villeneuve, scion of a rival retailing family, was after the same piece of real estate Megan had her eye on. Caught in the middle of a feud neither understood, they were powerless against the sizzling chemistry that overrode property, family and every shred of common sense.

Available in November

Here's a preview!

MEGAN LOOKED UP at her brother, her brow furrowed. At the same time, Gabe gasped. "Marriage? Is that what he said?" he shouted. "You're thinking of marrying him?"

"Yes," Philippe said, stepping away from her to stand in front of Gabe. "I asked Meggie to marry me."

She reached out and took his arm, drawing him back. "Philippe, this really isn't the right time to—"

"It's a perfect time," Philippe said. He took her trembling hand in his, then turned to Gabe. "I plan to marry her, with or without your family's blessing."

"The hell you will," Gabe said, stalking across the room and grabbing Megan's other arm. As her brother tried to pull her away, Philippe held fast. She looked back and forth at them both, then yanked her arms away.

"Stop it!" she cried. "Please!"

"Meggie, tell him," Philippe said softly. "Tell him how you feel. Tell him what you want."

Gabe held out his hand to stop her reply. "Don't bother, Megan. I'll make it easy for you. It's either Villeneuve or your family. Are you willing to give up your position at DeWilde's for this man?"

Megan stared at her brother in disbelief. "You can't do this, Gabe. You don't have the power."

"Dad gave me the power. It's either your job or him. You make the choice."

Megan frowned, her gaze shifting between the brother she'd always loved and the man she wanted so desperately to love. She knew in her heart that Philippe Villeneuve was a good and honorable man, a man who didn't deserve the wrath that her family had heaped upon him.

"Go ahead, Megan," Gabe taunted. "Choose. It's him or your family. Are you going to betray the family like Mother did?"

She bit her bottom lip and tried to stem a flood of tears. "Don't do this, Gabe. Please, don't make me choose. I can't."

"As long as you associate with a Villeneuve, you cannot be a part of DeWilde's."

"Stop saying that!" she cried. "I'm not going to choose. I'm not." The tears flowed freely now and there was nothing she could do to stop them. She stood between Philippe and Gabe, rent in two by emotions that welled up from deep inside her. A sob tore from her throat and she covered her face with her hands.

She felt Philippe's hands on her shoulders. "She won't have to choose," he said softly.

"She will," Gabe countered.

Megan looked up at Philippe through tear-clouded eyes. He smiled and shook his head, never taking his eyes from her. "See, that's the difference between us, DeWilde. I love your sister and I'd never do anything to hurt her. I'd never ask her to give up the family, or the job she loves. So I'll make the choice for her."

He reached out and cupped her cheek in his palm. His simple caress sent a frisson of joy through her and his words rang in her mind like cathedral bells on Christmas morning. He loved her! He had just said the words she wasn't sure she wanted to hear. And now that he'd said them, her own feelings came rushing forth. He loved her . . . and she loved him.

"You were right, Meggie," he said softly.

"Right?"

"We can't ignore the past. No matter how hard we try to bury it, it will always be there. And nothing I do can change that." He bent over her and brushed his mouth against hers. "Goodbye, Meggie."

HARLEQUIN®

Don't miss these Harlequin favorites by some of our most
distinguished authors!
And now, you can receive a discount by ordering two or more titles!

HT #25663	THE LAWMAN by Vicki Lewis Thompson	$3.25 U.S. ☐/$3.75 CAN. ☐
HP #11788	THE SISTER SWAP by Susan Napier	$3.25 U.S. ☐/$3.75 CAN. ☐
HR #03293	THE MAN WHO CAME FOR CHRISTMAS by Bethany Campbell	$2.99 U.S. ☐/$3.50 CAN. ☐
HS #70667	FATHERS & OTHER STRANGERS by Evelyn Crowe	$3.75 U.S. ☐/$4.25 CAN. ☐
HI #22198	MURDER BY THE BOOK by Margaret St. George	$2.89　☐
HAR #16520	THE ADVENTURESS by M.J. Rodgers	$3.50 U.S. ☐/$3.99 CAN. ☐
HH #28885	DESERT ROGUE by Erin Yorke	$4.50 U.S. ☐/$4.99 CAN. ☐

(limited quantities available on certain titles)

	AMOUNT	$
DEDUCT:	**10% DISCOUNT FOR 2+ BOOKS**	$
ADD:	**POSTAGE & HANDLING**	$
	($1.00 for one book, 50¢ for each additional)	
	APPLICABLE TAXES **	$＿＿＿＿
	TOTAL PAYABLE	$＿＿＿＿
	(check or money order—please do not send cash)	

To order, complete this form and send it, along with a check or money order for the
total above, payable to Harlequin Books, to: **In the U.S.:** 3010 Walden Avenue,
P.O. Box 9047, Buffalo, NY 14269-9047; **In Canada:** P.O. Box 613, Fort Erie, Ontario,
L2A 5X3.

Name: ＿＿＿＿＿＿＿＿＿＿＿＿＿＿＿＿＿＿＿＿＿＿＿＿＿＿＿＿＿＿＿＿
Address: ＿＿＿＿＿＿＿＿＿＿＿＿＿＿ City: ＿＿＿＿＿＿＿＿＿＿＿
State/Prov.: ＿＿＿＿＿＿＿＿＿＿ Zip/Postal Code: ＿＿＿＿＿＿＿＿

**New York residents remit applicable sales taxes.
Canadian residents remit applicable GST and provincial taxes.　　　HBACK-JS3

Look us up on-line at: http://www.romance.net

SPECIAL EDITION

Stories of love and life, these powerful
novels are tales that you can identify with—
romances with "something special" added in!

Fall in love with the stories of authors such
as **Nora Roberts, Diana Palmer, Ginna Gray**
and many more of your special favorites—as
well as wonderful new voices!

Special Edition brings you
entertainment for the heart!

Harlequin® Historical

If you're a serious fan of historical romance,
then you're in luck!

Harlequin Historicals brings you
stories by bestselling authors, rising new stars
and talented first-timers.

Ruth Langan & Theresa Michaels
Mary McBride & Cheryl St. John
Margaret Moore & Merline Lovelace
Julie Tetel & Nina Beaumont
Susan Amarillas & Ana Seymour
Deborah Simmons & Linda Castle
Cassandra Austin & Emily French
Miranda Jarrett & Suzanne Barclay
DeLoras Scott & Laurie Grant...

You'll never run out of favorites.

Harlequin Historicals...they're too good to miss!

HH-GEN

WAYS TO *UNEXPECTEDLY* MEET MR. RIGHT:

♡ Go out with the sexy-sounding stranger your daughter secretly set you up with through a personal ad.

♡ RSVP yes to a wedding invitation—soon it might be your turn to say "I do!"

♡ Receive a marriage proposal by mail— from a man you've never met....

These are just a few of the unexpected ways that written communication leads to love in Silhouette Yours Truly.

Each month, look for two fast-paced, fun and flirtatious Yours Truly novels (with entertaining treats and sneak previews in the back pages) by some of your favorite authors—and some who are sure to become favorites.

YOURS TRULY™:
Love—when you least expect it!

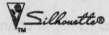

HARLEQUIN ◆ PRESENTS®

HARLEQUIN PRESENTS
men you won't be able to resist falling in love with...

HARLEQUIN PRESENTS
women who have feelings just like your own...

HARLEQUIN PRESENTS
powerful passion in exotic international settings...

HARLEQUIN PRESENTS
intense, dramatic stories that will keep you turning
to the very last page...

HARLEQUIN PRESENTS
The world's bestselling romance series!

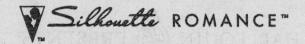

What's a single dad to do when he needs a wife by next Thursday?

Who's a confirmed bachelor to call when he finds a baby on his doorstep?

How does a plain Jane in love with her gorgeous boss get him to notice her?

From classic love stories to romantic comedies to emotional heart tuggers, **Silhouette Romance** offers six irresistible novels every month by some of your favorite authors!
Such as...beloved bestsellers **Diana Palmer, Annette Broadrick, Suzanne Carey, Elizabeth August** and **Marie Ferrarella,** to name just a few—and some sure to become favorites!

Fabulous Fathers...Bundles of Joy...Miniseries...
Months of blushing brides and convenient weddings...
Holiday celebrations... You'll find all this and much more in
Silhouette Romance—always emotional, always enjoyable, always about love!

SR-GEN